She thought her trip around the world would be fun, but she had no idea what she'd gotten into...

A tall, bearded man appeared. He stood still and gazed at her.

"Who are you?" She nervously watched the man enter the room. He looked familiar. He resembled one of the fellows she had seen on the street while walking to the bistro. A twinge of fear sent the beginnings of a scream to her throat.

"Me Caleb," he said and his tone of voice seemed pleasant and reassuring. "These yours." He raised his left hand holding her shoes and purse.

She swallowed her scream and her terror subsided. She felt relieved that her shoes would protect her tender feet from stones and gravel and that she would have her credit card. "Thank you," she murmured. "Where is Don Webster?"

"He held up." The man set the purse and shoes on the floor, closed the door, and walked toward her.

"Held up? What do you mean?" A twinge of fear returned.

Caleb pointed a clenched fist at her. "Pow."

She dashed past him, snatched her shoes and purse, and opened the door. In that instant, Caleb's arms circled her waist. Before she knew what was happening, he kicked the door shut, covered her mouth with duct tape, and held her arms behind her. She almost lost her balance as he taped her wrists together. As she kicked at him with her bare feet, he dragged her to the bed and tossed her onto it.

He grabbed her flailing feet and wound duct tape around her ankles.

Philomela Nightingale and her employee, Janice McGill, take the trip of a lifetime—around the world. They fly to amazing places, stay in lovely hotels, meet fascinating people, and experience different cultures. To their horror they also become involved with kidnapping and murder. Will Philomela's observational powers and intuition enable her to help the police solve these puzzling mysteries or has she finally bitten off more than she can handle?

KUDOS for *Odd Odyssey*

In *Odd Odyssey* by Benni Chisholm, Philomena Nightingale runs a monthly magazine. She and her employee Janice take a trip around the world, a month-long adventure. Unbeknownst to them, Janice has been targeted by people who want to kidnap her and force her wealthy father to ransom her. They send a guy on the trip with Philomena and Janice, and he tries time after time to hijack her, coming up with excuses for his odd behavior when the attempts fail. But sooner or later, he's bound to succeed. Isn't he? The book is a fun read, a cozy mystery. Odd Odyssey has an unusual storyline and an author whose voice is fresh and unique. ~ *Taylor Jones, Reviewer*

Odd Odyssey by Benni Chisholm is a mystery/adventure that defies genre classification. Janice McGill and her employer Philomena Nightingale work for a magazine *The Integrator* in Calgary, Canada. Philomena and Janice decide to take a month-long around-the-world cruise, just as Janice becomes the target of a group of bumbling kidnappers. Undaunted, our intrepid villains send their man on the tour. He's supposed to get Janice alone, in what she is supposed to think is a romantic escape, while his cohorts back home collect the ransom money. But things don't go quite the way anyone expects, resulting in a very odd odyssey indeed. Chisholm has a nice way with a story. Her voice is fresh and unique, her characters fun, realistic, and charming, and her plot is strong with plenty of twists and turns. A clever and fun mystery/adventure. ~ *Regan Murphy, Reviewer*

ACKNOWLEDGEMENTS

Thank you to the professor who instilled me with a bit of Greek Mythology.

Much appreciated are the keen eyes of Sandy and Elizabeth, my early readers. Their astute observations improved the story.

Thanks, Jessie, for sending me Spencer's photograph of Haley walking on the sand.

The discerning editors and artist at Black Opal Books dispensed encouragement and good advice. I owe them a debt of gratitude.

Merritt, your author photo minimizes my wise-woman wrinkles. Fantastic.

ODD

ODYSSEY

Benni Chisholm

A Black Opal Books Publication

BECAUSE SOME STORIES JUST HAVE TO BE TOLD

GENRE: MYSTERY-DETECTIVE/SUSPENSE/WOMEN'S FICTION

This is a work of fiction. Names, places, characters and incidents are either the product of the author's imagination or are used fictitiously, and any resemblance to any actual persons, living or dead, businesses, organizations, events or locales is entirely coincidental. All trademarks, service marks, registered trademarks, and registered service marks are the property of their respective owners and are used herein for identification purposes only. The publisher does not have any control over or assume any responsibility for author or third-party websites or their contents.

ODD ODYSSEY
Copyright © 2015 by Benni Chisholm
Cover Design by Benni Chisholm
Cover photo by Spencer MacCosham
Author photo by Merritt Chisholm
All cover art copyright © 2015
All Rights Reserved
Print ISBN: 978-1-626942-81-3

First Publication: JUNE 2015

Published by Black Opal Books **http://www.blackopalbooks.com**

DEDICATION

To the residents of Nepal:
May you and your beautiful land soon recover
from the devastation of the recent earthquake.

CHAPTER 1

A chill crawled up Don Webster's spine. What was he getting into? Clutching his glass, he gazed over the oak table at his two companions.

He watched Bob Evans glance around the room and heard him whisper, "McGill's daughter should warrant a high ransom."

"Janice?" Pierre Lalonde's voice croaked.

Don saw his face blanch and his hands almost knock over his glass.

"You know her?" Bob sounded surprised.

"She and my daughter are friends. Collette manages one of my gift shops and Janice works for *The Integrator.*"

"Damn." Bob furrowed his brows and clenched his fists. "The editor of that magazine is Philomela Nightingale. She's nothing but trouble."

Pierre placed his hands on his lap and slowly shook

his head. "I advertise my three businesses in *The Integrator*. Ms Nightingale is knowledgeable and helpful. She also has a great sense of humor."

Don glanced from Pierre's gentle eyes and relaxed hands to Bob's furrowed brow and clenched fists. He was intrigued. Who was this controversial woman? Why did one man admire her and the other dislike her?

"You obviously don't know her very well," Bob said. "Philomela's stubborn as a mule and snoopy as a terrier. If she starts to worry about a missing employee, she'll cause double trouble."

"Good reasons to drop Plan B—which, of course, is also illegal." Pierre's face blossomed into a smile. "Let's drop Plan A, too."

Don had arrived later than his two companions so hadn't heard about Plan A. He wondered if it was as edgy as Plan B. In all honesty, he couldn't understand why Bob wanted to kidnap McGill's daughter. It wasn't as if their investments with McGill Oil and Gas weren't doing well. Puzzled, he continued to look from one of his buddies to the other.

Bob Davis, a high flying accountant with a quick mind and a forceful personality, dominated the meeting. Pierre Lalonde, a successful owner of two gift shops and one sun-tanning salon, leaned back in his chair, apparently pleased with his rejection of Bob's two plans. Don knew from experience that Pierre liked things straight forward and legal. Bob, it seemed, liked twists and turns that stretched beyond the law.

Glancing nervously around the second level of the

Coyote Lounge, Don glimpsed oak tables and chairs while his eyes focused on nearby patrons. All appeared intent on private conversations.

He could hardly believe it was only a year ago that he'd left his job at Pierre's sun-tanning salon to become a ranch hand. Equally hard to believe was that six months ago he received Uncle Harry's inheritance—a joint-venture partnership with McGill Oil & Gas. His uncle's unexpected gift changed his life. It placed extra bucks in his jeans and put him on a par with sophisticated people like Bob and Pierre. The invitation to attend today's business meeting was based more on his recent windfall than on his financial expertise.

He drained his Canadian Club rye whisky and ginger ale, set his glass on the table and gazed at the two older men. Their subdued ties, button down shirts, and three-piece suits made his neat jeans and cowboy shirt seem overly casual. Having followed cowboy etiquette by placing his white hat on his lap, he fingered it uneasily.

"Service," Bob called and waved his arm in the air.

Lola glided over to the table. "What will you have, Mr. Davis?"

"Two more single malts."

"With water on the side?"

"Right. And a CC and ginger for the cowboy."

Don and Lola exchanged furtive smiles. As she walked away, he admired how her black tunic and tights clung to her slim waist and hips. Pierre's voice stopped his reverie.

"Your cowboy shirt's nice, Don, but aren't you rushing things? The Calgary Stampede doesn't start until Friday."

"These are my working duds, Pierre. I no longer work in your sun-tanning salon. This morning I rode horse-back and moved cattle from one pasture to another." With a mock sneer he added, "On Friday you'll be a cowboy too—an urban one."

Pierre grinned. "Touché."

Bob interrupted their jests by clearing his throat. "I think we should discuss Plan A," he said.

Don wondered if Plan A would involve what's-her-name Nightingale.

CHAPTER 2

With easy momentum, Janice McGill walked toward the house she shared with her dad. She thought of her forthcoming trip and how her employer had referred to it as *Janice's Odyssey.*

"Odyssey is a long eventful journey," Philomela had said "It dates back to Homer's classical account of Odysseus's ten year trip home after the Greeks won the Trojan War."

My trip, Janice thought, *will be much shorter.*

She gazed at red geraniums bordering the cement path and smiled. The bright flowers made her feel like dancing a jig. Conversely, a circular bed of white alyssum and pink petunias fostered a desire to sit down and relax. Colors always cheered or soothed her. Suddenly, they inspired an idea for a magazine article. The idea faded, superimposed by visions of her employer slashing poor grammar and bad syntax.

Philomela Nightingale was not a perfectionist, but she sometimes hovered close to it.

With a touch of whimsy, Janice recalled their first meeting. She had nervously pressed the doorbell of *The Integrator* office then jumped like a cat when a disembodied voice called, "Come on in." Breathing rapidly she had tip-toed into a small vestibule, peeked through an open door at a large desk, above which hung a mass of red hair. The voice said, "Good morning,"

Janice swallowed.

The hair ascended, exposing two green eyes, a nose, a mouth, and the upper portion of a trim figure. The right hand extended. "I'm Philomela Nightingale. You must be Janice McGill."

Janice nodded and took hold of the welcoming hand.

"A hundred thousand welcomes. Have a seat." Their hands separated and Philomela sat down behind her desk. "You have a BA and majored in English literature. You worked on the University year book. Do you have any other writing or publishing experience?"

Janice shook her head and sank onto a straight-backed chair. Her blue eyes met green ones that somehow instilled her with enough confidence to ask a question of her own. "Are you a descendant of Florence Nightingale?"

"Impossible. The lady with the lamp produced no progeny. She was too preoccupied with numerous nursing needs to bother creating children."

Hearing four alliterations, Janice stifled a giggle.

"Would you like to get excellent experience and poor pay here, instead of elsewhere?"

Janice nodded.

"When can you begin?"

"Right now, I guess."

"The office floor needs to be vacuumed. The vacuum cleaner is in the closet over there."

Walking to the closet, Janice wondered if she'd have to scrub floors, too.

The recollection made her smile. It was amazing how quickly the haphazard routines of magazine publishing had become second nature. Her tasks seldom involved vacuuming, only once involved scrubbing floors, and always involved mental stimulation. The publication of each issue provided—to use Philomela's alliterative phrase—"a satisfying sense of success."

After three months, Janice received a small raise. When t*he Integrator* changed from four to six publishing dates a year her salary jumped above the poverty line. A third increase allowed her to save heaps of money for the holiday of a lifetime—*Around The World In Thirty Days*.

Janice gazed at the red geraniums, white alyssum, and pink petunias. The article idea resurfaced in the form of emotional and mental powers of color-healing. Despite Philomela's eagle eye, Janice would start researching it Friday afternoon, after watching the Calgary Stampede parade.

CHAPTER 3

B ob's fingers formed a triangle in front of his nose. Above them, his dark eyes focused on Pierre. "I've given Plan A considerable thought," he said and shifted his gaze to Don.

Under Bob's mesmerising scrutiny, Don squirmed, unaware his movements accentuated his well-developed muscles and slim physique. He was aware, however, of Bob's tall skinniness and Pierre's short portliness and, that at age twenty-six, he was younger, fitter, and better looking than both his companions. Bob's mesmerizing spell ended as Lola set their drinks on the table.

Pierre and Don thanked her and Don's eyes lingered on her departing figure.

"As you know," Bob said, taking control as if presiding over an international business conference, "the purpose of this meeting is to discuss new money-making schemes."

He lowered his head and a shock of black hair fell over his left eye, softening his hawk-like face. "Plan A is an audit. I put a sharp pencil to a legitimate audit and concluded that if it goes to court we have one chance in three to come out ahead. If accounting errors are found in our favor, McGill Oil and Gas will pay the shortfall plus our court costs. If errors are found in their favor, we'll have to pay everything. If no errors are found, we'll still have to pay our audit costs. So you see the odds are against us."

"Spoken like an accountant imitating a lawyer," Pierre said.

Bob ignored Pierre's remark. "A legitimate audit is too iffy. We can't risk it. Myron McGill's accounting department isn't the best, but it's not the worst either. Major errors are unlikely."

"Let's forget the whole thing." Pierre ran his fingers through his hair. "Our joint venture oil investments are doing well. Let's be satisfied with them."

"I'm real happy with mine." Don grinned and it widened as Lola walked past balancing a tray of drinks high in the air.

"How old is Janice?" Bob asked.

"Mid-twenties." Pierre's shoulders slumped, portraying a lack of enthusiasm.

"When can I meet her?" Don paid more attention to Lola than to the conversation.

"You won't have to meet her," Bob interjected. "Not if we pursue a more or less legal audit."

Pierre shifted in his chair and cleared his throat. In a

strained tone of voice he asked, "What do you mean—more or less legal?"

Bob leaned over the table and quietly said, "We'll borrow a couple of files and do some creative accounting. Then we'll return the files to their original locations."

Pierre's eyebrows knit in obvious concern. Don's rose in puzzlement.

"After returning the files," Bob continued. "We'll call for an audit, a legitimate one. We'll innocently ask about the doctored files along with a couple of others as decoys. Lo and behold, the auditors will discover grievous accounting errors. We, the innocent joint-venture partners, will grow irate and demand retribution." Bob leaned back in his chair and the corners of his lips twitched upward.

"Only the actual audit will be legitimate?" Pierre asked.

Bob nodded affirmatively, picked up his glass, and sipped his whisky.

"Doctoring files, to say nothing of theft, is illegal." With a disgusted snort Pierre added, "I'd hate to be your enemy, Bob. You're a bit of an evil genius."

Don watched in awe as the recipient of Pierre's dubious compliment accepted it with a nod of the head. The charming, hawk-eyed man seemed to find little fault with vague words and unethical deeds. In a strange way, Bob reminded Don of his favorite birthday treat—dark devil's food cake hiding under pure white icing.

Was it just four weeks ago that he first met Bob at a lunch organized by Pierre? The three men had enjoyed drinks, dinner, and discussions about their joint-venture partnerships. Don had learned that Bob and Pierre had invested their own hard earned money. He, of course, had received his as a windfall from heaven.

Pump-jacks in east Saskatchewan pumped oil twenty-four hours a day, providing him with a small supplement to his mediocre salary. Thanks to the monthly checks, he was wearing a new pair of brown cowboy boots, a new white Smithbilt hat, and three months ago he started saving his money for the purchase of a one-ton truck. His long term dream, of course, was to buy an acre of land in the beautiful Rocky Mountain foothills.

He gave no thought to the two dry holes his Uncle Harry had helped finance before striking black gold. He simply enjoyed the goods the windfall enabled him to buy and the successful people it brought into his life.

As if accepting that he was an evil genius, Bob's lips smiled, though his eyes did not. Don watched him lean back in his chair.

Pierre mumbled, more to himself than to his companions, "McGill made a lot of money."

Don suspected Pierre was trying to rationalize details of Bob's audit plan. Physically, Pierre's small beady eyes, rotund body, and snorting laugh reminded Don of a pig enjoying a meal. Bob, on the other hand, had the dark head and piercing eyes of a hawk looking for prey. Don's heartbeat quickened and he felt uneasy.

Pierre waved his arm in Lola's direction and she glided over to their table. "Lola, could we have two more single malts with water and another CC and ginger?"

"Right away, Mr.Lalonde." She smiled then glanced at Don.

Don smiled warmly at her. Upon his arrival at the Coyote Lounge, he had invited her for dinner and a movie and she had accepted. Unfortunately, when starting to suggest a specific day and time, he was distracted by the sight of his two business associates. Instead of setting a date with Lola, he patted her shoulder, promised to talk with her later, then walked briskly to the corner table.

Now he watched her curvy figure and gorgeous brown hair float toward the bar. Bob caught his attention by leaning forward.

"I have a plan for the heist," Bob said. With the drama of a stage actor, he paused. Then he whispered, "Don will do it."

"Me?" Don's jaw dropped and he stared at Bob's face. "Pierre knows that, while working at his suntan salon, I didn't steal. I never took an unearned cent in my life." At least nothing much—three days ago he snitched several toonies from a cookie jar at the ranch house. But that didn't count because so far no one had mentioned the loss.

"You won't steal anything." Bob's voice was reassuring and oily smooth. "We simply want you to *borrow* a couple of files. I'll tell you which ones and where to find them. In a short time, you'll end up with extra, well-earned money. Just think of what you can do with it."

Well earned? Don wasn't so sure. He looked into his glass and slowly envisioned himself walking with Lola up a hill on his own foothill acreage. He warmed to Bob's idea. Could a successful company like McGill Oil & Gas Ltd afford to lose a few bucks without hurting anyone? Surely a small deceit on his part was worth obtaining his dream acreage.

"Umm," he murmured. "When would I do it?"

"During Stampede." Bob nodded his head as if the ten-day time frame was self-evident. He smiled and clasped both hands behind his head.

His companions watched Bob so intently they barely noticed Lola replace their empty glasses with full ones.

"Don," Pierre said, "beware of doing anything illegal."

Attending more to Lola's swaying hips as she walked away than to Pierre's remark, Don asked, "Does McGill work harder than the rest of us?"

"Give credit where credit is due," Bob said. "Myron McGill works hard and he's a good oilman. Fortunately for us, he's overly trusting." He moved his hands from behind his head, picked up his single malt whisky, and took a sip. Quietly he said, "Here's the plan. I'll phone and make an appointment to see McGill next week in his office. While we discuss unimportant items, Don will slip into the storage and file room and take the necessary files."

"What about staff?" Don asked. "Won't they see me?"

"Calgary Stampede," Bob said. "Everybody leaves early."

"How'll I get out?"

"When I leave McGill's office I'll whistle, 'How

You Going To Keep Them Down On The Farm?'" He whistled a few bars. "At that point you'll be on your own. Stay hidden and wait for McGill to leave. If the cleaning people arrive, don't worry. They'll think you work there."

"Sounds easy," Don said.

"Nothing can go wrong." Bob's penetrating eyes softened slightly. "Let's get down to the nitty-gritty. When are you free next week?"

"Monday's my regular day off at the ranch."

"I'll phone Myron McGill tomorrow and make an appointment for late Monday afternoon. You come to my office around three and we'll finalize the details."

CHAPTER 4

On Monday morning, Janice McGill clicked print, leaned back in her chair, and listened to the printer hum. She had worked all weekend on the three page article. Not even thoughts of Philomela's critical editing could dampen her feeling of accomplishment.

Her thoughts wandered briefly from the article to her forthcoming odyssey. Then the printer stopped humming and she sat up straight, plucked out the sheets of paper, and, with self-discipline, read them. Grammar and punctuation seemed okay. Clerical errors—or as her dad would say, "clergical" errors—seemed non-existent. Sentences flowed smoothly and made sense. Her article on color-healing was ready to face the world, or, more importantly, her editor.

She put the hard copy inside a used brown envelope, crossed out the original address, and above it wrote, *Philomela Nightingale*. Anticipating unending rewrites, she emailed the article as an attachment to her own computer in the office of *The Integrator.*

Raising both arms above her head, she felt the muscles in her upper back complain. Hunching over the keyboard all weekend had stretched her muscles in only one direction—bad for good posture. She sighed loudly, lowered her arms, and glanced at the Timex on her left wrist. Nine-thirty. Time to go.

ᘒᘒ

An hour later, adorned in her two year old Stampede attire of purple jeans, violet western shirt, tan cowboy hat, tan cowgirl boots, and purse, she strode into the familiar two-story frame house.

The main floor of the house encompassed the business office and working area of the eclectic magazine. Visitors, advertisers, free-lancers, and she—the one permanent employee—wandered in and out of the office at will during business hours. The second floor of the house was out of bounds. It privately housed the magazine's editor/publisher and her petroleum engineer husband, Brent Lark.

Janice's cowgirl boots clacked on the hardwood floor. She poked her nose around the door frame of her boss's office and tossed her cowboy hat onto a nearby chair.

Behind the desk, two green eyes peered over half-glasses. "You're late."

"I am. And with good reason."

"Were you out on the street eating a pancake breakfast? Or were you dancing with urban cowboys?"

Janice shook her head and with dramatic casualness dropped the used brown envelope on top of the desk. "*C'est fini.*"

Philomela lowered her head and Janice suspected she was trying to hide a smile. Sunlight glinted through the window on Philomela's startling red hair as she pulled the manuscript from the envelope. She flipped through all four pages then raised her head and looked intently at her employee. "So now you're an expert on color-healing."

"Of course." In the manner of a Scottish Highland dancer, Janice arched her arms over her head. "I see that my violet cowgirl shirt is helping to soothe your frayed nervous system."

"I used to call that color menopausal mauve, but an outer-fringe shopkeeper in Maui corrected me. Violet, she told me, is a spiritual color."

"She was absolutely right." Janice lowered her arms and leaned toward her boss. "And your blood-red hair, if used positively, will encourage compassion. If used negatively, it will increase a carnal desire, a longing for material things, and a heedlessness of brotherhood and sisterhood."

Philomela blinked and dubiously cocked her head. "That's good to know because right now we have a sisterhood problem. Half an hour ago our temporary help went home sick. She said she suffered from flu, but I diagnosed her illness as a hangover—too much stampeding. You'll have to start assembling this edition."

"No problemo."

"Why do our schools insist on partially teaching French and Spanish to every ignoramus?"

Janice giggled. "Mandarin and Arabic will be our next second languages."

"You're incorrigible."

Janice's tan cowgirl boots clicked through the doorway to the work room. At her desk, she turned on her computer and performed several repetitive tasks that allowed her mind to dwell on her forthcoming trip.

The itinerary for the exotic holiday had been created by Terrific Travel Company who then commissioned Peoples Airlines to supply a jet aircraft with three pilots, three flight attendants, and an engineer. Janice first learned about the trip from her dad who had taken a similar one the year before. So impressed was he with accommodations, food, staff, and tours that when news of another trip arrived he expressed a longing to go again.

"Unfortunately," he said to Janice, "my job of finding and producing the commodity that fuels those airplanes and coaches takes precedence. Maybe you could go."

The idea intrigued Janice. She already had a small savings account at the bank so, with an aim to pay now and fly later, she started to save in earnest. She refrained from purchasing fashionable outfits and accessories and made do with her existing wardrobe. She avoided dining in exotic restaurants with friends, brown-bagged lunches, and ate them inside the office on cold days and outside in a nearby park on warm ones. She ignored expensive gas-guzzling transportation by walking to and from work, an economy that added a bonus of keeping her body fit and trim. A large portion of her salary ended up in the savings account, designed to finance her exciting odyssey. If only the accruing bank interest was hefty, instead of paltry. Oh well, *c'est la guerre.*

Her biggest saving came from living rent-free while enjoying the comforts of home. Fortunately, her dad liked her company and her cooking experiments. The arrangement proved symbiotic.

She often discussed the trip with him. As the departure date drew closer, she sometimes mentioned it to Philomela. Her mentor always responded in a practical manner.

"Keep a journal then write an article about your odyssey for *The Integrator.* Save receipts for income tax. You don't want your partner in Ottawa grabbing too much of your money."

"Why don't you join me?" Janice once asked.

"What? Be your peripatetic partner? I couldn't possibly leave Brent for a whole month."

Janice continued to plan on travelling alone within a group. It would prepare her for the day she moved from the family home to a place of her own. After all, a girl her age couldn't live with her dad forever.

Sitting in front of her computer, she focused on the virtual advertisement for the Coyote Lounge. Concluding that it could be better, she suspected she was turning into a near perfectionist like her boss. She studied the picture of Lola carrying a tray of drinks high in the air and recalled how at the photo shoot she had been amazed at the strength and balance of the girl's wrists, hands, and shoulders. Amazing as they had been, it was Lola's pretty face and figure that would attract customers—especially male ones.

Janice shook her head. What did the layout lack? She printed the advertisement and studied the picture on the sheet of paper.

Unable to determine what was wrong, she tossed the page on the table near her desk. Her back ached and her stomach growled so she changed positions, picked up a glass from her desk, and sipped some water.

In another lifetime, the workroom had been a living room with velour sofas, wingback chairs, and fringed lamps. She knew this because a picture of it hung on the wall. Now the room contained a work table, a desk with a computer, a comfortable office chair, a book case, and three straight back chairs.

The sound of cowgirl boots clicking on the hardwood floor made her look toward the door.

"How's it going?" Philomela asked, walking toward her.

"The Coyote Lounge advert needs work." Janice pointed to the sheet of paper on the table. "Something's wrong."

Philomela surveyed the paper. "Mmm…let's see. The picture of Lola should be enlarged and set to the left of the page. The heading should be bigger and the rest of the print shifted right."

Janice set her water glass on the desk, made the

changes on the computer, then said, "Omigod. That really is better."

Philomela gazed at the monitor. "Lola is such an attractive young girl."

"She was two grades behind me in high school."

"I didn't know that."

"She was a good kid," Janice said. "Capable, kind, and considerate."

"Qualities that make her good in the food and beverage business. How's the advert for Mr. Lalonde's gift shops?"

"It's okay." Janice clicked the mouse and brought up the advertisement.

"He'll be happy with that." Philomela looked up at the ceiling then, with dramatic nonchalance murmured, "I read your article on color-healing. It's outer-fringy."

Janice cringed. *Here it comes*, she thought.

"If there's space, I'd like to put it in the August issue," Philomela continued.

Janice could not believe her ears. She cranked her head around and looked unbelievingly at her boss's face.

"The theme will fit hand in glove with my short bio of a naturopath."

Janice remained speechless.

"I didn't revise any punctuation. Nor did I find any spelling errors."

Basking in her boss's praise, Janice felt her face flush. "An article that requires no editing is a first for me."

"It deserves a celebratory lunch."

"Oh…"

"You're saving money."

"How did you know?"

"You've only mentioned it three hundred times."

Janice hadn't realized she'd been so obsessive. "That often?"

"Perhaps only two hundred and ninety-nine times. I suppose you forfeited fun and frivolity during Stampede weekend in order to complete your article."

"Philomela, your perception is uncanny."

"Don't worry. Lunch is on me. But we must support our advertisers. Do you want to drive to Coyote Lounge or walk to Fourth Street Rose?"

"The weather's beautiful. Let's walk."

༄༅༄

Fifteen minutes later, they strolled through the open door of the restaurant and nearly collided with a group of western-attired young men. Philomela and Janice leaned against the wall so the group could make their way out-side. The last man held his brown Smithbilt hat above his curly brown hair and moved past Philomela. As he eased by Janice, his elbow brushed her bosom.

"Oops. Sorry." With obvious embarrassment, he glanced down at her face then abruptly stopped walking.

She gazed into two gray eyes twinkling beneath shaggy brown eyebrows. She noticed his straight nose and how his brown moustache and beard couldn't quite hide his smiling mouth.

"I hope I didn't hurt you," he said.

"Not at all." Her knees developed an unwelcome weakness, but she managed to say, "This entranceway is very narrow."

"It is. Thanks for letting us pass."

"You're welcome." And like an idiot she added, "Anytime."

The moustache and beard had even less hope of hiding his widening smile. "This is a good restaurant. I've never been here before."

"It's my favorite." Their conversation was incredibly mundane but she wanted it to continue forever.

For a few seconds, they gazed into each other's eyes. Then the young man murmured, "I think my friends have gone on without me. I'd better go."

They moved in opposite directions. Janice, trying for one last glimpse of his pleasing countenance, turned her head. At the same moment, he looked back at her. Their eyes locked and the weakness in her knees increased. He waved his brown hat, placed it on top of his head, and disappeared out the door. She sighed and moved forward. Her knees regained strength.

Normally, she avoided eye contact with unknown males, but for some reason this occasion seemed different. But what did it matter? She'd probably never see him again.

Catching up with Philomela, Janice watched the long denim skirt of the hostess swish toward them. The hostess's friendly smile was as cheery as the provincial wild rose embroidered on each pocket of her white shirt.

"Welcome," she said and led them to a table by the front window. She placed two menus on the pink tablecloth.

"The hostess is wearing the dress-of-the-day," Janice remarked as the long denim skirt swished away. "Or should I say dress-of-the-week."

"Her figure and long blond hair are almost as nice as yours."

Janice giggled. "Do your powers of observation never cease?"

Philomela ignored her employee's jest and looked up at a young waitress whose outfit resembled the hostess's, except her denim skirt stopped mid-thigh.

"Would you like something from the bar?" she asked.

"We're celebrating an important event," Philomela replied. "I think we should have some wine." She looked at Janice and asked, "House white okay?"

"Perfect."

Philomela ordered two glasses of the house Chardonnay.

"Would you like to order lunch now?" the waitress asked.

"We need a minute to menu meander," Philomela said.

Janice saw the waitress's eyes go blank and, apparently, Philomela did too for she explained, "We'd like to study the menu."

The waitress departed and Janice said, "Brent jokes about your overuse of alliteration. But I think it's awesome."

"It's phonetically pathetic. The words just pop out." Philomela scanned the menu then turned her attention to the waitress who was setting two stemmed glasses on the table. "I'd like the Greek salad and garlic toast," she said.

"Soup and beef sandwich for me, please," Janice said. The waitress nodded and again moved away. Philomela picked up her glass, sniffed the bouquet, and took a tiny sip. She nodded appreciatively. "So you're a professional sommelier," Janice said.

"Hardly. But I'd like to propose a toast to your first unedited article."

"I'll drink to that."

They clinked glasses and sipped daintily.

Philomela set her glass on the pink tablecloth. "Your article on color reminds me of how Radiant Red hides my sprinkles of white. Brent likes it. Romantic, don't you think?"

"Hair dye romantic?" Janice giggled. "I don't think so. But Brent is—romantic, I mean. How come he wasn't romantic enough for you to take his name?"

"The magazine was well established before I met him so I kept my surname when we married. If we'd had children, I might have changed it to Lark. As it is, our marriage, our names, and our vocations fit well together. What more could I ask for?"

"For you—nothing. For civilization—a continuation of your exotic genes."

"Flattery will get you everywhere." Philomela smiled pensively. "Did you know my grandmother had second sight?"

"Yes, you mentioned it before. I'm not psychic, but while researching the color-healing article, I ran into a few things that seemed mind-bending."

"Delve into whatever you want, Janice: Astrology, numerology, meditation. Just don't become so airy-fairy that you have no earthly value."

The waitress placed their food on the table and conversation lagged. After a few moments of concentrating on the earthly task of eating, Janice looked over at her mentor. "Do you like Greek salad because of your ancestry?" she asked.

"No, I just like black olives, tomatoes, green peppers, onions, oregano, and feta cheese.

"Do you know anyone else whose name was based on a Greek myth?"

"My sister, Procne. The mythical Procne was turned into a swallow. Philomela was turned into a nightingale."

"I confess to not knowing the entire myth."

"There are at least three versions. All involve lust, rape, revenge, and murder. The story is horrid, but my mother liked the names of the sisters."

"Awesome. My name is so boring. I was named after my Aunt Janice, a spinster school teacher."

Philomela chuckled and glanced at her wristwatch. "Let's forfeit coffee and return to the office. We should leave work early and enjoy a bit of the World's-Greatest-Outdoor-Show."

"I'd love to see the horse barns," Janice said. "Instead, I'll probably end up helping my dad."

Philomela nodded, opened her purse, and paid cash for lunch.

℘℘℘

Outside on Fourth Street, Janice stopped at a florist shop and studied a window display. "Wow," she said, "look at the flowers in that tall glass vase. I'm going inside for a better look." She skipped through the open door of the shop and left her boss standing alone on the sidewalk.

"Hi, Philly."

Hearing her hated nickname, Philomela pivoted and stared at a shiny black BMW convertible parked at the curb. She recognized the driver's shock of black hair and dark piercing eyes. She walked over to the vehicle.

"Bob, you've bought a fancy new car. The accounting business must be good."

"No complaints. How's the magazine?"

"Limping along and paying its way."

"Are you enjoying the Stampede?" he asked.

"So far, I haven't seen much. How about you?"

"I'm going to the rodeo this afternoon." He started the engine. "Take care, Philly."

Philomela grimaced and watched the convertible pull away from the curb.

"Who's the dude?" Janice asked, coming up to her boss.

"He used to advertise in *The Integrator*. I annoyed him a few times by refusing to twist the truth in his accounting adverts. Now he's too busy and too rich to advertise. Like the Greek god, Zeus, he's clever, cunning—and charming when he wants to be."

"Nice car," Janice said as the black convertible eased into moving traffic and sped away.

CHAPTER 5

Philomela sat at her desk, reached inside a drawer, and took out a check book, intending to pay electrical, water, and sundry other bills. Picking up her ballpoint pen, she heard the front door open and shut. She held the pen in midair and listened to footsteps stride across the vestibule floor. Gazing above her half-glasses, she saw a familiar figure appear in the doorway of her office. She smiled, rose to her feet, and extended her right hand.

"Detective O'Malley. What a splendid surprise."

The tall, muscular man took her hand and shook it vigorously. "Hi, Philomela. How are you and Brent doing?"

"Very well, thanks. Right now Brent's in Saskatchewan, completing an oil well. Fortunately it wasn't a dry hole."

"Good. Our cars and planes keep guzzling the black

stuff. Am I too late to run a notice in your August, 'Upcoming Events' section?"

"We're working on the August edition right now."

"The Police Chorus is doing a show at the end of August. Here are the details—date, time, place, etc." He handed her a sheet of paper.

She scanned it and nodded. "I'll give it to Janice right now." She walked to the door of the workroom and saw her employee leaning back in her chair, obviously trying to catch sight of the visitor with the deep, resonating voice. Philomela grinned and handed her the paper. "Can you insert this notice in 'Upcoming Events?'"

"No problemo." Janice took the paper and whispered, "Who's the hunk?"

"Detective O'Malley. He's the spark plug for the Police Chorus. Come and meet him."

Janice leaped to her feet and followed Philomela to her office. After introductions were performed, O'Malley suggested that Janice attend the show.

"Are all the chorus members as good looking as you?" she asked, gazing with admiration at his thick fair hair, pearly smile, and muscular physique.

"Better looking," he replied.

"Then I'll attend for sure." Janice giggled and gazed at his suit and tie. "Don't you wear a uniform?"

"Not as a detective."

"O'Malley is happily married and has two children," Philomela said, purposely pouring cold water on Janice's apparent interest in the man.

After his departure, Janice returned to the workroom

and Philomela stayed in her office to finish paying bills. While writing checks, she mentally weighed the advantages of moving into the modern world and paying bills on line. After the last check was written and stuffed in an envelope, she glanced at her watch.

"Good grief." She leaped to her feet and hurried to the workroom. "Janice, cancel your concentration. You were supposed to leave half an hour ago."

"I'll just finish putting the police chorus notice in Upcoming Events." A few minutes later, she strode into Philomela's office, plunked her tan cowboy hat on her head, and waved her hand. "Farewell, boss. See you Tuesday morning,"

"At five a.m. sharp."

"Dreamer." Janice's face wreathed in a smile. She sashayed to the door and, over her shoulder, said, "Thanks again for the celebratory lunch."

"You're welcome." In Philomela's mind, Janice was the daughter she never had.

CHAPTER 6

Feeling elated about her article, Janice strode briskly past Central Park, turned east on Twelfth Avenue, then entered a glass-and-concrete building. She walked into an elevator and zoomed up to the tenth floor. The moving box stopped, the door slid open, and her cowgirl boots moved silently over the plush carpet of a long corridor. The building seemed as empty as the Stampede Grounds during a winter blizzard.

At the sign of *McGill Oil and Gas*, she opened the door, stepped inside, and gazed at the receptionist's empty chair. No surprise here. Receptionist, secretary, accountants, land personnel, engineer, geophysicist, and geologist would spend part of the week participating in pancake breakfasts, street dances, crazy rides, interesting exhibitions, infield rodeos, chuck wagon races, and evening grandstand performances. Even though cattle ranching no longer ruled the city's economy, locals as well as tourists made the ten-day celebration a huge success. She smiled to herself, thinking of the numerous occasions her dad had said, "Too much stampeding and too little work."

She made her way toward his office and heard the sound of voices. At least one other person besides her dad was still here. She stopped at his open door, knocked on the doorframe, and peeked around the corner.

He saw her and said, "Janice, are you finished work?"

She nodded, entered his office, and looked at a dark-haired man sitting in the chair across the desk from her dad. He unfolded his long legs and politely stood up. Boots with heels, tight denim jeans, and dark cowboy shirt accentuated his tall, slim build.

"Janice," her dad said, "this is Bob Davis. He owns Davis Accounting Firm. He's one of my joint venture partners. Bob, this is my daughter, Janice."

Bob stepped toward her and extended his right hand. "It's a pleasure."

She shook his hand and looked up at his hawk-like face. His dark eyes pierced hers and she felt a chill scamper down her spine. Quickly dropping his hand, she looked over at her dad. "Are you two the only ones here?"

He frowned and nodded. "Real work won't get done until next Monday." A smile replaced his frown and he asked, "Would you have time to do some photocopying for me?"

"Sure," she replied.

"Next year, I'm going to make everyone take ten days of their holidays during the Stampede."

"I've heard that song before," she said and rolled her eyes.

"He sounds tough," Bob said.

"He's a pussy cat." She grinned. "And members of his staff know it."

Bob smiled and lowered his head to one side. A shock of black hair fell over his left eye, making him appear less intimidating and more approachable. His coal black hair, pale skin, dark eyes, and hawkish nose portrayed an elegance that at first had not been apparent. The curve of his full lips promised sensuality that no female could ignore. He leaned toward her.

Automatically, she stepped back. His closeness and height overpowered her and, for some reason, his entire presence was disturbing. Did he exude an air of sexuality? She wasn't sure. Did he give an impression of willful power? She didn't know. But she did know he oozed with magnetic attraction that seemed to bode ill.

Bob turned from her to her dad. "Myron," he said. "You didn't tell me you had such a gorgeous daughter."

"You didn't ask." Her dad's voice was light and easy, but it intensified with his next words. "Bob, is there anything else we should discuss?"

"I don't think so." Bob glanced at his watch. "It's nearing five. I must be on my way. I'll phone you when the Stampede is over and we'll get together for lunch. It's been a pleasure meeting you, Janice. I hope we meet again." Glancing over at Myron, he said, "I'll let myself out." He walked into the hallway and started to whistle.

Recognizing the tune, "How You Going To Keep Them Down On the Farm?" Janice looked her dad a query. "Is he a good friend of yours?" she asked.

"A joint-venture partner. Our only social contact is the company's annual Christmas party."

"What do you want me to photocopy?"

"Farmout and lease agreements. They're right here." He pointed to a pile of documents sitting on top of his desk.

She carried the papers to the accounting area and turned on the photocopier. After it warmed up, she copied three pages of the first document. Then the machine ran out of paper.

She walked across the hall to the storage and file room. The door was shut which surprised her. During working hours it was left open because staff walked in and out obtaining and returning files and office equipment. She turned the knob, opened the door a crack, and saw that the ceiling light was on. Someone must have neglected to turn it off. She opened the door wider.

"Omigod!" she gasped.

An unknown man, wearing a white cowboy hat, stood in front of a filing cabinet. He looked as startled and surprised as she felt. Not knowing what to say or do, she gazed from his clean shaven face to the snaps on the front of his western style shirt and down his jeans to his brown cowboy boots. Along the way, she noted that both his arms were behind his back.

"Who are you?" she asked.

The man raised his right hand and placed it on the side of his head. He blinked as if confused. His fingers scraped the fair hair under the edge of his hat while his left hand remained at his back. "I think I'm in the wrong place," he muttered.

"Do you work here?"

"No."

"What are you looking for?"

"I um…I'm sorry I startled you." He glanced around the small room in apparent dismay then politely took off his cowboy hat.

She could not help noticing how handsome he looked, how his eyes matched his pale blue western shirt, and how his thick, straight, fair hair framed his handsome face. "Do you have business to transact with McGill Oil and Gas?"

"No. I…I'm looking for the law firm of Brown, Jones, and Young."

"Oh." Having gotten over the initial shock of seeing an unexpected stranger, she giggled. "You've risen too high. That office is on the floor directly below this one."

From down the hall, her dad called, "Who are you talking with, Janice?"

"A guy who wants the law firm on the ninth floor."

"What in the world?" Myron marched down the hall and looked through the open door of the filing room. He stared questioningly from his daughter to the interloper. "What's this all about?"

"Sorry, sir. I'm really embarrassed. Too much stampeding, I'm afraid."

Myron studied him. "Young man, let me give you a few words of advice. Drink alcohol less and read signs more."

"Yes, sir."

"Are you sure you understand?"

"Absolutely. Sorry again to have disturbed you." He lowered his head, gave Janice an admiring glance, and walked out of the file room.

Janice and her dad stepped into the hall and watched him put his hat on his head and weave his way unsteadily down the hall and out the main door.

"Strange," Myron said, shaking his head. "Very strange indeed. I didn't hear him come in. How could someone who was lost end up in our filing and storage room?"

"He must have been awfully drunk to close himself in there."

"The door was closed?"

"Yes."

"Stranger and stranger. Did he take anything? Staplers? Pens? Pencils? Files?"

"He didn't seem to be carrying anything."

"Probably not a thief. Just an over-enthusiastic party animal." He again shook his head and muttered, "Stampede Week." He walked back to his office.

Janice re-entered the storage and filing room and noticed the partially open drawer of a filing cabinet. She looked inside, concluded nothing was amiss, and closed it. Dismissing the intruder from her thoughts, she took a package of paper from a shelf, carried it across the hall to the accounting area, filled the paper tray of the photocopier, and pressed the copy button. When the task was finished, she carried the originals and the copies to her dad's office and set them on his desk.

He looked up from the document he had been studying and grinned. "Thanks, Janice, I really appreciate this."

"You're welcome. Anything else I can do?"

He shook his head.

Inside the rectangular box, she zoomed by her lonesome down to the main floor and proceeded to walk home. It was partly uphill, but she was young and healthy so made good time. As usual, she admired the area's lovely gardens and recalled happy times when her mother was alive.

She unlocked the back door, walked to the kitchen, and compared the silence of the house to the silence of her dad's office during the Calgary Stampede. She stopped in front of the refrigerator and took out three lamb chops, some fresh asparagus, and a jar of mint sauce. A few minutes later, while scrubbing potatoes, she recalled the fair haired stranger in the file room.

The illegitimate visitor had no reason to be in the file room and, though he must have been tipsy, he was sober enough to be embarrassed. Strange that he caused her no more discomfort than her dad's legitimate visitor. What was his name? Oh yes, Bob Davis. If she remembered correctly, her dad said Bob owned an accounting business and was a joint-venture partner with McGill Oil and Gas.

Holding a potato in midair, she gazed at it and tried

to visualize the dark eyed man who had looked down from what seemed a great height. Instead of seeing him, she fleetingly saw O'Malley, the handsome police detective. Philomela had been quick to point out that he was happily married with children. Then her mind drifted to Fourth Street Rose and the gray-eyed man who had made her legs feel weak.

What a strange afternoon it had been. In a matter of a few hours she had been in contact with four interesting men, none of whom she knew and none of whom would likely re-enter her life.

CHAPTER 7

Don heard the western music before he reached the dimly lit second level of the Coyote Lounge. Glancing at the musicians playing piano, guitar, and mandolin, he wondered if their gentle tunes would minimize the chance of anyone eavesdropping on secretive conversations. Then, seeing his two investment buddies, he took a deep breath. With an unconscious slump of his shoulders, and a conscious air of reluctance, he walked slowly past the musicians. Reaching the corner table, he sat down, took off his cowboy hat, and placed it on his lap. His blue eyes met Bob's dark ones.

"You didn't succeed," Bob said. "I can tell by the expression on your face."

Intimidated less by Bob's words than by his accusing eyes, Don lowered his gaze to the table. "I found one file right away." Shifting his eyes up to Pierre's, he hoped to receive support. None came, so he sighed and looked over at Bob. "When you started to whistle, I closed the door of the file room to make sure no one would see me and I found the second file. Then, as bad luck would have it, the door opened and in walked a good-looking clerk. I stood with my back against the filing cabinet and managed to drop both files into the open drawer. The clerk was so surprised to see me, she didn't realize what I was doing. I leaned against the drawer and partially closed it. The whole time I stared at her like an idiot."

"What did the clerk look like?" Bob asked.

"She was slim and wore western duds—purple jeans, I think. Her blonde hair was shoulder length."

Bob groaned. "Janice McGill."

"Really? She's a looker."

"Did Myron see you?" Bob asked.

"Yeah. He heard us talking so he came into the file room. I pretended to be a drunk, looking for the law offices on the floor below them."

"That was quick thinking," Pierre said.

Grateful for the compliment of having done something right, Don explained, "On my way up to the tenth floor the elevator door had opened on the ninth floor. I noticed the law firm's sign."

"If Myron saw you," Bob said, "we won't have a second chance to steal files. We'll have to chuck the audit plan."

Don frowned and thought: *Surely Bob meant to say borrow, not steal.*

"Good." Pierre's facial expression registered relief. "I didn't like Plan A from the get-go."

"Damn that girl," Bob muttered. "Why did she have to show up at that specific time? If only she'd come earlier or later." He drained his Scotch whisky and set the empty glass on the table. "We'll have to resort to plan B."

Pierre placed both elbows on the table and pursed his lips. "Bad idea."

Bob seemed not to see or hear him. "I haven't worked out any details for Plan B. Kidnapping won't be easy. It needs more thought." He waved to Lola, who quickly came over to the table. Pointing to the three musicians, Bob complained, "I can't stand that loud noise. The second level of the lounge is supposed to be a quiet retreat."

"Ten days during Stampede is the one exception." She kicked up her left cowgirl boot to show she was part of it.

"Two more single malt whiskies and a CC and ginger," Bob growled.

Watching Lola's retreating figure, Don experienced an unexpected feeling of longing. He wished he hadn't postponed setting the dinner and movie date with her. Oh well, he would do it soon. He shifted position and looked over at Bob.

Bob sat like a statue, his dark eyes closed as though lost in meditation. Don wondered what he was thinking. Finally his eyes opened and he stared darkly at Don.

"Well, Don, what about nabbing Janice? Could you manage it?"

With a lack of self-confidence, Don murmured, "I don't know. She's a looker and she's—"

"A rich looker," Bob said, finishing the sentence. "Where could you keep her...until the ransom money is delivered?"

Silently, Don considered the entire idea. Though kidnapping was serious business, he was confident no one would get hurt. McGill Oil and Gas could afford to lose a few bucks and the acreage in the foothills was still for sale. With a mitt full of cash he could purchase it.

He leaned forward. "There's an old shack in the forest-reserve past the ranch," he whispered. "No one ever goes there. It's pretty dilapidated, but it could easily serve as a summer hideout for a day or two."

"Could you blindfold her and take her there in your truck?" Bob asked.

"Absolutely." Don hoped he sounded more confident than he felt.

"Could you keep her hidden until Myron forks over the money?"

Don nodded. "The shack is hidden in the trees so no one would find us. I'd stress the abundance of cougars and bears in the area. That would make her afraid to run away."

"I don't like it." Pierre shook his head vigorously. "It's too dangerous for Janice. And for Don, too."

"No more dangerous than stealing files," Bob said.

Don felt uncomfortable. Again, had Bob meant borrowing instead of stealing?

Pierre gazed steadily at Don. "Don, kidnapping is a criminal offence—"

"The important thing," Bob interjected, "is that the girl doesn't get hurt."

Don felt insulted that Bob could even think such a thing. "I wouldn't hurt her."

"Don, there's something else to be considered." Pierre continued to gaze at him. "You will take all the risks. You'll be the front man. If you're caught, you'll be blamed for everything."

"I could always say you two made me do it."

"You could say that," Pierre said, "but who would believe you?" Don frowned and Pierre continued, "Give this a lot of serious thought, my boy. If it backfires you could be in deep trouble."

Lola delivered the drinks. The two older men picked up their glasses and took long swigs of the amber fluid. Don gazed at Lola's retreating back, sipped his rye and ginger, and contemplated Pierre's words. Would the money and excitement be worth the risk? He gazed at his silent companions and felt the air grow heavy and oppressive.

Bob broke the silence by telling a stupid blonde joke.

Don realized he was trying to be funny but, like a failed stand-up comedian, his humor fell short. Don smiled weakly.

"Going back to Plan B," Bob said, looking at Pierre, "does Janice have a set routine?"

"Ms. Nightingale allows flexible hours," Pierre said. "As a result, Janice sometimes works at home and sometimes at the office. No set routine."

"I have a strategy," Bob said, holding up one hand. "I'll invite her out for dinner."

"Dinner?" Pierre looked surprised. "Are you trying to rob the cradle, Bob? Or are you just tired of being a happy divorcee?"

Bob ignored Pierre and turned to Don. "Because Myron and Janice saw you in the file room, we'll need to get you a Lone Ranger type mask and a black wig or toque. You'll wear them and hide in the shrubbery outside the McGill residence. When I take Janice home after dinner, you can nab her as she walks from the car to the front door."

Don grinned with slowly growing enthusiasm. "With duct tape, I'll cover her mouth and tie her hands. I'll get her in the truck, blindfold her, and drive out to the shack."

Bob nodded approval. "Then you'll phone Pierre who will phone Myron and in a disguised voice provide him with all the necessary details—the amount of ransom money and where to leave it. Pierre, you'll warn Myron—contact the police and his daughter will die."

Pierre yelped. "Kidnapping is terrible. Murder is too much."

"None of us is prepared to commit murder," Bob said. "But Myron won't know that. I'll phone and invite Janice out for dinner the day after tomorrow. Is Wednesday evening okay with you, Don?"

"Absolutely."

"I'll phone you Wednesday afternoon and we'll decide what time I should bring her home."

Don nodded, feeling nervous yet pleased to be able to redeem himself. Snatching Janice in the dark might be easier than stealing files during the day. Besides, this plan would involve all three of them—he would kidnap Janice and take her to the shack. Pierre would phone Myron and in a disguised voice ask for ransom money. Bob would…What would Bob do? Oh yeah, he'd take Janice out for a nice dinner.

CHAPTER 8

Holding the landline to her ear, Janice nearly fell off her chair. This phone call was the last thing in the world she expected.

Firstly, Bob Davis was a good twenty-five years her senior. Secondly, she was not attracted to him. Thirdly, she figured the feeling was mutual. His departure from her dad's office had given her the impression he considered her another pretty face in a city full of pretty faces.

Yet here he was on the phone, inviting her out for dinner.

"We could go to the Coyote Lounge," he suggested. "They know me there so the service will be good."

"They know me, too. They advertise in *The Integrator*." She cleared her throat and, trying to sound sophisticated, she added, "In fact, we recently did a photo shoot at the restaurant."

"That's settled then. I'll pick you up five minutes ago."

"Omigod!" Her attempt at sophistication dropped to artlessness. "Umm, that's pretty short notice."

"How about forty-five minutes from now?"

She sucked air into her lungs. What should she do? Should she decline his offer rather than admit to being dateless? Was he a harmless, middle-aged man, trying to recapture his youth? Or was he a secret rapist or a serial killer? It had been months since she had been out for dinner, and restaurants during Calgary Stampede were always fun. She expelled a lungful of air.

"Okay," she replied, dropping all attempts at sophistication. "Forty-five minutes will give me time to powder my nose and put on my cowgirl boots." She didn't wear powder, but she did wear cowgirl boots—her bit to help the Calgary Stampede maintain its reputation as the World's-Greatest-Outdoor-Show. If worse came to worst, her pointy toed boots could serve as weapons. "I'll tell Dad to get his own dinner," she said.

"I'm sure he's capable of doing that."

"Actually, he's quite a good cook."

"Great. See you in forty-five minutes."

The phone went dead so she hurried to the kitchen and informed her dad about her sudden and unexpected date with Bob Davis. A faint look of displeasure flashed across his face. He said nothing so she assumed his displeasure resulted from his having to prepare his own dinner.

Dashing upstairs, she recalled how on Monday her

dad had rather abruptly concluded his meeting with Bob. It wasn't as if he had another appointment or that Bob wasn't a legitimate joint-venture partner, it just seemed that something about the man had made her dad uneasy. Or was her imagination working overtime?

She had met Bob only two days ago so she tried to visualize him. She vaguely saw his tall, skeletal frame and his dark piercing eyes. After meeting him, she had thought of him once—while scrubbing potatoes at the kitchen sink. What was there to think about? They had nothing in common, except her dad. They enjoyed no mutual friends or acquaintances and their age difference was considerable. She had no real desire to see him again, either at a large social function or alone on a date. She suspected he felt the same about her. All this should make dinner an interesting experience—for both of them.

She touched her eyelashes with mascara, pierced silver cowboy boot earrings in her earlobes, put on a four year old, ankle-length denim dress with a plunging neckline, and stuck her feet in her tan cowgirl boots. She plunked her tan cowgirl hat on her head and wondered if this dress would adorn her body again during the remaining days of the Stampede.

Hearing the zoom of a car, she peeked out her bedroom window. A black BMW convertible pulled to a stop in front of the house. Where and when had she recently seen a similar vehicle? No place or occasion came to mind. She watched Bob Davis get out of the car and stride with surprising vigour between the red geraniums up to the house. She heard the doorbell ring, briefly studied herself in the full length mirror, and then dashed downstairs. Slowing her pace she stopped at the front door and nonchalantly opened it.

"You're very prompt." With a dramatic flourish, she glanced at her wristwatch. "Forty-five minutes precisely."

"Ah, the beauty of cellphones." His eyes swept from her hat down to her boots and up again. "But a cellphone's beauty cannot compare with yours."

She had not expected him to have a sense of humor. Maybe the evening would be fun, as well as interesting.

"Cellphones have other advantages," he said. "They save time and money. Both of which are valuable. I consider myself lucky that you weren't busy tonight. Are you ready?"

She nodded, turned to the inside foyer and called, "G'night Dad."

"Goodnight. Have a good time."

He did not make an appearance, which was unlike him. Usually he chatted with her dates and made them feel welcome. He also made them aware that his one and only daughter should be treated like a lady.

Janice felt Bob's hand gently cup her elbow. Like an old-fashioned gentleman, he guided her to the black convertible and opened the passenger door. After she eased inside, he closed the door and walked around the front of the car to the other side.

He drove within the speed limit then slowed down to twenty kilometres at the area once known as Electric Avenue.

People clustered in groups on the sidewalks and three rickshaws waited curbside for passengers.

"Look at the line-ups," he said. "Too many people and not enough food outlets. Coyote Lounge will be better."

୧୨୧୨

They left the BMW in a parkade and walked to Bob's favorite watering hole. At the top of the stairs they stopped, appalled. At least twenty people stood waiting for a table.

"There's Lola." Janice waved at her and the girl responded by gliding over to them. "Lola," Janice said, "you should see the advertisement layout. That picture of you is awesome. It's bound to attract customers, especially the masculine variety."

"At the moment, we don't need more customers." Lola glanced around at the lineup of people then looked at Bob with an expression of sincere apology. "Mr. Davis, as you can see we're jammed to the rooftop. I hate turning away good customers. If you come back in an hour the crowd might be less."

Bob said nothing, took Janice's arm, and turned sharply toward the stairs.

"Lola," Janice said, glancing back at her. "It's good to see you again."

Outside, Bob asked, "How do you know Lola?"

"I told you earlier. The Coyote Lounge advertises in *The Integrator*. We recently took pictures of Lola carry-

ing a drinks tray for the advertising display. She's a natural model. Besides, I knew her in high school."

"As they say, it's a small world. Well, what will we
do now? How about Buzzards?"

"I've never been to Buzzards."

"Good. That's where we'll go."

They walked a block and a half and entered the restaurant. Bob led the way around attractively placed bales
of hay out to the patio. "The evening's warm," he said.
"There's no wind so we'll be comfortable out here."

"As everyone knows," Janice said, "Calgary has two
seasons—winter and Stampede week."

They sat at a table and hardly had time to glance
around before a waiter, wearing blue jeans and cowboy
shirt, stopped at their table and asked if they would like
something from the bar.

Bob looked questioningly at Janice. "Beer okay?"

"Sure. It's the Stampede drink."

"A pitcher of beer," he said to the waiter.

When the pitcher and two pilsner glasses appeared
on the table, Bob looked up at the waiter and ordered a
vegetable platter with dip and a plate of barbeque ribs.
The young man nodded and disappeared. Bob picked up
the pitcher, poured the amber fluid into both glasses, and
set the pitcher back down on the table. He raised his
glass.

"Cheers, Janice. Happy Stampede."

"Cheers." She clinked her glass against his then
sipped the cool liquid. "It's amazing how refreshing beer
can be on a warm day."

"You've probably had your fair share this week."

"This is my first. I had a celebratory lunch with my boss on Monday and we each drank a glass of wine."

An ear-piercing screech prompted him to turn his head toward a small stage. Looking back at Janice, he said, "One doesn't have to go to Electric Avenue to be electrified."

She giggled. "The performer's electric guitar does the job."

They listened to the entertainer tune his guitar and, when the screeching stopped, his musical skills became apparent. They nodded approval and listened to a song about being lonesome and then to a happy rendition of "You Are My Sunshine." During the latter tune the entire atmosphere brightened. Urban cowboys and cowgirls joined in the singing and many leaped onto a postage-size hardwood square and danced.

"Who needs to go away for a holiday?" Bob asked.

"Ten days of happy decadence takes its toll," she replied. "A holiday is needed after Stampede."

"Employers have to provide pay checks even though less work gets done. I'm lucky because I employ three older ladies who only attend the evening grandstand performance." He leaned back in his chair and smiled. "Speaking of holidays, do you take one during the summer?"

"No." She sat upright and returned his smile. "However, come October I'm going on an exciting trip."

"Two weeks?"

"Thirty days." She grinned and added, "I can't take any longer."

"Because you're indispensable?"

"Because my money will run out." Bob quizzically cocked his head, so she explained, "I've avoided the Stampede this year because I'm saving money for the holiday of a lifetime."

"I see. And where are you going on this holiday of a lifetime?"

"Around the World."

He stared at her briefly then asked, "Airplane or ship?"

"Airplane. Terrific Travel organized the trip. Dad went on it last year. He still raves about it."

"Is your dad helping you finance it?"

"Indirectly." She grinned. "I clean house for my rent and cook food for my groceries. It saves me a heap of money."

"Let's hope oil prices don't drop any lower. That could affect your dad's income."

"I'm glad nothing like that stopped Dad from going on the trip last year. It was the best thing that's happened to him in four years."

Bob gazed at her, obviously puzzled.

"He was awfully depressed after mom died," she said.

Bob lowered his head and a shock of hair fell loosely over one eye. He looked at her with a sympathetic expression. "I'm sorry. I'd forgotten."

"He still misses her. But thanks to that trip he's starting to enjoy life again."

"No lady friend?"

"He's fifty-six years old." Realizing Bob was close to her dad's age, she put her hand over her mouth. "I suppose that's not too old…"

"Not too old at all," Bob assured her. He grinned, picked up the pitcher, and topped their glasses. "I'd like to go around the world with you."

For a few seconds she felt self-conscious. Was he serious? No, he was kidding.

"You going alone?" he asked.

"Alone with fifty other people."

"You'll have a single hotel room?"

"Yes."

"You might be able to persuade me to join you." His smile oozed with charm.

Confident he was speaking in jest, she giggled. His dark eyes gleamed in a friendly way, not sharp or mesmerizing, and Janice suddenly remembered where she had first seen him. It was not in her dad's office. It was after her celebratory lunch with Philomela. He was the dark haired man in the black BMW convertible, the man who Philomela compared to the Greek god, Zeus—clever, cunning—and charming when he wanted to be.

Janice's recollection faded as vegetables and ribs arrived. The beer pitcher was empty and Bob ordered another one.

"I can't drink anymore beer," Janice said.

"You'll want it to cool the ribs. They're spicy hot."

Laughter rang loudly near the patio entrance and a foursome dressed in western gear headed toward them. They greeted Bob and gazed questioningly at Janice. He introduced her and after a bit of small talk all four made their way to an empty table.

"Bob," another voice said, "are you stampeded out?"

Janice looked up at two newcomers. Much to her surprise, she recognized Mr. and Mrs. Lalonde.

"Not yet, Pierre," Bob replied.

"You've got stamina, my boy. More stamina than I've got."

"I'm younger than you."

Pierre burst out laughing then turned and greeted Janice. He asked if she was still enjoying her job at the magazine and she replied affirmatively.

"Janice is a friend of our daughter's," Mrs. Lalonde said to Bob, unaware that at the Coyote Lounge Pierre had already explained the relationship.

"Bob and I are joint-venture partners with your dad," Pierre said to Janice, unaware that she already knew it. "We're happy with the investment. Your dad is a good oil finder."

Having heard that compliment before, she nodded and smiled. The conversation moved to Collette's job in the gift shop. A fresh pitcher of beer was delivered to the table then the Lalondes said goodbye and joined their friends.

Bob refilled both glasses while Janice nibbled a crisp cauliflower. After biting on a sparerib she sputtered. "Ooh, spicy hot." She heeded Bob's warning and took a long drink of beer to cool her mouth and throat. In what seemed a short time, the spareribs disappeared and the pitcher emptied. She had drunk far more than she normally did, possibly because Bob kept topping up her glass, or possibly because the food was so hot. Maybe because Bob was a charming companion who made time flow quickly. He consumed more alcohol than she did and doubtless absorbed it better because he had larger bones and more flesh.

The decibel rate on the patio increased so it was almost a relief to leave Buzzards. Inside the quiet car, Bob turned on the ignition and glanced at his watch.

"I think we should stop at the Cannery and listen to a bit of jazz. It will be a change from all that western music." Before she could point out her need to be at work at eight o'clock next morning, he said, "We won't stay long. Fifteen or twenty minutes."

He drove the car from the parkade and, a few minutes later, stopped at a curb near the Cannery. Inside the restaurant, he ordered a brandy and Janice ordered coffee.

"Put Drambuie in the coffee," Bob told the waitress. Janice tried to negate the order but he insisted. "It'll help you sleep."

Janice doubted that theory so, after the waitress brought the coffee, she sat back and sipped it gingerly. The taste of liquor was evident. The band started to play a jump jive number and it was so lively, she felt an urge to leap up and dance.

Glancing at her escort, she realized he felt no such

urge, so she tapped her feet and bobbed her head in time with the music.

True to his word, twenty minutes after arriving, Bob drained his glass and suggested they leave. She stood up, leaving most of the coffee and Drambuie in the mug. If Bob noticed, he said nothing. He seemed sober, but because he had imbibed so much she offered to drive.

"I'm fine. Besides, it's not far."

He drove the BMW carefully up the hill, passed a parked truck, and stopped in front of her house. Though he had driven as well as lots of non-drinkers, she felt relieved to get home without experiencing an accident or police interference.

"Thanks for a lovely evening," she said, smiling at him. "It was fun." She opened the car door and stepped outside.

"Goodnight, Janice. I enjoyed your company."

She half expected him to escort her to the door but, as his car eased from the curb and slowly drove down the street, she walked between the red geraniums toward the house. A rustle of leaves on a lilac bush caught her attention. No breeze stirred the air so she stopped in wonderment and stared at the moonlit foliage.

"Anybody there?" she asked.

No response.

Tabby, she thought. *The neighbour's cat is out hunting.* She stepped over a geranium and moved on the lawn toward the lilac bush. Suddenly, the front yard blazed with light. Startled, she looked at the porch. The door opened and her dad stepped outside.

"You're home," he said. "Did you have a pleasant evening?"

"It was fun. What are you doing up so late?"

"I fell asleep in front of the TV. Car lights shone in the window and woke me up. I figured it must be you and Bob."

"He just left. Are you spying on me?"

"Perhaps a little."

She went up the front steps and stopped beside him. "We ate at Buzzards then listened to a jump-jive band at the Cannery. They were good."

"I'd forgotten about that jazz group."

"You'd like it—" She turned toward the lilac bush. "Did you hear that?"

"It's just Tabby hunting for mice."

She chuckled, glanced one last time at the lilac bush, then went inside the house. Her dad followed and turned off the outside light.

CHAPTER 9

Don's spirits were low. He shuffled up one step at a time to the second level of the Coyote Lounge. His eyes adjusted to the subdued lighting and he looked at a new musical group on the small stage. A pianist tinkled the ivories, a guitarist strummed a guitar, and a contortionist hit the drums. Electronic equipment made the trio sound louder than a seventeen piece big band—too noisy even for Don, and he liked loud music.

Spotting his two cohorts sitting at the table at the far end of the room, he wanted only to turn around and run down the stairs.

He hesitated a moment then thrust his shoulders back and moved forward. Carrying a heavy weight of reluctance, he slumped into an empty seat across from Bob. He nervously took off his white hat, set it on his lap, and silently looked down at it.

The music stopped and, in the reign of silence, Bob

growled, "Don, your body language tells me you failed again."

Don raised his eyes and sighed. "Sorry, Bob. There was nothing I could do about it."

"What went wrong?" Bob abruptly turned to Lola who had stopped at their table. Gruffly he said, "Two single malt whiskies with water on the side. Make mine a double. Rye and ginger for the cowboy."

"Coming right up, Mr. Davis." Lola glanced with concern at Don then gave him a tentative smile and departed.

Bob's eyebrows knit together. "Well, Don, what went wrong this time?"

"I almost got caught."

"By whom?"

"Janice's dad."

Bob's right hand slammed his forehead. His flashing dark eyes reminded Don of a wild stallion's.

"Don't be too hard on the lad," Pierre said.

Ignoring Pierre, Bob glared at Don. Then he cleared his throat. "Everything was going perfectly. I got Janice to drink more beer than she should have so she'd be easier to control. I left her standing alone on the curb outside the house at the predetermined hour and drove off, figuring you'd nab her. Were you not at the right place at the right time?"

"I was hiding behind a lilac bush when she got out of the car. I think she heard me brush against some leaves and, by the light of the moon, she came toward me. Everything was perfect. I made ready to leap out and grab her when the whole front yard lit up like a ballpark. Myron McGill stepped out on the front landing. He told Janice he had been dozing in front of the TV when car headlights woke him up." With a note of satisfaction, Don added, "Your headlights, Bob." He paused dramatically then continued, "They chatted about a jazz band at the Cannery then walked into the house and turned off the light. There I was—empty handed, except for a roll of duct tape, an eye mask, and a tight fitting black toque."

"Damn Myron." Bob shook his head like a dog worrying a rag doll. "It could have worked out so well."

"It was bad timing on Myron's part," Pierre said. "It wasn't your fault, Don." He reached over and gave Don's hand a pat. Then he said, "I didn't like the idea anyway. We'll just forget it."

But Don didn't forget it. The dream of owning a parcel of land in the foothills was becoming more and more important. "Maybe we could go back to the audit idea," he suggested.

"Myron and his daughter saw you in the file room so that won't work a second time." Bob pursed his lips. "More importantly, Stampede is the only time to get inside the office unobserved. Next week the staff will be conscientious to a fault. Another attempt to steal files would be pointless. Too many people will be compensating for their laxness during Stampede."

Don and Pierre remained silent.

"Since Myron and his daughter didn't see you last night," Bob said, "we could try a revised plan, a different kidnapping approach."

Like a rider bucked off a Brahma bull, Don prepared to move sideways. How could a revised plan possibly succeed?

"I have a new idea," Bob announced, looking pleased with his brilliance. "Janice is planning a trip around the world."

"That doesn't sound promising." Don slumped in his chair.

Bob studied Don for several seconds. "She's travelling alone with a tour group in October. That's about two and a half months from now. She'll be gone thirty days. Here is Plan C." He gently tapped his temple with his right forefinger and smiled. "Before I develop the details, do either of you have any other suggestions? Something we could do before October?"

Don shook his head.

"I'm against any plan that's illegal." Pierre said.

Ignoring Pierre, Bob focused on Don. "In two months, Janice will forget the drunk in the file room. If you wear different clothes, dye your hair brown, and grow a moustache and beard, she'll never recognize you. You could go around the world on the same tour as Janice."

Don's eyes expanded to the size of saucers. "I've never been off the North American continent," he said.

"That will add to your adventure." Bob smiled. "At the first opportunity, you'll nab Janice and hole up with her in a hotel room. Myron will pay the ransom money quickly because he'll be anxious to get his daughter out of a foreign country and back home."

"The plan is too dangerous, the trip is too costly, and kidnapping is illegal." Pierre leaned back in his chair, stared at his two companions, then watched Lola place fresh drinks on the table.

Bob paid her with cash and, as she walked away, he turned to Don. "You've always wanted to travel, haven't you?" he asked.

"Well, sort of." In truth, Don had never thought about it. All he wanted was a foothill acreage.

"Could the income from your uncle's investment pay for a holiday?"

Don thought a moment. "Well, I've saved a bit to help buy a new truck. I could use that, I suppose."

"Pierre and I could contribute a few bucks, just to help out. When the kidnapping is completed, we'll divide the ransom money in three. We each should receive more than three hundred thousand dollars."

"You're going to ask for a million?" Don gulped.

"Maybe we should ask for more," Bob said. "I'm sure Myron's daughter is worth it to him."

"A million is a lot of dough." Don figured his third would pay for the entire foothill acreage.

"What would you do with your share, Bob?" Pierre did not wait for a reply. With unusual sarcasm he asked, "Pay alimony? Set up a mistress?"

Bob ignored Pierre and gazed intently at the potential kidnapper. "This morning I phoned the travel company and learned that food, hotel rooms, and most tours and tips are included in the initial price. You won't need to fork out much money after the main trip is paid for. Unless, of course, you want to buy fancy drinks and souvenirs."

For Don, the mention of hotel rooms, tours, and fancy drinks put things in perspective. Until then he had been unable to imagine flying, eating, and sleeping around the world. It had been too far beyond his dreams, much like an inexperienced astronaut soaring through outer space. Now he could actually imagine himself sitting in a plane and sleeping and eating in fancy hotels.

"Do you want to make your own arrangements?" Bob asked, as if his suggestion had already been agreed upon. "Or do you want me to do it?"

"Well, I don't know."

"I'll contact Terrific Travel Company for you. By the way, the trip is called Around the World in Thirty Days."

"Awesome." Don's eyes were wide and he felt flabbergasted.

Pierre pursed his lips and said nothing.

Bob raised his glass, drained it, and beckoned to Lola. He ordered refills then turned to his companions. "Maybe we should hire someone as backup for Don. If something goes wrong, two heads are better than one. But that, of course, would mean a four-way split."

Don tried to calculate if his share of a four-way split would be large enough to buy the acreage.

"A three-way split is better," Bob said and smiled at Don, as if the deal were finalized. "You'll have thirty days to do the deed. When you have her locked up, phone Pierre and he'll take it from there."

Lola set the drinks on the table and Pierre said, "I'll

buy this round." He handed her his credit card.

When Lola's business transaction with Pierre was finished, she gave Don a lingering, somewhat puzzled glance. He responded with a nervous smile, watched her walk away, then sat back and listened to the music. The tune ended and the guitarist announced a twenty minute break.

"Thank god," Bob said. "Now we'll get some peace and quiet." He leaned over the table toward Don. "We still have lots of time to plan various strategies. But we might as well think about some right now. A gun will be too difficult to get past airport security. Instead, you should have a knife."

Shocked, Don stared at Bob. "Why would I want a knife? Let alone a gun?"

"As a threat, that's all. The sight of it would make her go where you want her to go, do what you want her to do. It would encourage her to be quiet."

"This is crazy," Pierre muttered. "He'll never get a knife through airport security."

"He'll pack it in his suitcase, not in his carry-on. Or he could buy a knife during the trip at a souvenir shop." Bob studied Pierre a moment then took a long sip of whisky. Setting his glass gently on the table, he turned to Don. "The blade doesn't have to be much larger than a fingernail file." Gazing at the young man's glassy-eyed expression, he quickly explained, "The knife is only for show. You won't use it."

"I won't have it on the plane."

"You won't need it on the plane. You might need it

as a minor threat in a hotel or on a sight-seeing tour. Or wherever you decide circumstances are right for kidnapping."

"I couldn't use it anyway," Don said. Then he thought of the other problem. "What if she recognizes me? She stared hard at me in the file room."

"As I said earlier, brown hair, moustache, and beard will change your appearance. And if you don't dress like a cowboy, she's even less likely to recognize you."

"Cowboys go on trips, too, you know." Don suspected he sounded more petulant than he intended.

"Of course, they do," Bob said. Then as if soothing a fussy baby, he added, "You were wearing western gear when Janice saw you in the file room. Clothes, as well as facial hair and hair color, can change a person's appearance. A casual outfit of shorts and bright shirt or a preppy look with button down shirt and tie will make you look entirely different."

"You make him sound like a buyer of exotic trivia for a gift shop," Pierre murmured.

Bob's eyes lit up. "Good suggestion, Pierre."

"What places do I visit?" Don asked, starting to feel a touch of enthusiasm.

"Janice mentioned Kuala Lumpur and Kathmandu," Bob replied.

"Never heard of them. Where are they?"

"Somewhere in the far east. The weather will be warm. You'll get brochures and information from the travel agency."

The trip sounded like something in another universe.

Don's touch of enthusiasm grew. It was almost as exciting as riding a Brahma bull.

"Janice is a nice girl," Pierre murmured. "Take good
care of her."

"Absolutely."

CHAPTER 10

It was late in the afternoon when Janice stood by Philomela's desk, leafed through a pile of snail-mail, and picked up a large envelope addressed to Ms. McGill. In multi-task fashion, she opened it while describing her date with Bob Davis the previous evening.

"We listened to jazz at the Cannery and ate dinner at Buzzards. We couldn't get in the Coyote Lounge because it was too busy. I told Lola that her picture would bring in new customers. Mind you, last night they had more customers than they could handle."

She pulled colorful brochures from the envelope and flipped them like a deck of cards. "Wow," she exclaimed. "Fiji, Australia, Indonesia, Malaysia, Nepal, Seychelles, Jordon, Turkey, Austria, and Ireland. A real geography lesson—better than a classroom lecture. It's so cool."

"Sounds hot to me," Philomela said. "Except for Austria and Ireland.

"I wasn't referring to temperatures," Janice chided. Gazing at two more pictures, she said, "It's so thrilling. I can't believe I'm going to visit the exotic cities of Nadi, Perth, Bali, Kuala Lumpur, Kathmandu, Victoria, Aqaba, Istanbul, Vienna and Dublin. They used to be nothing but vague names on a map and now they're coming to life." She tossed a picture on Philomela's desk. "This is Petra, a ruin in Jordan. It's one of the new Seven Wonders of the World."

Philomela picked it up and stared at a building carved into a colorful mountain. "It's more interesting than listening to you rant about saving money."

Janice giggled. "Why don't you come with me?"

"*The Integrator* has to be published in October and I can't leave Brent for a whole month."

"Maybe he'd like to come."

"Perhaps."

Janice raised her eyes and stared at her boss. Had she heard correctly? Was Philomela actually contemplating going on the trip?

❧❧❧

Next morning, Janice hunched over her keyboard, putting final touches on the August edition when Philomela walked into the workroom.

"Brent declined," she announced. "An oil well is scheduled to be drilled in early October and it will need his close attention. However, he suggested I travel around the world without him."

Speechless, Janice almost fell off her chair.

"Four weeks is a long time to be apart," Philomela mused.

Janice regained her voice. "I'd be thrilled to have you as a travelling companion."

Philomela nodded her head.

☙☙☙

Three weeks later the topic resurfaced. Again, Janice sat at her computer. This time she held her breath as Philomela verbally pondered the timing of the trip.

"The magazine's publishing deadline is the first of October. I have to be here to make sure distribution goes according to schedule."

"The magazine," Janice said, "could be sent out a day or two before we leave. After our return we'll have a whole month to finalize the next edition."

Philomela bit her lower lip and looked pensively at her employee. Janice reached over to the worktable, took a brochure from the envelope and tossed it in the air.

Philomela caught it then read aloud. "The Captain's Cocktail Party will be held in the Shangri-La hotel in the city of Kuala Lumpur in the country of Malaysia." Her eyes rested on pictures of exotic foliage, modern high-rise buildings, beautiful people, and delectable food.

Recognizing a note of longing in her mentor's voice, Janice said nothing. Peripherally, she watched Philomela gaze at other brochures. She kept her tongue silent by concentrating on her computer and googling *Philomela*.

Up came a few versions of the Greek myth. She learned that the mythological Philomela and her sister Procne were born in Athens. Procne married King Tereus of Thrace who had a son, Itys. The king wearied of his wife so he hid her away, plucked out her tongue, and married her younger sister. Unable to talk or write, Procne wove the story into a piece of tapestry and a faithful servant delivered it to her sister. Appalled, Philomela freed Procne, helped her kill Itys, then cook and feed him to his father for dinner. When the king discovered the ghastly deed, he tried to kill both girls, but the gods on Mount Olympus took pity on them and turned all three into birds. Procne became a swallow, Philomela a nightingale, and King Tereus a hawk forever chasing them.

Gazing at the monitor, Janice moved her tongue around her mouth and licked her lips. *How could one manage without a tongue?* Not having an answer, she looked at Philomela who was replacing the brochure in the envelope.

"I just brought *Philomela* up on my computer. Now I know the story of your namesake."

"Grim and ghastly, isn't it."

"That's an understatement. Procne and Philomela were murderers." Janice stared at her mentor. "Why in the world did your parents base their daughters' names on such a horrid story?"

"My mother claimed the girls acted under duress. More importantly, she liked the names and thought Philomela fit nicely with her married name—Nightingale."

"Murder doesn't fit your persona."

"Well, I was involved with two murders on the island of Maui."

"Unlike your namesake, you were on the correct side of the law."

"I'm the inverse of the original Philomela." She looked up at the ceiling and, in a soft tone of voice, surprised Janice by saying. "Last night, Brent admitted he would like to heli-ski for a week in January. He figures a world trip would be a fair exchange."

Janice's mouth dropped.

"In eleven years, we've never taken separate holidays." Philomela said.

Janice moved her tongue against the roof of her mouth and swallowed. "Would you rather heli-ski down a steep cliff or fly in comfort around the world?"

"The latter, of course. I'm not daring and dauntless like Brent."

"Anyone who could start *The Integrator* from scratch must be daring and dauntless." Janice grabbed the envelope, pulled out another brochure, and handed it to her boss.

"I could cash an RRSP to pay for the trip." Philomela gazed at a glossy photograph of the Down-Under Winery. "For a similar amount, Brent could pay for a heli-ski week plus buy a second-hand Jaguar he's been lusting after."

"You want Brent to be happy." Janice emphasized the point by adding, "Being my travelling companion will give him the perfect excuse to splurge on a week of heli-skiing, plus buy an old Jaguar."

Philomela smiled. "He thinks an organized tour will prevent me from getting involved with the sleazy side of life."

Janice burst out laughing. "You mean he doesn't want you to get involved with another murder."

"True." Looking wistfully at her employee, she said, "But the tour's probably fully booked."

"I talked with the travel agent yesterday. There are three airplane seats left. Hotel rooms are no problem because you could share with me. You'd be doing me a favor. Double occupancy is cheaper per person than single occupancy."

"Could we stand rooming together?"

"Of course." Janice stood up and gazed directly at Philomela. "Let's think of what must be done. You need a Visa to get into Nepal. Do you have a valid passport?"

Philomela nodded. "While insanity reigns, give me the travel agent's phone number. Don't ever accuse me of being deaf to verbal persuasion."

During the next two weeks, they bounced plans off each other and every day excitement increased. Snail-mail documents arrived, giving specific dates and times of arrivals, departures, hotels, and tours that were included in the package price. Optional tours would cost extra. Janice signed up for all included tours plus a few optional ones.

"I look forward to the optional tour of the Down-Under Winery," Philomela said, ticking off most of the same tours as Janice. "I don't think I'll take the boat trip to the small island near Fiji. After flying over the Pacific,

I suspect jet lag will get the best of me. I'm longer in the tooth and less resilient than you."

"That's okay. I'll take that tour all by my lonesome."

CHAPTER 11

Three days after receiving the travel documents, Janice accepted an invitation from Bob Davis for dinner at the Rancher's Pub. She knew it would be an interesting evening, not just because Bob was an intriguing companion, expecting only youth and scintillating conversation from her, but because she had never been to that particular pub before.

Sitting across the table from him, she smiled as he asked how her holiday plans were progressing. "Super," she replied. "I found a travelling companion." Surprised to see his lips form a thin line and his brows furrow, she wondered what had annoyed him.

"Who is your travelling companion?" he asked.

"My boss, Philomela Nightingale. She's a good old stick, a bit outspoken at times, but lots of fun." In jest, she added, "Maybe you should join us."

"Could I handle travelling with two lovely women?"

He lowered his head and a shock of black hair fell over one eye, softening his facial expression.

"Bob, you're too smooth by half." Glancing around the room, she said, "Look, one wall displays ranch brands and another is filled with pictures of cattle, horses, and cowboys. No wonder the place is called Rancher's Pub."

Bob turned the conversation back to her trip. "Will you and Philomela take all the optional tours?"

"How do you know about optional tours?"

"Oh…well, I've looked into organized trips before. Most have a few optional tours."

"I suppose they do. Philomela intends to skip the first one—a boat tour from Fiji to the small island of Mana. She thinks the weather will be hot and she'll be too tired after the long flight."

"It's a good idea to go on separate tours occasionally," Bob said. He looked so wise and agreeable that she paid close attention to his next words. "You don't want to get sick of each other's company. Familiarity can breed contempt."

She found Bob's apparent concern about her plans and personal welfare flattering. This personality trait had been unapparent on the previous date.

Later, as she made her way to the necessary room, she gazed at other customers and found their relaxed attitudes reminiscent of patrons at Fourth Street Rose. The lunch celebrating her color-healing article came to mind as did Philomela's mention of disagreements between herself and the owner of the black, BMW convertible. If she remembered correctly, the trouble had started with his accounting adverts in *The Integrator*. Janice washed her hands at the sink and suddenly realized Bob had never acknowledged knowing Philomela. She wondered why.

Was it because he had bad memories of their disagreements? Or had he simply forgotten them? Maybe he suspected Philomela disapproved of his relationship with her young employee.

The latter certainly could be true. Philomela had once remarked about her dates with Bob by stating the obvious: "Janice, there's a large age gap between you and Bob Davis."

Her reply had also stated the obvious. "At least twenty-five years. But it doesn't matter. We enjoy dinner and each other's company. Nothing more."

"He's divorced."

"I didn't cause it."

Her boss had said no more, apparently knowing when to zip her lip.

Drying her hands and staring at her reflection in the mirror, Janice wondered if Philomela's only concern had been age difference. Did she think their relationship involved more than exchanges of anecdotes and listening to each other's views on numerous subjects?

Bob was worldly and experienced. He obviously basked in showing off her youth to his middle-age friends. Strange how his friends often appeared at each watering hole.

Males seemed envious of him and women frequently glanced at her with suspicion. She knew the January-June situation flattered his ego. She doubted he wanted anything more.

Back at the table, she verbally compared the Rancher's Pub to the Coyote Lounge. In the middle of her dissertation, Mr. And Mrs. Lalonde came by and Mr. Lalonde asked about her trip. She informed him that Philomela was joining her. He seemed more pleased than she would have expected. She asked if his tanning salon was as busy as ever.

Mr. Lalonde shook his head. "Too much talk of skin cancer."

Because of a previous dinner reservation, they declined Bob's offer of buying them drinks.

ოჯო

Later, at home in bed, Janice wondered about the amount of alcohol Bob consumed. One glass of wine usually lasted her all evening while he drank three or four glasses of whisky. Was he trying to deplete healthy liver and brain cells as well as lessen the contents of his wallet? If she paid for that many drinks her Around the World Odyssey would be unaffordable.

She often felt like the proverbial outsider, mainly because Bob and his friends were older. Once she tried to keep up with their drinking ritual and she became dozy and rather incoherent. Falling asleep in a restaurant was not her idea of a good time. Because Bob and his friends seemed immune to this problem, they tried to encourage her to drink more than she could handle.

"Eat more, Janice, and you'll hold your liquor better," Bob once said at the Coyote Lounge.

Overhearing him, Lola had whispered, "I'll dilute your white wine with water."

She rolled over and smiled. Lola had saved her from experiencing more than one hangover.

CHAPTER 12

The last day of September, and all had been done that could be done. Autumn breezes had cooled the temperature and, in the manner of cowboys rounding up cattle, Janice and Philomela had moved every which way. They had written articles, compiled pictures, collected advertisements, edited texts, checked printing, and helped with distribution. Before month's end all deadlines had been met.

Their creation was out of their hands. Like a child they had lovingly produced and nurtured to maturity, the magazine spread its wings and flew into the arms of daily newspapers and local shops to fend for its self and spread across the city.

e/ɔe/ɔ

With unhidden excitement, Don greeted his two cohorts at the corner table on the second level of the Coyote Lounge. He sat across from Bob, who behaved like a wise old hawk, and Pierre, who nervously twisted his paper napkin. Lola glided up to the table and cheerily asked, "The usual?"

As she moved away, Pierre turned to Don. "Well, tomorrow's the day you leave. I still find the kidnapping plan repugnant, but I hope the trip itself will be a wonderful experience for you."

"The plan is foolproof," Bob said. "Don will do just fine."

Pierre sipped his drink, set his glass on the table, and cleared his throat. "I want Don and Janice to enjoy the trip. I don't want either of them to get hurt."

"They won't be hurt," Bob snapped. Then his voice grew soft and smooth. "Don is a capable, sensible young man. He won't do anything stupid." He handed a small bottle to Don. "These are sleeping pills. Ativan. Keep them in your suitcase—to be used in case Janice needs to be sedated."

Pierre frowned and shook his head. "I don't like the sound of that."

"Pierre, you worry too much. Don will only sweet talk the girl. But being forearmed makes good sense. Did you buy more duct tape, Don?"

Don nodded and Pierre's frown deepened.

Bob craned his neck and glanced around the room. "I say, look over there." He flung out his hand and pointed to the other side of the room. "Is that Philomela Nightingale?"

His two companions looked in the direction his hand indicated.

"I wouldn't know Philomela if I saw her," Don said.

"That's definitely not her." Pierre said. "That girl's figure has more generous proportions."

"My error." Bob bowed his head in homage to Pierre and then raised his glass. "Let's drink a toast to Janice." All three drank then set their glasses back on the table. Bob raised his glass again. "A toast to you, Don. May you have a pleasant and successful trip." Shortly after drinking the second toast, Bob suggested they order more drinks.

"I should head home," Pierre said. "I'm tired."

Bob ignored Pierre. "Don, there's one more thing to remember. We shouldn't contact each other with emails or phone calls until after you've secured the hostage. It'll help control costs. It will also prevent anyone from getting wind of our plans."

Don nodded and glanced around.

Bob stood up and the other two followed. Don led the way to the stairway and went down two steps. Suddenly, something hurtled past him. Startled, he watched the thing tumble down the entire flight and crumble in a heap at the bottom. Glancing back, he saw Bob. Where was Pierre? He jerked his head around and stared in disbelief at the body lying at the bottom of the stairs.

He dashed down two steps at a time. At the bottom, he squatted beside the crumbled body and with relief saw his former employer's chest rise and fall. Someone knelt beside him. Don turned his head and saw Lola. Her mere presence made him feel better. "He's alive," he said.

"Look at the blood around his head. I'll phone 911." She leaped to her feet and hurried to the manager's office. A minute later, she returned and sat on her heels beside Don. Their eyes met. "I'm fond of Mr. Lalonde. I hope he's okay."

"He's like a second father to me," Don said.

The paramedics arrived and checked their patient. As if in a funeral cortege, Lola and Don followed the stretcher outside. When it disappeared inside the ambulance and the double doors closed, Lola asked a paramedic, "What hospital will you take him to?"

"Rockyview."

Don was silent, too dismayed to speak. He watched the ambulance drive away, carrying his friend and substitute father to the hospital. He finally murmured, "I should cancel my holiday."

"There's nothing you can do," Lola said. "He's in good hands."

Don lowered his head, embarrassed because tears were filling his eyes.

Bob, who stood near the entrance talking with the manager, strolled over and rested a hand on his shoulder. "Pierre will be fine," he said reassuringly. "I'll visit him and make sure everything is taken care of." He gently patted Don's back. "Don't worry about him. Just enjoy your trip. That's what Pierre would want you to do."

CHAPTER 13

Janice sat beside her dad in the front seat of his Kia Soul and paid no attention to the soft music issuing from the car radio. In the trunk of the car were two suitcases, a medium sized bag for sunny climes and a small one for cooler Vienna and Dublin.

"This is good real estate," her dad said, glancing at the two story frame building.

"It's a nice place to work." Janice peripherally saw Philomela and Brent come out the front door of *The Integrator* office and walk toward the parked vehicle.

Brent pulled a suitcase on wheels and carried a smaller one. Philomela, with a large purse slung over one shoulder, walked beside him. Myron climbed from the driver's seat, moved to the back of the car, and opened the trunk. He greeted Philomela then extended his hand to Brent.

"My wife has learned to travel light," Brent said, shaking his hand.

"That's a real skill." Myron closed the lid of the trunk. "Especially for a woman travelling on her own."

Brent moved close to Philomela, and Janice watched her melt into his arms. When they finally separated, he opened the back door of the car and she climbed inside.

"Have a good time," Brent said and slowly shut the door.

The closing click sounded so final that Janice wouldn't have been surprised to see Philomela open it and bound outside. However, her dad prevented such action by putting the gear in drive and guiding the car away from the curb.

"You girls are wise to go to Vancouver this morning," Myron said, speaking above the drone of the radio. "The afternoon weather forecast is rain in Calgary and fog in Vancouver." Suddenly he reached down and turned up the volume of the radio.

"...down a flight of stairs," a newscaster said. "Pierre Lalonde owns a tanning salon and two gift shops and is well known around the city. His condition is serious and his wife, son, daughter, and son-in-law are with him at the Rockyview Hospital."

"Omigod," Janice exclaimed, "that's Collette's dad."

"He's one of my joint venture partners," Myron said.

"He advertises regularly in *The Integrator*." Philomela leaned toward the front seat. "I wonder what happened."

"He fell down a flight of stairs," Myron said, glancing back at Philomela. "I didn't hear the newscaster say when or why or where. But it sounds serious."

After the car stopped in front of the departure terminal, the women grasped their suitcase handles and forgot Pierre Lalonde. Janice kissed her dad on the cheek, and Philomela shook his hand.

"Bon voyage, girls," he said. "Have a good time. I'll see you in a month."

Inside the terminal, they moved quickly through the ticket line. Getting through security was more of a trial but, fortunately, they triggered no whistles or alarm bells.

The flight to Vancouver lasted an hour and ended with a fog-free landing. They climbed aboard a shuttle bus that whizzed them through the city to their hotel. A receptionist informed them their room would be ready in an hour so they left their suitcases with the concierge and went outside to a seaside walkway.

"The air smells so soft and salty," Philomela said, inhaling deeply. She extended her arms and drew in another lungful of air. "I love the way it soothes and softens my skin."

Ignoring her mentor's alliterative excesses, Janice gazed at the water. "This is different scenery from what we're used to." She watched several large boats churning through the water and a float plane rising from the waves into the air.

An hour later, in their hotel room, Philomela put her toiletries beside the sink and hung her favorite dress in the closet. The dress was chocolate in color and lived up to the label she had given it: fantastic frock. It was the perfect travel dress—light weight, wrinkle free, and stain resistant. She intended to wear it this evening at the departure gala and she planned to wear it at other social functions such as the captain's reception in Kuala Lampur.

Janice was not so pleased. "Look at my blue dress," she cried. "It's a wrinkled mess."

"Turn on the hot water in the shower. When the bathroom is steamy, hang the dress on the shower rod. While we eat lunch the moist air might smooth out a few wrinkles."

Janice followed Philomela's suggestion.

Back in their room after lunch, they stretched out on the two beds and quietly read. A short while later both nodded off and slept.

Philomela woke up first and stared at her wristwatch. "Good grief. It's time to tart ourselves up for the reception and dinner."

Janice jumped off the bed and dashed into the bathroom. "It worked," she called. "My dress has fewer wrinkles than before." She came out of the bathroom and looked sadly at her employer.

"For some reason, I just thought of Mr. Lalonde. I hope he's okay."

"I hope so, too," Philomela said.

A short while later, Philomela, adorned in her fantastic frock and brown pumps, and Janice, in her partially unwrinkled blue dress and high-heel sandals, entered the cocktail area.

Groups of casually attired people dulled their eyes,

and the sounds of high and low voices struck their ears.

"Buzzing bees are bombarding my eardrums," Philomela said. "Good grief. I think fancy fashions are forbidden. We're overdressed."

"Don't worry." Janice pointed across the room. "We're not alone. See that tall slim lady near the bar. Her gold flecked dress is awesome, way more fashionable than anything we own."

Philomela looked toward the bar and saw a vision of gold and black. "Yes," she agreed, "her outfit is smashing. And her black hair is—"

Her remark was cut short by a petite woman stopping in front of her. "Hello, I'm Fran Moleski, one of the tour guides."

Philomela looked into the friendly face and introduced Janice and herself.

"I recognize your names," Fran said. "This is your first trip with Around the World in Thirty Days."

Philomela nodded, impressed that the guide had done her homework.

"I'm happy to say you're with me—the red group. Just watch for the red maple leaf on the front of the coaches." Glancing over at two couples, loudly greeting and hugging and kissing each other, Fran explained, "Those four people are taking the world trip for the third time."

"That's quite a recommendation for the tour company," Philomela said. "Those travellers must be well-heeled."

"They're careful in how they prioritize their money.

All four are retired Ontario school teachers. Oh—" Fran held up her hand. "There's another newcomer. He seems totally lost. I must rescue him. Enjoy yourselves."

Philomela watched her hurry toward a young man who stood alone, apparently not knowing what to do. His brown beard and moustache were neatly trimmed and his navy jacket and gray pants made him look quite preppy. A waiter distracted her by holding a tray of drinks in front of her and she took a glass of white wine and thanked him. He then turned to Janice.

Sipping her wine, Philomela glanced toward the bar but saw no sign of the lady in the gold and black dress. Then her peripheral vision glimpsed a shimmering panther glide toward her and Janice. Black ringlets framed the woman's face and twisted and twirled in all directions. The ringlets reminded Philomela of Medusa, one of the three Greek mythological Gorgon sisters whose hair consisted of writhing snakes and whose eyes turned onlookers into stone. Philomela was confident this modern day replica lacked that scary ability. However, as the woman glided closer her dark, penetrating eyes made Philomela wonder if perhaps she might be able to perform the dastardly deed.

"I'm Miranda Gordon," the woman said, stopping in front of Philomela. "I hope you don't think I'm being presumptuous, but I noticed you two smartly dressed ladies and wanted to meet you."

"How kind of you." To avoid the risk of being turned to stone, Philomela avoided looking directly into the woman's dark eyes. She introduced herself and, while introducing Janice, accidently did focus on the dark eyes. Thankful to remain flesh and blood she chuckled. "I confess that we admired you from afar. Your gold flecked dress and tall figure are an entrancing combination."

"Thank you," Miranda replied, as if accustomed to receiving compliments about her appearance. Glancing at a nearby foursome clad in scruffy shirts and jeans, she asked, "Are we overdressed? Or are they underdressed?"

"The latter," Philomela replied.

"Good. For special occasions, I'd rather dress up than dress down."

"Not everyone thinks that way," Philomela said.

"Since we have something in common, it will be a pleasure to rub shoulders with you two." Miranda proceeded to tell her life story, at least part of it. "I took early retirement from teaching high school and now own a modelling studio in Toronto. So you understand why clothes interest me."

"They interest me, too," Philomela said, "but for a more simplistic reason—they can be fun."

Aspects of the fashion world were left behind as Janice, Miranda, and Philomela moved into the elegant dining room. Like three birds on a clothesline, they sat down at a table covered with a white linen tablecloth. They looked over gleaming glasses and shining cutlery at their young dinner companions.

Captain Sanderson, the chief pilot, introduced himself and his aircrew. As the meal proceeded, he proved an expert raconteur and kept them well entertained. Philomela found him especially interesting when he related

how he had used a simulator in Ontario to practise landing a 747 in Katmandu.

"The Nepal airfield is in a bowl between high foothills and towering mountains," he explained. "The pow-
ers-that-be want their pilots to know what they're doing."

"That's reassuring," Philomela said. "I also want my
pilot to know what he's doing."

Captain Sanderson chuckled. "So do I."

When the dinner ended, Fran distributed passports
that had been used to obtain visas. Travellers chatted with
each other then began to disperse. Clutching their valuable, identification booklets, Philomela and Janice headed
toward the elevator.

Philomela noticed Fran introduce the preppy young
man to a group of seasoned travellers. The tour guide obviously had great empathy. Under her tutelage, the young
man no longer seemed lost.

CHAPTER 14

Sitting in her comfortable, business class seat, Philomela squinted at the printed form the flight attendant had just handed her. She held it close to her eyes then at arm's length. Finally she placed it in front of her young companion's face.

"Janice, is your form the same as mine?"

"Yes. Except for our names."

Philomela examined the sheet of paper again. It was heavy in weight, eight by eleven inches in size, gray in color, and embellished with the picture of a curly haired man around whom various words were printed in dark ink. "My reading glasses are in my purse," she said. "Would you read yours out loud?"

"It's a certificate with a picture of Zeus."

"What's the Greek ruler of the celestial realm doing here?"

"He's gracing the 'Order of Equatorial Air Crossings.'" In a clear voice Janice read: "'Be it known by all in the universe that Janice McGill, having this day gallantly crossed the Equator in a Boeing 737-400, becomes a Free Spirit of the air, and all Rights, Benefits, and Perquisites reserved for those who cross between the Hemispheres in Airliners are hereby bestowed. All ye Powers and Dominions subject to his most puissant Majesty, Zeus, take note. Sunday, October second.' It's signed by Captain Sanderson."

"And to think I didn't even know we had crossed the equator."

"Me neither." Janice chuckled. "Perquisites are things people get above and beyond their salaries. But what is puissant"

"Powerful. Mighty. You must have skipped the English class that taught puissant."

Philomela saw Janice's attention shift from the certificate in her hand to a young man walking down the aisle. His straight brown hair, trim moustache, and chin beard belonged to the young man Fran had befriended at the reception last night. In a tee-shirt and jeans, he now looked casual, not preppy. Janice watched him with apparent interest and he seemed equally interested in her.

"Do you know that young man?" Philomela asked after he had passed by.

"No, but he looks vaguely familiar. I didn't see him last night at Terrific Travel's reception and dinner. Did you?"

"Yes, he was all by himself until Fran rescued him." Philomela's train of thought filtered back to the gala. "I didn't speak with him. But I did speak with people who had been on the trip before. They had nothing but good to say about the travel company, the staff, and the airline crew."

"Last night at dinner I had an interesting chat with a flight attendant and the flight engineer," Janice said. "They were fun, but today they're all business, doing their jobs."

"Good. They'll ensure our comfort and safety."

"Did you notice a couple of handicapped fellow-travellers?

"I did. The initial information package stressed in bold print that only the fleet of foot should go on this trip. The cane-lady must have missed that page."

"How is she going to walk long distances and climb dozens of stairs?" Not waiting for a reply, Janice adjusted her seat and leaned backward. "This is comfortable. You should try it."

Philomela brushed lunch crumbs from her green jogging suit. Following Terrific Travel's advice to dress comfortably on the airplane, she felt as if the suit was a favorite old nightgown. She adjusted her seat and leaned back. Soon her eyelids fluttered and closed.

"*Allo, Madeline. Comment ca va?*"

With a start Philomela opened her eyes. Was she dreaming?

"*Bien, merci.*"

For an instant, she thought she was back in her high school French class.

"*Quoi de neuf?*"

"*Pas grand'chose.*"

Not much new. What nonsense, everything was new—airplane, crossing the equator, napping on a business class seat. Philomela adjusted the back of her seat and sat upright.

The voices belonged to a woman sitting in front of her and to one standing in the aisle. They conversed in French and apparently knew each other quite well.

Eavesdropping was something Philomela had done in excess when trying to solve a murder on Maui, but there was no need to do it now. She turned to Janice who also was awake. "Did you have a nap?

"Yes," Janice replied.

"I suspect the couple in front of us live in Montreal or Ottawa."

"Besides being bilingual," Janice mused aloud, watching the elegant lady walk toward her own seat, "French Canadians dress well and are self-assured. They make me feel like a country bumpkin."

Philomela gave her employee's arm a motherly pat. "No one can make you feel like a bumpkin without your consent."

Janice abruptly sat upright. "Omigod. The cane-lady's going to crash into that man."

Philomela watched the man thwart a crash by falling on top of a lady sitting in an aisle seat. Seemingly oblivious to her near collision, the cane-wielding lady sailed past the surprised couple trying to disentangle themselves.

"She expects everyone to stand aside for her," Janice

said, "and she uses that cane like a weapon, not a walking aid."

"In attire she's the inverse of the French Canadian ladies."

"Well," Janice said, "she may dress badly but she's self-assured."

"Or is she just a self-centered bully?" Philomela asked.

Suddenly a deep voice boomed over a loud speaker, "This is your captain speaking. We have started our descent and will arrive in Nadi, Fiji, in twenty minutes. All passengers should return to their seats and buckle their seat belts. Happy landing."

Hooking up her seat belt, Philomela peripherally saw the young man with straight brown hair, moustache, and chin beard stop beside Janice and lean toward her.

"I understand you two ladies are from Calgary," he said.

"Yes, we are," Janice replied.

"I'm from Calgary, too."

"You look familiar. Have we met before?"

"I don't believe so. Fran Moleski pointed you out to me last night at the reception. But I didn't get a chance to speak with you. My name is Don Webster. "

"I'm Janice McGill and this is my friend, Philomela Nightingale."

Philomela leaned over Janice and extended her right hand. "Nice to meet you, Don. I'm sure we'll see quite a bit of each other."

"Absolutely." He smiled and shook her hand. "Here

comes a flight attendant. I'd better dash to my seat before she gives me what-for. See you later."

Philomela watched him pass another young man going in the opposite direction. The second young man paused and he too stared at Janice. A flicker of recognition seemed to register on his face, but he said nothing and walked on.

"Those two fellows could almost be twins," Philomela said. "They both have brown hair and are about the same height and build. Don, however, has fashionable facial hair whereas the second chap is clean shaven. And the second man's hair is curly and his eyebrows look like shaggy awnings."

"Philomela, you're so observant."

"I observed that both men showed an interest in you. They'll certainly spice up your trip."

"Ridiculous." Janice gave her companion a mock frown then concentrated on checking her seat belt.

❧❧❧

Back on Mother Earth they boarded a coach that took them to a sprawling hotel. After receiving room keys, Janice and Philomela walked on a cement path amid colorful trees and shrubs. Philomela pointed out frangipani and hibiscus flowers to Janice.

In their room at the extreme end of the building, they freshened up then returned to the core of the hotel. They found the dining room, ate a light supper, and returned to their room. A small bottle of brandy rested on each pillow and they decided to sample it. After pouring the contents in two glasses, they took them outside and sat down on patio chairs. Janice kicked off her flip-flops.

Philomela brought out her i-Pad and read a message from Brent. "Good grief," she exclaimed. "Do you remember the radio newscast we heard on our way to the Calgary airport?"

"You mean the one about Mr. Lalonde falling down stairs?"

"Apparently, the flight of stairs was at the Coyote Lounge. He either tripped or lost his balance. He was taken by ambulance to the Rockyview Hospital and the next afternoon he died."

"Omigod. He died while we were in Vancouver." Janice remained silent. Then, as if holding a wake, she praised the deceased man's good nature and entrepreneurial spirit. She concluded by saying, "He was always nice to us kids."

"He was the most genial client my magazine ever had. I'll miss him."

Besides feeling sad, they both felt the atmospheric strain of the long flight and the 1166 metre drop in altitude from Calgary to sea level. They finished their nightcaps, went inside, and climbed into bed.

"I can't stop thinking about Mr. Lalonde's accident," Philomela said.

Half asleep, Janice murmured, "Poor Collette. Poor Mrs. Lalonde."

CHAPTER 15

Janice awoke to the sound of birdsong. Still in her nightgown, she stepped out on the patio and listened to their joyful trills. Life was good. She picked up a flip-flop and looked around for the other one. She couldn't find it. Who would take one flip-flop? Then she remembered last night's sad news and the birdsong turned into a funeral dirge. She wandered into the room and lamented to her employer about Mr. Lalonde's unexpected demise.

"His fatal fall is terrible," Philomela said, gazing at her employee. "But we can't do anything about it. We can't even express sympathy to his relatives, not until we get home. We'll have to push the sad news to the back of our minds and do our best to enjoy the holiday."

Janice cleared her throat, forced a weak smile, then described the weather on the patio. She proceeded to dress accordingly—walking shorts, tee-shirt, and white runners. On their way to the dining room, she said, "Maybe a bird took my flip-flop,"

"Probably a rat," Philomela said.

In the now familiar dining room, Janice gazed out a window, over a terrace to a lawn sloping down to the sea. While eating breakfast, she felt like a fairy princess. Then Mr. Lalonde came to mind and a wan smile spread across her face.

"A penny for your thoughts," Philomela said.

"They're worth more than a penny. I just recalled how Mr. Lalonde told Collette and me that we were prettier than fairy princesses. We were dressed in clothes way too big for us and probably looked stupid. But he made us feel like princesses."

Later, as they lounged by the pool and swam in the warm water, the deceased man frequently came up in their conversation. After lunch, they silently walked toward their room.

"Hello, ladies."

Startled, Janice turned sharply and saw the young man called Don Webster walking behind them. She remembered his name. Was that a good or a bad omen?

"Are you going on the tour this afternoon?" he asked.

Janice nodded. "Are you?"

"I was tempted to sit by the pool and drink beer, but a walk around an orchid farm will probably do my poor body more good. Who is this Raymond Burr anyway?

"He was a Canadian actor," Philomela said. "He starred in two popular TV detective series, *Perry Mason* and *Ironsides*. And he created the orchid farm on Fiji."

"I bet none of his plants would survive the freezing temperatures in Calgary," Janice said.

"Freezing temperature? What's that?" Don raised his hands in mock disbelief.

Philomela chuckled. "Snow and cold are not on my radar screen, either." She strode ahead, allowing the two younger people to walk side by side.

"Did you find a small bottle of brandy on your pillow last night?" Don asked.

"Yes. We drank ours out on the patio before going to bed." She refrained from mentioning the sad news about Mr. Lalonde that had appeared on Philomela's i-Pad. She didn't want to dampen his holiday spirit, especially since he wouldn't know who she was talking about.

"I drank mine, too. It was a nice touch." He moved closer to Janice and, when she increased her pace, so did he. "Have you seen any sign of the insurrection that recently occurred on the island?"

"Not a thing," she replied.

"This morning, I talked with a night watchman. Though he had a gun in his holster he was pretty relaxed about it. He said the troubles won't affect us."

They parted company, he to his room, and she to catch up with Philomela. Hurrying forward, she felt branches laden with flowers brush her head and shoulders. Though tropical and beautiful, she found them spooky and invasive. She caught up with Philomela who was inserting her key in the lock.

"Don didn't waste any time," Philomela said.

"What do you mean?"

"Young, attractive, single girls on this trip are at a premium." Philomela opened the door and walked inside their room. "Most of the females are like me, north of middle age. He's making sure he latches onto the best of the lot before anyone else does."

"Don't be silly."

When they later waited outside the hotel reception area for the coach, Janice saw Philomela nod to Don who stood in the shade of a large tree. Janice smiled politely at him then the cane-lady distracted her as she waved her cane like a baton. Janice took a few steps forward and stopped behind Philomela. Trying to see who her employer was chatting with, Janice shifted to one side and recognized the young man. Even though a Tilley hat protected his head and sunglasses hid his eyes, he still bore a resemblance to Don. She noted his jaw was square compared to Don's rounder one. He seemed calmer than Don who often bounced with nervous energy. She must be spending too much time with Philomela—she was becoming far too observant. She stepped closer in order to hear his words.

"We live in the same city," he said to Philomela, "and we had to come half way around the world to meet."

"Crazy, isn't it." Philomela's chuckle was contagious.

He responded with a laugh. His laugh was contagious, too.

"Did you attend the departure party in Vancouver?" Philomela asked.

"No, but I hear it was a good one. I stayed with my sister in West Van. She drove me to the airport this morning."

"Wasn't that fuel stop in Oahu dreadful?" Philomela shook her head. "We deplaned, stood in line at customs, made our way to the departure area, stood in line for security, and then stood in line to re-board. As far as security was concerned, it seemed a farce."

They continued chatting and Janice listened, wondering if her mentor even noticed her. Or did Philomela wish to keep the young man's company to herself? Two coaches pulled up to the curb and Fran Moleski announced that stragglers would be left behind. She directed her group to the one with a red maple leaf in the window. The cane-lady pushed her way to the front of the queue and everyone politely waited as she ambled up the steps. She swung her cane and glared at a woman who dared to sit in the seat behind the driver. The woman moved on and left the cane-lady to take possession of it.

Philomela and her male friend sat down on the second last row of the coach. Janice sat in the row in front of them.

"Janice," Philomela said, leaning toward her, "I thought you were with Don. I'd like you to meet Frank Smith. Like us, he's from Calgary."

Janice turned in her seat and they exchanged pleasantries. Frank said in a low voice, "I've seen you somewhere before."

"I probably have a look-alike," Janice said. "You have one, right on this coach."

"I do?"

"That chap over there." She nodded her head, indicating Don who sat across the aisle a few seats in front of them. "He's also from Calgary."

"You think I look like him?"

"Same build, except your hair is curly and his is straight. Otherwise, the similarity is remarkable."

"You flatter me."

"No," Philomela interjected, "she's flattering the other man."

Frank chuckled and studied Don a moment. "You know, I had a moustache and beard similar to his. I found them a nuisance so shaved them off."

"Good thing," Janice said. "Otherwise we might not be able to tell you two apart."

The coach started to move. A guide stood up and introduced himself. He welcomed the visitors and asked if they had noticed the nearby hills. When the responses subsided, he elaborated: "We call them the Sleeping Giants."

"A lot of places have a sleeping giant," Philomela whispered. "I know of two others. Thunder Bay, Ontario, and the Hawaiian island of Kauai."

The guide told a few jokes and, in no time, the coach arrived at Raymond Burr's orchid farm. The cane lady got off first and Miranda Gordon, looking gorgeous, followed close behind. When all the passengers were on the ground, they mingled a few minutes then walked haphazardly behind the guide.

Don fell in step with Janice and, after a few moments, asked, "Are you enjoying the tour?"

"It's interesting. And I love the weather."

He stayed beside her for the initial walkabout and said little until they stopped under a greenhouse made of black mesh. He reached up and touched it. "Who would think of greenhouses being designed to keep the sun out?"

"Not very Canadian, that's for sure." Janice grinned at him then glanced back at Philomela who walked with a sprightly white-haired lady. Glancing farther back, she hoped to see Frank but saw no sign of him.

"Are you going on the boat trip to the island of Mana?" Don asked.

"Yes, I am."

"Is Philomela going, too?"

"Funny you should ask. She's taking tomorrow off to recuperate from our flight."

"She's probably the smart one." He placed a hand under Janice's elbow and guided her up a steep incline. Reaching the top of the incline, he said, "Maybe we could go on the boat together."

"That might work."

"I'll pick you up at your room after breakfast."

"Okay." She gave him the room number.

That evening, after she and Philomela had discussed the day in general and the orchid farm in particular, Janice suddenly felt guilty. She had enjoyed the busy afternoon tour and not once had she given a thought to Mr. Lalonde. She knew his wife and daughter would be suffering inconsolable grief and here she was having a wonderful time.

Well, she and Philomela had agreed to try and do exactly that.

CHAPTER 16

Don Webster locked the door of his room, pocketed the key in his Tilley shorts, and adjusted his backpack. A nearby bush with white flowers released a heady perfume but his nostrils hardly registered the scent. His thoughts were too busy swirling with exciting, half-made plans.

He had attained the first step of his goal—charming Janice McGill. Because of her attractive appearance and pleasant manner, the work had been effortless and fun. The fact that her father was comfortably rich helped, of course. Normally his taste in females ran to a more outgoing, flamboyant type of girl but, under the circumstances, he could not complain. Janice was the best-looking female in the tour group and certainly the youngest. She also was easy to be with.

Her travelling companion was another matter. Philomela Nightingale was friendly and had some of the flamboyance he admired, especially in general appearance, though her scarlet hair was a bit of a wonder. He didn't know whether he agreed with Bob Davis, who thought she was a snoopy bitch, or Pierre Lalonde, who thought she was pleasant and helpful. At the orchid farm she had purposely walked with other members of the group, leaving him alone with Janice. Maybe she was a closet romantic who liked to aid and abet romance in others. However, he had been warned by Bob to watch her. Already he had witnessed her easy way with people and her capable street-smarts. Yes, if there was anyone to be wary of, it was Philomela Nightingale.

Fortunately, one bit of knowledge Bob had gleaned from Janice was coming true: Philomela intended to pass on the boat trip to the island of Mana. Though early days in the trip, this might be his best opportunity to kidnap Janice and hole up with her—just the two of them in a love nest on a tropical island. His thoughts bubbled with romance, passion, and ransom money.

He strode along the path and his backpack brushed against a flowering shrub. Its fragrant aroma along with a few serenading birds failed to penetrate his concentration. He was too busy formulating a plan. He wondered if accommodations on Mana consisted of a thatch-roofed shack on a beach of yellow sand. No matter, his basic idea was to rent a room and entice Janice into it.

The method of enticement would depend on circumstances. He hoped he wouldn't need the small knife or duct tape or sleeping pills that hid inside a red plastic pouch in his backpack. He mulled over what to do after his sweet talk had enticed Janice into a hotel room. Chat? Make love? Gag her? Tie her up? Put her to sleep? He knew they would have to remain hidden until the boat departed back to Fiji.

His major concern centered on the vigilance of the tour guide. With luck, the guide would not miss them and Janice's absence would not be detected until Philomela searched for her at dinnertime. Then all sorts of speculations would occur, especially when someone realized that he, too, was missing. Everyone would ask logical questions: Had they returned to the town of Nadi? Had they fallen overboard en route from the island of Mana? Had they decided to elope? Or had they simply shacked up together on the tiny island? Everyone would be puzzled and confused.

Meanwhile, on Mana, he would rent a motor boat and under the darkness of night take Janice to Suva, another town on Fiji. When the search eventually got back to the small island of Mana, they would be long gone. Who would think to search for them in the town of Suva?

His plan was as cunning as any devised by Bob Davis. Was that good or bad? The thought of his wily mentor reminded him of Pierre. He hoped Pierre had recovered from his fall down the Coyote Lounge stairs. If he was still in hospital, Don hoped Lola and Bob visited him.

Reaching the last room of the hotel wing, he knocked on the door and Philomela opened it. He gazed at her startling red hair and mauve cover-up and decided she looked pretty good for an old broad.

"Good morning, Don," she said. "It's a beautiful day for a boat ride."

"Yeah, it is."

"Janice is almost ready. Come on in."

Don entered the room and Philomela guided him past two single beds to a chair in front of a large window. At her invitation, he dropped his backpack at his feet and sat down.

"If you look out the window," she said, "you can see the boat. Members of our group are gathering on the beach."

He turned to the window. "The boat's quite big. It'll hold a lot of people."

The bathroom door opened and Janice, wearing navy blue shorts and a white tee-shirt, entered the room. She smiled. "Good morning. Don."

"Hi." He stood up. "You look ravishing."

"In this old thing?" She laughed then graciously thanked him. "Do you have your bathing suit?" she asked.

"In my backpack."

"Could I put my few things with yours?"

"No problem." He opened the bag and she dropped her bathing suit, small make-up kit, wallet, and sun-glass case inside. "Is that everything?" he asked.

"I hope so." She hung her camera around her neck. "Do you have sun-tan lotion?"

"Absolutely. I never leave home without it."

"I've already slathered some on. If I need more after swimming, maybe I could borrow yours."

"As long as you return it." He chuckled at the lame witticism.

Janice looked over at Philomela. "Will you be bored while we're gone?"

"Not a bit. I'll read by the pool and maybe take a nap. I emailed Brent last night to let him know we're enjoying ourselves. He should get back to me soon. Have a good time and don't do anything I wouldn't do."

"Does that mean we can do absolutely anything?" Don asked. "Short of murder, of course."

Philomela rolled her eyes and deigned to reply.

The two young people walked outside. Janice glanced at the undergrowth surrounding the patio. "I left my flip-flops out here two nights ago. Yesterday morning one was missing."

"Did someone steal it?"

"I thought a Myna bird took it. Philomela figured it was a rat. The thief must like stinky feet." She giggled. "I'll wear these white runners until I buy a new pair of flip-flops."

They crossed the lawn, reached the beach, and stopped at the jetty where fellow travellers watched the empty tender glide from the tour boat. It stopped at the jetty and, along with dozens of others, Janice and Don climbed aboard. The tender returned to the tour boat, disgorged its human cargo, and the two young people ran with ease up the stairway to the top deck. They found two seats shaded from the tropical sun by a large orange canopy and Don claimed both by spreading his towel on one and his backpack on the other. They strolled over to the railing and watched the tender bring the last of their group to the tour boat.

Don noted with satisfaction that no one seemed to keep track of the number of passengers boarding the vessel.

The tour boat started to glide through the water and they watched the hotel and its attractive landscaping decrease in size then fade from sight. Their view consisted of misty sea and sky until a small island floated by. It disappeared, leaving nothing but more sea and sky.

"Water, water everywhere," Janice said, "and not a drop to drink."

"We can drink beer."

"Alcohol in the morning? How decadent."

He wheeled around and ran down the steps to the bar on the lower deck. After several minutes, he returned with two cans of Coors-Light and with a broad smile handed one to Janice. They left the railing, sat down on their saved chairs, and opened the cans.

"Maybe Philomela should have come," Janice said. "This is relaxing." She sipped the cool liquid and added, "I'm developing island lethargy."

"I could spend a lifetime living like this. Would you join me?"

"I'm too lazy to make a decision."

Don felt optimistic despite Janice's vague reply. Voices speaking in a foreign language caught his attention and he glanced around then leaned close to Janice. "Those four people two rows behind us. Are they French?"

She surreptitiously glanced around. "Yes. One couple sat in front of Philomela and me on the plane. As usual, they're smartly dressed. You've heard the saying: 'French people work to dress while the rest of us dress to work.' Oh, look on the other side of the aisle. There's the glamorous lady from Toronto. Wow, her outfit is so sophisticated—dove gray pants and top, pink and gray jacket, and silver earrings. I don't see the cane-lady."

"She's probably on the lower deck, or maybe she didn't come."

A white haired man sitting on Don's other side leaned toward him and asked where he was from." Don told him and he said, "I'm a retired teacher from Owen Sound in Ontario. This is my fourth world trip."

"Wow," Don said. "You must have a good pension."

"Could be worse." He glanced at Janice. "Where's your red-haired friend?"

"She's having a day off."

"Is this your first trip around the world?"

"Yeah," Don replied.

"Enjoying it, eh?"

"Absolutely."

At that moment, a voice over the loud speaker announced: "We are approaching Mana on our port side."

Everyone moved to the left side of the boat and looked over the railing at a circular piece of sand pinched at the waist and surrounded by water. As the boat drew nearer, they could see palm trees and manmade structures. A crew member tossed food overboard and their attention shifted to fish gobbling up the food and swimming in circles, waiting for more. Janice and many others busily clicked their cameras.

The tour boat slowed in momentum, its engines reversed, and crew members tossed stern and bow lines to men on a wharf. The wharf was larger than the little jetty near the Fiji hotel. A smattering of people stood and watched passengers disembark.

Janice and Don made their way along the wharf to the beach then followed fellow passengers to a small pavilion whose palm frond roof was supported by wooden pillars. The guide told them a few details about the island.

Again, Don noted with satisfaction that no one seemed to pay attention to the number of individuals who got off the boat. A person strolling away from the wharf could easily get lost and later be missed by no one but a close companion.

The guide led them along a sandy, double-track road past a few houses built on short wooden stilts. They ended up at a long, low building.

"This building," the guide explained, "is the hotel. It has a reception area, gift shop, bar, dining room, guest rooms, and lavatories. If anyone wants to swim before lunch please feel free to do so."

Like sheep, they followed him to a tiled patio that extended from an open air-bar on one side and overflowed with tables and chairs onto white sand on the other. Nearby, palm trees bordered a shower and a swimming pool. Sand stretched down to the sea.

Don thought the hotel would make a perfect hideaway.

Janice identified the necessary rooms, male and female. They entered the appropriate ones and emerged attired in swim trunks and bikini. Don stuffed their clothes in his backpack, set it under a long buffet table on the patio, then dashed toward the beach. Janice was close behind. Together, they ran straight into the warm water. The sandy bottom dropped off quickly, encouraging most swimmers to stay fairly close to shore. Two hardy souls swam farther out and discovered a sand bar on which they could stand and view the world. Don swam out to them and Janice followed. All four stood on the sandy hill and, with water barely reaching their hips, carried on a brief conversation. The discoverers of the underwater hill dived in and swam back to shore. Janice and Don remained alone.

"Another island must be forming here," she said.

"A tropical storm will probably wash it away." Don glanced behind them and muttered, "What's that?"

She turned and squealed in alarm. "Omigod. Is it a log with an upright branch? Or is it the dorsal fin of a shark?" She raised her arms. "I'm not taking any chances. I'm going back."

Don watched her swim toward shore and, after a quick backward glance, followed her. He caught up with her just as something brushed against his foot. Expecting a shark to bite off his leg, he felt his heart beat a military tattoo. Breathlessly, he scrambled after Janice onto the beach. Realizing that his foot was intact, he felt his heartbeat slow down. From the safe vantage point, he looked out to sea and saw nothing ominous.

"The shark must have realized we'd taste bad," Janice said."

"It could have been a bunch of flotsam." Don sniffed the air and turned toward the hotel. "I smell food. Lunch time."

"Let's take a quick dip in the pool and wash off the salt," Janice said.

They stepped under an outdoor shower, jumped in the pool, and found the water too warm for swimming. They floated on their backs for a few minutes then climbed out, showered again, and reclined on chaises-longue. When their swimsuits were partially dry, they walked up to the buffet tables now laden with salads, breads, fish, and fruit. Don retrieved his backpack. From it, he removed his clothes and a red plastic bag then handed the backpack to Janice. They separated and, several minutes later, reunited and hung their swimsuits on two chairs to let the sun complete the drying process. Don put his red plastic bag in the backpack and they walked to the bar.

"Let me buy this time," Janice said.

"Certainly not."

"I earn money, too, you know. You've already bought me a beer. You shouldn't pay for everything."

He succumbed, outwardly pretending to be cha-grined, but inwardly pleased because he might need his money later on.

Carrying a beer, Don followed Janice to the table where the four French Canadians sat. In his best high school French, Don said, "*Bon jour*," and started to ask if he and Janice could join them. At that moment, the cane-lady moved close to Don and swung her stick toward him. Startled, he stepped back and she plunked down on the very chair he had intended for Janice. With only one empty chair left, he raised his eyebrows. Janice giggled and moved over to an empty table. He followed and another foursome joined them. They chatted and wandered up to the buffet tables. Food took precedence over conversation.

Don cleaned his plate then stood up. "I'm off to see a man about a horse."

Janice grinned at him. "Don't let one of those cute local maidens gallop you away."

"Do you think one might try?"

"You never know your luck."

Inside the airy building, he found the necessary room and the gift shop. He strolled over to the registration desk and asked the clerk about a room.

"I'm hoping for a romantic evening," he said. "If it doesn't pan out, could I cancel my reservation?"

The clerk laughed. "I'll get your name and credit card number and give you a key." He glanced at his wrist watch. "It's two-thirty. If you return the key before four, I won't charge you."

Handing the clerk his credit card, Don felt confident he would use the room. He imagined a passionate evening of drinks, conversation, and who knew what else. But the female he envisioned surprised him. It was not Janice McGill. It was Lola Grieve.

CHAPTER 17

Janice glanced at the interior of the hotel and saw no sign of Don. Eating a slice of papaya, she listened to her four lunch companions discuss previous holidays. All were older than she, probably retired, yet healthy and active enough to make age guessing impossible. She concluded that old and young travellers had two things in common: a sense of adventure and an interest in everything around them. She had read that age is a state of mind and now the reality of it seemed evident. Of course, reasonably good health was necessary.

"Did you enjoy your lunch?" a voice behind her asked.

Startled, she turned and gazed up at the gray eyes and bushy eyebrows of Frank Smith. "Yes," she replied, "but I ate too much."

"That's a common problem. We're too well fed."

She glanced at Don's empty chair. "Have a seat."

He sat down beside her. "I don't see your red-haired friend."

"She stayed at the hotel to rest after the long flight."

"Smart lady. And your boyfriend?"

"He's not my boyfriend." Her voice was louder and her words quicker than she intended. As if making amends for the outburst, she belabored the point by saying, "We met on the airplane."

"Ah, a holiday romance."

"It's not a romance." Under the beginnings of a suntan, she felt an annoying blush.

"Part of the fun of a trip is meeting new people." His smile started with his lips, shone through his eyes, and ended with a chuckle. She found his chuckle contagious.

"Well, aren't we cosy?" Don's voice broke through their laughter.

She almost wished he had delayed his arrival so she could have a few more minutes alone with Frank. As Don dragged a chair from an empty table, she thought he looked annoyed.

Frank extended his right hand. "I'm Frank Smith."

"Don Webster." Taking hold of the hand he asked, "What business are you in?"

"Veterinary medicine," Frank replied. "I've been working at a clinic in High River."

"I know the area well. I thought large animal vets were too poor to travel around the world."

"Partly right. For two years before going to university I worked up north on oil rigs. The pay was good, so my savings and summer earnings eliminated the need for a student loan. After three years working as a vet and with no family to support, here I am. When I return from this trip, I start working in a clinic in southwest Calgary. The owner is almost ready to retire so I hope to eventually buy his business." He looked at Don. "What do you do?"

"I have an import business. During our travels, I intend to scout around for unique things to buy and later sell back home."

"Will that give your trip a legitimate tax deduction?"

"I hope so. I was thinking of asking Janice to help me check out the merchandise here. She has a good eye for style."

Frank nodded and glanced appreciably at Janice.

"Don," she said, feeling rather flattered, "you never mentioned you had an import business."

"You didn't ask. I must say the gift shop here looks interesting. Would you mind telling me if anything appeals to you? From a woman's point of view."

"I'd love to do that." She jumped to her feet and reached for the backpack. "I'd better get my wallet in case I find something I want to buy."

She unzipped the backpack and took out the red plastic bag. Don lunged toward her and grabbed it. With a nervous laugh he said, "My money and stuff."

"Oh, sorry." She again dug in the backpack, found her wallet, and held it up. "My worldly wealth." Oh no, she thought, an alliteration. She definitely was spending too much time with Philomela.

Don took the backpack from her, put his red plastic

bag inside, then slung the pack over his shoulder. He put his hand under Janice's elbow, bade Frank goodbye, and guided her from the table toward the airy building.

"We have to go through the bar and reception area to get to the gift shop," he explained.

Just as they entered the bar area, she turned around and called, "Frank, do you want to come to the gift shop with us?"

"I'd like to." Frank stood up and hurried toward them.

"This way," Don growled.

Janice glanced at him, surprised to see his lips form the reverse of a happy face. Knowing he was annoyed about something, she silently followed him through the bar area, past the registration desk, and into the gift shop. Frank walked behind them. Inside the shop, they looked at different items and she expressed views about Calgary sales appeal or lack thereof. "These shirts wouldn't sell at home," she said. "They're strictly tropical wear."

"Would it be difficult to get local handicrafts from here to Nadi's international airport?" Frank asked.

"Probably," Don replied.

They examined and discussed several other items then Janice made a purchase for herself—a pair of flip-flops to replace the one that had gone missing on the patio. After leaving the shop, they walked into the reception area and heard the tour guide loudly call for attention. "It's time to regroup and get on the boat," he announced.

Don abruptly left his companions and strode to the desk in the reception area. Janice watched him speak to the clerk, shake his head, and hand the man a key. The clerk seemed overly sympathetic as he accepted the key and gave Don a sheet of paper which Don promptly ripped to shreds. She found the entire transaction bizarre. The key was especially odd. Where did Don get the key and what would it unlock? She turned questioningly to Frank and he wordlessly shrugged his shoulders. They waited a moment then, side by side, strolled out to the patio. Don caught up with them and all three walked to the wharf.

On the upper deck of the boat, Don dropped his backpack on the floor and sat down on a chair. He leaned back and closed his eyes and Janice asked if he was tired. When he failed to reply, she wondered if he was sick.

Sitting between the two men, she turned to Frank who asked if she planned to attend the social function this evening.

"I don't know," she said. But one thing she did know—at the moment, Frank was far better company than Don.

❧❧❧

Back in the hotel room, Janice bubbled with enthusiasm about her day on the island of Mana. Philomela listened with interest to her descriptions of boat, sand, water, food, buildings, and people. When Janice's chatter slowed to a stop, the older woman smiled and described how she had spent her day dozing, reading, sunbathing, and strolling around the garden.

Her smile faded when she mentioned exchanging emails with Brent.

"The police are looking more deeply into Mr. Lalonde's death. They want an inquest."

Janice found the news ominous. "An inquest? Why?"

"Brent said a judicial inquiry is necessary because the death was sudden and apparently accidental. The word, 'apparently,' worries me. Do they think his death was not accidental?"

With eyes wide Janice stared at her mentor. "What's the alternative?

"Suicide. Or murder."

CHAPTER 18

Don felt tired. Entering the dining room, he gazed at the buffet table and wondered if food would revive him. He walked slowly to the sumptuous display, shunted along it, and filled his tray with a full English breakfast—bacon, sausage, egg, tomato, and toast. Looking around, he spied Philomela and Janice sitting at a table for four. They gazed out the window, chatted with each other, and nibbled fresh fruit and muffins. They seemed oblivious to his presence. The two empty chairs beckoned to him so, carrying his laden tray, he moved toward them. Drawing near, he heard Janice's words.

"His death is so tragic. He was old, but not ancient."

Philomela moved her head slowly from side to side. "He had several years to go before reaching retirement age."

"He was such a kind man." Janice gazed at Philomela for several seconds. "Will the inquest affect the family?"

Don's ears perked up. Death? Inquest? Someone they knew must have died under suspicious circumstances. He cleared his throat and politely said, "Good morning."

Philomela looked up at him, studied his laden tray, and, not so politely, asked, "Do you always eat such a high cholesterol breakfast?"

"I try to. Does it offend you?"

"Not a bit. Please join us." Philomela watched him unload his tray and place it on a nearby empty table. He sat down across from her and she stood up. "I'm leaving," she announced, "not because of your abundance of cholesterol, Don, but because I've finished eating and still have packing to do."

Sure that she was aiding romance, he winked at her.

She ignored the wink, turned to Janice, and pointed to her wristwatch. "Don't forget the time." With a wave of her fingers, she walked briskly to the dining room exit and disappeared.

"What's this about an inquest?" Don asked, raising a forkful of sausage to his mouth.

"Philomela's husband emailed her. A friend in Calgary died quite suddenly and an inquest will be held."

"Anyone I know?"

"I doubt it. I've known him for a long time and would rather not talk about it." Changing the subject, she asked, "Did you sleep well?"

"Absolutely. And you?"

"Like the dead." She cringed. "Bad choice of words. Yesterday's abundance of fresh air made me tired."

"I went to a mini casino after last night's cocktail party. It was a private function with a small roulette wheel and a black jack table. Not many people. You should have come."

"I would have had more fun flushing a ten dollar bill down the toilet."

He laughed. "That describes it pretty well."

"Did many of our group go?"

"Captain Sanderson and his wife Rose shared a taxi with Frank and me. They didn't stay long. They were sight-seeing more than gambling." Don raised his glass of orange juice and drained it. With a sigh of contentment, he set the glass on the table. "All I need now to feel human again is a cup of coffee."

"Have some of this." She reached for a coffee pot sitting in the center of the table and filled his cup. "Did Frank win any money?"

"Actually, he did. But then he lost it." Don started to cut his bacon. He paused with knife in air because a disturbing recollection entered his mind. He had bragged to Frank about solving all his money problems. More disturbing, he could not remember his exact words. What if he had blurted out the plan to kidnap Janice? There was no question he had drunk too many cocktails and too much beer.

Janice broke into his thoughts. "You mean Frank lost all his money?"

"Just his winnings." He put a forkful of bacon into

his mouth, chewed, swallowed, and took a second bite. Every bite tasted better than the preceding one. The emptier his plate became the more human he felt. He was relieved not to be suffering a hangover.

"Did you and Frank share a taxi back to our hotel?"

"No. I think losing his winnings psyched Frank out. He said he'd walk back. Rather a long walk in the dark of night."

She sipped her coffee and gazed over the lawn at the ocean.

"Did you and Philomela do anything special after the cocktail party?" Don asked, wondering if she was thinking about her dead friend.

"We watched some local entertainment in the hotel then went to bed. Are you going on one of the tours tomorrow?"

"No. I'm not interested in wine-making or in sheep ranching. I think I'll get a taxi and check out beautiful down-town Perth. How about you?"

"Philomela and I are booked on the winery tour." She glanced at her wristwatch, placed her serviette on the table, and pushed back her chair. "Our flight leaves at eleven-thirty. I'd better go. Like Philomela, I'm not completely packed."

"How about having dinner with me tonight in Perth?"

She shook her head. "A group dinner with entertainment is planned. See you on the coach." She stood up and moved quickly from the table.

Don admired her yellow walking shorts, matching

tee-shirt, and blonde hair falling in a single braid to her upper back. She reminded him of a canary. She was colorful and pretty. Almost as pretty as Lola—

"Hello, Don."

Startled, he looked up at the most striking woman of the entire tour group. Her ringlets of black hair bounced and twisted around her head as if alive. Her dark eyes focused intently on him with what seemed like hidden meaning. But what kind of meaning?

"We haven't met. I'm Miranda Gordon." He politely started to rise from his chair and she said, "Don't get up, Don."

"You know my name—"

"It's in the booklet and I've seen you around. I commend you for latching onto Janice. She's a lovely young girl." She sat on the chair to his right and leaned toward him.

He could smell her perfume and found it sickly sweet. He leaned away from her. "Unfortunately, I haven't latched onto Janice."

"I can tell she likes you. I saw the two of you yesterday on Mana. You had a nice swim in the ocean."

They discussed yesterday's tour and all the time her dark eyes continued to focus on him. Finally, she mentioned last minute packing and stood up.

With relief, he watched her glide out of the room. Her appearance was stunning, her movements were graceful, but her manner and words were disconcerting. She was much too interested in him. Surely, she wasn't on the make. After all, he was half her age.

He re-filled his coffee cup and quietly sipped the dark brew. He admitted to himself that last evening Frank turned out to be good company. After the gift shop fiasco, he had blamed Frank for ruining his kidnapping plan and cheerfully could have killed him. However, in actual fact, Janice had been the guilty party. She was the one who asked Frank to join them.

Suddenly, a dismaying thought leaped to mind. Had Bob Davis hired a backup person to come on the trip? Someone who might spy on him? He recalled Bob suggesting that two kidnappers might be better than one. He'd replied that he wouldn't need any help. Now, he wasn't so sure. There were so many variables and so many unexpected outside influences.

Could Frank be part of the kidnapping plan? In the Coyote Lounge, Bob had concluded that the ransom money should be split only three ways. Could he have changed his mind?

Half the fun of this whole activity had been making plans with Bob and Pierre and being served by Lola. The fact that Pierre disliked the scheme was a downer, and his fall down the stairs was terrible. Hopefully, he was fully recovered and back home with his family.

Don glanced around the dining room and saw no one from the world tour group. It was time to go. Hurrying to his room, he wondered if he should phone or email Bob and tell him about yesterday's failure. That way he would learn how Pierre was doing.

No, Bob had been adamant that phone calls or emails should not be used until after the hostage was secured. He had worried that someone might catch wind of their plan. As far as Pierre's recovery was concerned, no news was good news.

He entered his room and tossed his cellphone in his suitcase.

CHAPTER 19

H ere we are," Philomela said, "on the opposite side of earth."

"Awesome." Janice hooked up her seatbelt.

"And we're on our way to the Down-Under Winery."

Sitting aboard a six-passenger Piper Cherokee, Philomela gazed at Janice and grinned. When the plane soared up from the runway, tilted sharply over farmlands, fields, roads, and houses, she nervously clutched her armrests.

"Look at those two big trees with purple flowers," Janice said.

Philomela gazed out the window and decided the trees were too close for comfort. Clutching the armrests even tighter, she said, "Jacaranda. They must be the most spectacular trees on earth."

She relaxed as the airplane flew higher and levelled

out, leaving the flowering trees far behind. They soared over grasslands, sandy beaches, and the azure ocean. In less than an hour from departure, the plane descended and Philomela glimpsed a dirt runway surrounded by a forest of strange trees. Olive colored leaves rippled above white tree trunks.

"Watch for kangaroos," the pilot announced. "They sometimes run amongst the Eucalyptus trees."

The two women gazed intently at the wooded area near the runway but saw no sign of wildlife. They continued to watch for kangaroos as they climbed from the small plane and jumped onto the dry earth. Their feet created small dust storms that flew up to their knees, but kangaroos remained hidden.

"This Eucalyptus forest smells like a dusty desert," Philomela said. "And the bright sun intensifies it. Oh look, here comes our transportation."

A mini-coach created a magician's cape of dust as it sped on a dirt trail toward them. It stopped abruptly and a petite driver jumped out. She greeted the travellers then ushered them inside the vehicle. Philomela glanced out the window as a second plane roared from the sky to the runway.

The mini-coach driver maneuvered the vehicle along the winding dirt trail and briefly pulled onto a lay-by to let another mini-coach pass by. A few minutes later, she turned the coach onto a paved highway and passed through a town that reminded Philomela of ranching towns in Western Canada.

"Why are those metal bars on the front of all the vehicles?" she asked.

"Roo bars," the driver replied. "Kangaroos are prevalent around these parts so people install bars to protect their cars and trucks." She turned the vehicle onto a narrow road and pointed to rows of grapevines randomly interspersed with large yellow flowers. "Parrots eat fruit and flower seeds," she explained, "so sunflowers are planted to lure them away from the grapes."

They rounded a corner and entered a scenic area of cascading lawns, rock gardens, and colorful flowerbeds. Nestled between two flowering shrubs, a large sign displayed the letters: *Down-Under Winery.*

As the mini-coach pulled to a stop, Philomela studied a rambling, frame building. Except for white cement stairs leading to the front entrance, the building blended with the sandy colored soil.

"What a pristine place," she murmured, gazing at the well-kept grounds. "The climate may be semi-desert but the vines and gardens look lush and lovely."

They climbed from the mini-coach, walked along the edge of the curving driveway, and admired gorgeous flowers. The driver beckoned and led them up the white steps.

At the top of the stairs, Philomela watched Janice take her camera from her purse and snap pictures. The second mini-coach rounded the corner, pulled to a stop behind the first one, and allowed fellow travellers to pour onto the driveway. She recognized Frank as he walked to a flowerbed and bent down to study it. Though a veterinarian specializing in fauna, he also seemed interested in flora. Strange that he came on the wine tour instead of the sheep ranch tour. Then again, his veterinary clinic was in southern Alberta where cattlemen sometimes scorned sheep, partly because they cropped the grass so short.

"There is no way those exotic grapes could grow in my small garden," Philomela said to Janice. "Cold snow and warm Chinook winds would kill them before they ever had a chance to get established."

Inside the building, Philomela noted a counter on her left. Behind it, floor-to-ceiling shelves were filled with wine bottles lying on their sides. To her right, she saw an elegant dining room whose far wall consisted of a long row of expansive windows. Outside the windows, a large deck swept the entire length of the room.

"Welcome to Down-Under Winery." She turned and gazed at a young man who had appeared from nowhere. Standing behind the counter he said, "My name is Alistair and I'll be taking you on a tour of the cellars and grounds. We'll wait for the rest of your party to join us."

Fellow travellers from the second coach straggled through the front door and, as their eyes adjusted from the outside glare to the inside dimness, they glanced from the bottle-filled shelves to the dining tables adorned with white serviettes and stemmed glasses.

Alistair introduced himself to the newcomers and continued his spiel: "Before we begin, you'll receive a small sample of one of our best wines. Believe it or not, it won the international wine contest in France, besting wines from France, Germany, and Italy. You'll now have the pleasure of tasting our award winning Sauvignon Blanc."

He removed the cork from two bottles. A young girl came up beside him and the two of them filled tiny wine glasses one quarter full and placed them on a tray. The girl distributed the glasses to the guests.

"The bouquet is distinctively pungent," Alistair said. "The taste is fruity yet has enough glycerine for smoothness and if you look closely you will see what we call legs. The color is pale, yet rich looking."

Each visitor studied the legs, breathed in the bouquet, and sipped the liquid. Everyone agreed it tasted delicious. They placed the empty glasses on the counter and Alistair led the group through a hall and down a short flight of stairs. They entered a room that, compared to the heat outside, was freezing cold. They walked past large stainless steel tanks to an adjacent room full of oak casks. Philomela found herself standing beside a French Canadian gentleman and, glancing back, she saw Janice chatting with Frank Smith.

As they followed Alistair up a different flight of stairs, she heard Janice ask Frank if he was enjoying the tour and heard him admit he particularly liked the wine he had just tasted.

Alistair overrode all conversation by pronouncing, "We will now go to the deck outside the dining room and view the vines."

After studying rows of grape vines and learning how they were planted, pruned, netted to keep birds out, and harvested, they followed Alistair back inside.

At the counter, everyone gathered around him. "You'll have a chance to taste another award winning wine," he said, "a Chardonnay. Then we'll go to the dining room for lunch."

This time the girl behind the counter filled the tiny glasses three quarters full.

Philomela was thirsty so she emptied hers quickly. In an unexpected silence, her voice sounded loud and clear. "This wine tastes more-ish."

Alistair chuckled, picked up a bottle from the counter, walked over to Philomela, and, with a dramatic flourish, filled her empty glass to the rim.

"You understood that non-word perfectly," Philomela said, feeling rather embarrassed at her gauche remark.

"Wine and more-ish go together." Alistair gave her a jovial smile. "Anyone else want more?" He held the bottle above his head and several guests raised their glasses which he proceeded to replenish.

After entering the dining room, Janice sat down beside Frank at a circular table. Philomela sat across from them beside the French Canadian gentleman.

"Janice and Frank," she said, "this is Andre Bouchard."

In unaccented English, Andre greeted them. "Unfortunately," he said, "my wife Madeline succumbed to a severe headache and stayed back at the hotel. She was sorry to miss this tour. She knows more about wine than I do."

"Maybe you could buy a bottle and take it to her," Philomela suggested.

"I probably will."

Seeing the two pilots sitting on the deck outside the large windows, Philomela felt reassured. They were eating food and apparently drinking water. Designated drivers.

Inside the dining room, wine flowed freely. With each course a new one appeared, making conversation grow easier and louder. When dessert was being served, the man sitting beside Janice turned and leaned his white head toward her.

"There is good news and bad news," he said.

Puzzled, Janice gazed at him and waited.

"The bad news is I have aids." Janice abruptly leaned back from him. He smiled and continued, "The good news is I have Alzheimer's so I'll soon forget it."

The joke, though old and worn, was greeted with hilarity. Everyone within hearing distance laughed merrily. Philomela knew the wine accentuated the humor and, glancing around, she noted that older travellers laughed the hardest.

Doubtless, they knew a bit about aids and a lot about Alzheimer's.

A new wine accompanied dessert and, like a river, it flowed into glasses. Frank, possibly abetted with liquid courage, cleared his throat, leaned over the table, and said, "Philomela, I'd like to ask you a personal question."

"Yes?"

"Is your lovely hair color natural?"

"Young man," she replied, "that's for me to know and for you to wonder." She smiled and added, "For your ears only, this color is professionally known as Radiant Red."

"Radiant it is." Frank's gray eyes sparkled and his lips curved in a wide grin. "You know, I just remembered where I first saw you two ladies. During Stampede. Lunch at Fourth Street Rose."

"Omigod." Janice put her left hand up to her mouth. "You were going out as we were coming in. You had a chin beard and a moustache. I like you better without them." She lowered her eyes with apparent modesty.

"Good, I won't re-grow them."

When lunch finally drew to a close, Philomela glanced at her watch and the numbers blurred slightly. She blinked, stretched her arm as far as it would go, and read aloud, "Twenty minutes after four. Can you believe we've been eating lunch for more than three hours?"

Frank burst out laughing. "The company made time go fast."

"Perhaps the wine helped." Philomela chuckled. "Speaking of wine, I think I'll take a bottle back to my husband."

Along with several others, Frank and Philomela purchased award-winning wines then carried their well-packaged purchases down the white stairs to the driveway.

The petite mini-coach driver asked them to ride in the same coach and the same airplane they had occupied on the trip out. "That way no one will be left behind."

"Well," Frank said, "this is where we part company."

Janice nodded. "It's been an awesome day."

Settled in their seats in the Piper Cherokee, Janice and Philomela verbally relived the delightful tour and the lovely lunch. After the little plane ascended, Philomela said, "The altitude, not the wine, is slurring my speech." Janice did not reply. Philomela turned and gazed at her in astonishment. "You've fallen fast asleep," she murmured. With no more ado, she leaned back and followed suit.

When the wheels of the plane landed on the paved runway, Philomela's upper eyelids fluttered open. They were back in Perth. The hour flight had taken only minutes. Janice stirred beside her then woke up. They prepared to disembark.

In the hotel lobby, Frank joined them. "Nice flight. I suppose everyone is too tired to go for a walk."

Janice yawned and nodded her head.

"Tomorrow will come early," Philomela said. "In the lingering light of dawn, we'll float down the Swan River to the town of Freemantle." She moved ahead so the two young people could stroll side by side.

Still feeling full from lunch, Philomela placed her hands on her abdomen. The action brought to mind Pierre Lalonde's portly figure. He would have enjoyed today's lunch. His life span had been only a few years longer than hers. Too young to die, especially from a freakish accident. If it was an accident.

Her abdomen contracted and she stopped walking. Something about Pierre's fall nagged at her. She visualized him at the top of the Coyote Lounge stairs and wondered why he had fallen.

Had he tripped on a loose carpet? Had he experienced a brief case of vertigo? Had he experienced a minor stroke?

Or had there been a more sinister reason for his death?

She hurried to their hotel room to check her emails.

CHAPTER 20

The cruise down the Swan River was scenic, the town of Freemantle was charming, and Janice couldn't ask for more pleasant companions. Frank noted that the ambience of the town was enhanced by having been the center for an America's Cup sailing race. Philomela mentioned that the beach looked ideal for swimming. Like a true importer, Don suggested they explore the town's attractive boutiques.

Inside a shop, Janice saw Philomela grab Don's arm and heard her whisper, "This place is a tourist trap." It was true. The small area overflowed with stuff. Philomela pointed out a few items that were good and many that weren't. Don laughed and actually seemed to pay attention to her.

"Are you being inundated with import ideas?" Janice asked him.

"My head's spinning," he replied.

It was four-thirty when they arrived back at their hotel in Perth, an hour before they were due to board coaches for another adventure. Warm weather, early mornings, and busy sight-seeing schedules were taking their toll. Inside their room, Janice flopped on the bed and closed her eyes.

Forty minutes later she opened them to see Philomela in panties and bra standing in front of the closet, contemplating her meagre wardrobe.

"Did you have a shower?" Janice asked, raising her head and rubbing her eyes.

"Yes. Did you have a good sleep?

Janice sat up and nodded her head.

"You'd better shake a leg. You've got twenty minutes to get ready."

Janice took a quick shower, donned her yellow skirt and shirt, and dabbed lipstick on her lips. "I surmise," she said, "that Pioneer World in Perth will resemble Heritage Park in Calgary."

∽∾∽

Her surmise proved correct. With historical accuracy, both places contained wooden buildings of frontier designs. The visual impact of Pioneer World immediately took both women back in time to the early settlers, circa 1880. Local guides and shop keepers wore period dress and, adding to the time-frame, was a large bosomed, yellow-haired lady adorned in a long orange gown and a big red hat. She greeted them with a loud, cockney accent.

"Welcome, welcome. My name is Madame and I am so pleased to see you. You can play two-up, shop, or come with me and have some fun." Her eyes zeroed in on Frank who walked several paces behind Philomela and Janice. Madame strolled over to him and took his arm. "Come with me, you darlin' man. I want to chat you up."

"Is chatting all you do?" Frank asked.

"Mercy no." She chuckled. "I have numerous tricks to show you. You two ladies go up the road to the beer hall and leave me to look after this gentleman. Take your time and look at the shops. This darlin' man and I have stories to tell and things to do." She chuckled again and, holding Frank by the arm, led him along the center of the road.

Janice watched Frank a few seconds then shrugged. Surely he would survive Madame's clutches. All she could do was walk with Philomela toward the beer hall. En route they stopped at two shops, admired clothing and accessories, but bought nothing. At the third shop, they were tempted by two didgeridoos, but knowing the large musical instruments would make difficult travelling companions, they settled on purchasing two small boomerangs.

"Easier to pack than didgeridoos," Janice said as she paid the cashier.

Outside on the road, they heard the tinkling sound of piano music. It increased in volume as they neared the beer hall. Janice peered inside the hall and saw Madame sitting on a stool playing the upright instrument. She saw no sign of Frank, but she spotted Don standing at the bar with other members of their group. He was holding a glass of beer.

Madame began to sing and several people surrounded the piano and joined her in song. Not everyone knew the words, but that did not stop them from humming the familiar tunes. Philomela and Janice made their way to the bar, ordered iced tea from the bartender then found an empty table and sat down.

"Madam's music is melodious," Philomela said. "She must be a professional entertainer."

Madame suddenly quit playing the piano and stood up. "He is here," she announced in a loud voice and pointed toward the entranceway. "Thomo the Outbacker is here."

A wild looking man with straggly hair leaned against the doorframe. "Who wants to come outside and play a game of Two Up?" he yelled. "I'll even provide the betting money." He held up a wad of bills.

"Play-dough," Philomela said. She stood up, smiled encouragingly at Janice, and started to walk toward the door.

Janice followed her outside. Don joined them and, with four other people, they formed a circle. Thomo distributed funny money, held up a disc, gave instructions, and then proceeded to play a form of Heads or Tails.

Philomela and Janice quickly lost all their play-dough. Don lasted the longest and ended up being the big winner.

"This is my lucky day," Don announced to a group

of onlookers. He raised his glass to his lips and drained it. "I need another beer," he said.

A new man appeared. Holding shears in one hand and a shaggy sheep in the other, he explained that he was a sheep-shearer. Near the main door of the beer hall, he gave a rapid demonstration of the art of relieving sheep of several pounds of wool. As the animal ran off, everyone applauded. The sheep-shearer then directed them to a larger building where they were given a small tin cup of billie and a hunk of damper. They drank the tea and tried to eat the damper.

"Damper is something I can live without." Janice surreptitiously threw her small piece of heavy bread into a nearby garbage can.

A drunk dressed in a shabby black suit and bowler hat staggered up to her. "Don't you like dampeh?" he asked in a very British accent.

"Not particularly," Janice replied.

"Do you deem it a delicacy?" Philomela asked.

Seeming rather tipsy, he nodded his head. "I am a remittance man and I eat great quantities of dampeh. My name is Archie." With classic dignity, he raised his hat then lost his balance and almost fell over. With no dignity at all, he staggered away.

"There's Frank," Janice said, waving at him. She hurried toward him but Madame was faster.

"You darlin' man," she said in a strident voice. "Come this way. A beautiful buffet dinner of lamb, prawns, and salads is waiting for us in the dining hall." She took Frank's arm and led him to the buffet table.

"Sounds good," Janice said. "I'm starving."

"Even after eating that big lunch at Freemantle?" Philomela asked.

"That was hours ago," Janice replied.

After filling her plate at the buffet table, she sat down beside Philomela and Don and ate heartily. Finishing her meal, she watched Archie the remittance man wander amongst the tables, smile foolishly at guests, and unsteadily chase young serving wenches.

"Do you think Archie is really drunk?" Janice asked.

"I don't think so." Don laughed as Archie bumped into the table adjacent to theirs and nearly fell on top of one of the guests. "But he does remind me of a few drunks I have known."

They were eating desert when Archie staggered up to the stage. They soon realized he was a tried and true professional entertainer. He gave a monologue that kept them laughing for more than thirty minutes. The only times he stopped speaking were when hilarity drowned out his voice, and those times were frequent.

When the show was over, Janice's sides were sore and her jaw ached. It had been a long time since she had laughed so hard and so long.

Don stood up. "I have to see a man about a horse." He headed toward the men's room.

The two women wandered outside and Philomela philosophically observed, "Light has lost its fight with dark." She started at the sight of a man appearing from the shadows. "Oh, Frank, it's you. What did Madame do with you? Or is it a secret?"

"She took me to a shop and ditched me," he replied. "So I walked up that hill to a pen that held two large kangaroos. After I returned, she caught me again and pushed me first in line at the buffet table. Then she ditched me again."

Philomela chuckled. "Madame was obviously all talk and no action."

"Right on." He laughed and gazed over at the small hill. "Did you see the kangaroos in the enclosure at the end of that trail?"

"No," Janice replied, her eyes following his gaze.

"If you like, I'll take you there now."

Philomela declined the offer and walked over to a bench.

Janice, eager to see kangaroos, accepted the invitation. She strolled beside Frank up the trail under street lamps that were far apart and then petered out completely. They walked a short distance by the light of a gibbous moon and a million twinkling stars. Two rows of tall Eucalyptus trees suddenly obliterated the moon, making the trail darker and seemingly steeper and narrower. In the heavy gloom, Janice walked single file behind Frank.

"Even if kangaroos are there," Janice said, "how will we see them in the dark?" She tripped on a root and almost fell. Feeling increasingly nervous, she suggested, "Maybe we should turn around."

"The trees are thinning out. There's moonlight up ahead. We're almost there."

"Are there poisonous snakes here?" she asked.

"Hopefully, they're asleep."

Janice didn't find that particularly reassuring. Suddenly, a male voice yelled from far behind them, "The coaches are leaving. Janice and Frank, you'd better get back here right now."

"Too bad," Frank said. "The kangaroos are worth seeing."

With mixed emotions, she stopped walking. She wanted to leave the creepy path, yet at the same time, she wanted to see the kangaroos. Did she also want to continue enjoying Frank's company?

"We don't want to miss the coach," Frank said. He squeezed past her and started to retrace his steps.

She followed him until the trees thinned out and the gibbous moon reappeared. As the path widened, he waited and they walked side by side. When street lamps welcomed them, they headed for the coaches and saw several figures milling around. Like a guard on duty, one figure marched up to them.

"You sure took your time," Don growled.

"We went up the hill to look at kangaroos," Janice said.

"An unlikely story." Don chugalugged a beer. "How could you see them in the dark?"

"The hilltop is lit by the moon," Frank explained. "But we didn't get that far."

"I guess not." Don's voice rang with sarcasm. "I went up there when we first arrived. Even in daylight that trail is treacherous with several steep drop-offs." He frowned and in a zealous tone of voice said, "One of you could have fallen and been injured."

His words dismayed Janice, not because she feared injury but because Don was so loud and so critical. Was it beer talk or was he really worried about them? People gathered around as he loudly continued his reprimand.

"Frank, you were foolhardy. If you saw the kangaroos earlier, you must have been aware of the dangers."

"I walked there when it was light," Frank said. "I didn't notice any steep drop-offs."

"You must suffer from tunnel vision." Don glanced with a smirk of satisfaction at his growing audience.

Janice suspected his uncharacteristic words and behaviour resulted from too much beer so she tried to change the subject. "Are the coaches ready to leave?"

"One has already gone," Don said. "The last one is waiting for stragglers like you and Frank."

She hurried to the remaining coach and saw Philomela sitting beside Madeline Bouchard. Janice sat down in the seat directly in front of Philomela.

"Janice," Philomela said, leaning toward her, "did you find the kangaroos?"

"No. We didn't have time to go all the way up."

Don strode down the aisle and stopped beside Philomela. "Frank foolishly took her up a dangerous path in the dark."

"Were you the hero who rescued her?" Philomela asked.

"You might put it that way."

Janice thought he was puffed up with importance but when Philomela snickered he diminished in size. He turned and walked toward the front of the coach and sat down beside Miranda Gordon.

Feeling miffed by his words and behavior, Janice listened to Philomela chat with her seat companion.

"Madeline, did you enjoy tonight's British music-hall entertainment?"

"Is that what it's called? I must remember the name so I'll never have to attend another one."

Janice stiffened. Turning, she witnessed Philomela's faint smile.

"It takes all kinds to make a world," Philomela said. "I'm one of those who enjoy that type of comedy, especially when it's well done."

Compared with the boisterous entertainment and Don's loud reprimands, the coach ride back to the hotel was serene and quiet. Silence continued until Janice and Philomela entered their room.

"Madeline is very snooty," Janice said.

"Slapstick humor isn't everyone's cup of tea."

Janice put on her nightgown and hung up her yellow skirt and shirt. Stuffing her underclothes into her small laundry bag, she was surprised when Philomela stepped out of the bathroom and abruptly asked, "Do you like Frank?"

"Yes, he's nice."

"As nice as Don?

Suspecting the questions were more than idle conversation, Janice watched as her mentor climb into bed. "Do you think Frank was wrong to take me up the hill in the dark?"

"The question is—were Don's acerbic accusations based on fact?"

"Frank said he didn't see any steep drop-offs. Nor did I."

Lying in bed in the dark, Janice thought about Don's exaggerated concern for her safety. His loud annoyance with Frank had been embarrassing and unhelpful.

She no longer felt like a princess in fairyland. She felt more like Alice in the rabbit hole. Things were getting curiouser and curiouser. In fact, they were getting downright odd.

CHAPTER 21

Children darted to and fro. They held necklaces, bracelets, and small articles of batik under the noses of tourists, forcing them to stop and listen to their songs: "One American dollah. One American dollah."

Janice turned her attention from the energetic children to a few attractive women standing silently in front of a row of tents.

They had smooth dusky skin, sleek dark hair, and nary an ounce of excess fat on their trim bodies. With practiced eyes, they studied tourists walking through the market and, every so often, one glided forward and zeroed in on a likely customer.

"This way, this way," called male hawkers who also stood near the tents. "Come, come."

Each merchant focused on the flow of moving tourists, as if planning to write a psychology thesis, then, for no apparent reason, one would move forward and latch onto a potential buyer.

"This is awful," Philomela said. "The children chant and the hawkers hoot. I'd rather walk through a mass of marauding mosquitoes."

"Don't look at them," Janice said. "Madeline said eye contact makes them think they have you."

"Five American dollahs." A beautiful young girl brushed up against Janice and held a gold and red piece of cotton batik in front of her face.

Taken by surprise, Janice gazed at the fabric. She could not help but admire the startling colors and the intricate designs.

"Five American dollahs," the girl repeated in a singsong voice, her large dark eyes looking hopefully at Janice's face.

"Come on, Janice." Don grabbed her arm. "We're not shopping. We're on our way to the Holy Springs Temple."

The young girl clutched Janice's other arm. "Five American dollahs."

"Don't show any interest," Don said, moving between the girl and Janice.

"But I was interested," Janice said, looking back at the young girl who now targeted Philomela.

Vigorously shaking her head, Philomela hurried forward and the young girl zeroed in on another unsuspecting tourist. Her singsong voice again rang like a melody, "Five American dollahs."

Janice, Don, and Philomela stared straight ahead and

followed their guide between the two rows of Balinese market tents. The market thinned out.

"This is better," Philomela said.

She spoke too soon. Like a swarm of locusts men surrounded them and hollered, "Sashes for the temple. One American dollah."

Earlier, on the coach, their guide had warned them about the gold sashes. They would not be allowed to enter the temple without one.

"Why did we bother getting Balinese rupiahs?" Janice asked. "These people only want American dollars."

"What will happen if the American dollar drops in value?" Philomela asked. No one answered so she dug in her purse and brought out a green dollar bill.

Each of their fellow tourists rented the required accessory from one of the sellers and within minutes every waistline was encircled by a yellow sash.

As Janice finished tying a bow in hers, their guide strode up to her and pointed to a large sign by the entrance gate. Her eyes followed the direction of his finger and she read the sign: *Menstruating Women Not Allowed To Enter.*

She felt her mouth open in a surprised, "O." With a giggle of embarrassment, she looked at the guide, shook her head and said, "I'm okay. This isn't my time of month."

Apparently satisfied, he glanced questioningly at Philomela who also shook her head. He moved quickly over to the gate of the Holy Springs Temple.

"You're one of the few in our group who is young enough to have to worry about that," Philomela said.

"Don't you?" Janice asked.

"Less and less. It's called menopause."

They followed the guide along cement pathways and saw no specific temple, just a series of monuments protected from the elements by thatched roofs. At a pool of water—large and murky—the guide stopped.

"These are the healing waters from the holy spring," he explained. "The spring is over there." He pointed to a small rock outcrop.

Unable to see the actual spring, Janice studied the murky pool. She hoped she wouldn't get sick and have to rely on its healing powers.

When they walked back toward the entrance gate, Philomela approached the guide and asked if the temple was Hindu, Buddhist, or Muslim.

"Hindu," he replied.

"Does that religion concentrate on healing rather than on proselytising and killing?"

He nodded and led them through the open gate of the temple compound. From out of nowhere, the salesmen reappeared, snatched back their sashes, and hurried toward a new crowd of tourists. The call went up, "One American dollah."

In amazement, Janice watched them. "They must rent those grubby things again and again all day long," she said.

"Do you think those sashes ever get washed?" Philomela asked.

The question remained unanswered. They walked apprehensively toward the double row of tents. At the market, they again were greeted by swarms of children, a few male hawkers, and several dainty women.

"I'd like to buy a table cloth," Janice said to Philomela, "for my hopeless chest."

A delicate-looking lady who obviously understood English heard her. She grasped Janice's left wrist and very sweetly said, "I have beautiful table cloths. Come."

"I'll just be a minute, Philomela." Janice said. "You go ahead. I'll see you at the coach." She smiled expectantly at the petite lady and walked with her to the wide entranceway of a tent. They went inside, where Janice saw shelves overflowing with fabrics and ornaments. Still grasping her left wrist, the lady pulled her deeper into the mysterious dimness. Suddenly, Janice felt uncomfortable. She relaxed slightly when the thin little lady smiled, released her wrist, and pulled a large swatch of pink batik from a shelf.

"You like?"

In the dim light, Janice studied the fabric and shook her head. "No, I want to buy a white table cloth, not a piece of colored fabric."

The lady pulled out a red and white roll. "This good quality batik."

Janice fingered the thin fabric and shook her head again. "Too much red and it's not bound on the sides."

The lady pulled out another piece of batik, blue and white. Except for the color, it was the same as the one Janice had just touched.

"Thank you, but this isn't what I'm looking for." She turned to leave and the thin fingers again gripped her left wrist. Janice stared at her in amazement.

With one hand the delicate-looking lady held her fast, and with the other hand she pulled another swatch of fabric from the shelf. "You buy. Only twenty American dollahs."

"Please let go of my wrist," Janice said.

"You buy. Only twenty American dollahs."

Janice tried to pull free, but could not. She yanked her arm backward and the dainty fingers tightened like a vice. She was prepared to kick the woman in the shins when a movement at the entrance caught her attention. She saw a man standing like a statue with arms folded in front of his chest. His sturdy legs were wide apart and his feet were firmly planted on the ground. He watched tourists outside the tent and occasionally glanced at the two struggling women. Janice knew that even if she got away from the woman's vice-like grip, she would have trouble getting past that formidable looking man.

She didn't know what to do.

CHAPTER 22

Don stood with Philomela and Miranda outside the coach. They discussed Janice's absence and made suggestions on what was keeping her. Philomela said she might be making other purchases besides the tablecloth.

"A merchant may have gone to another tent to get correct change," Miranda said. "That would take time."

"Maybe Janice got caught in the crush of people," Don said.

Philomela's concern became obvious as she started to pace back and forth. "Have you recently seen Janice," she asked anyone who came nearby. "The girl with long blond hair?"

No one recalled seeing her.

"Why doesn't she come?" Philomela gazed toward the market. "Purchasing a tablecloth shouldn't take this long."

Miranda turned to Don and smiled. "Why don't you go back to the market and search for her? Philomela and I will stay here in case she returns. We'll let the driver know she's missing and that you're looking for her."

Don nodded, secretly pleased with Miranda's suggestion. Doubtless, she had no idea she was setting up a perfect opportunity for him to hide out with Janice, provided he succeeded in finding her.

He left the group by the coach and hurried toward the double row of market tents. Walking along one side of the tents, he slowed his steps at each opening and glanced inside. At the end of the row, he turned and proceeded to walk along the tents on the opposite side. Again, he paused at each one and scanned its interior. He even stepped inside a few for a better look.

While inside one of the tents, he recalled not seeing Frank near the coach. Could the veterinarian have something to do with Janice's absence? Was he up to no good? In Australia, Frank had enticed her up the hill to look at kangaroos, maybe because he planned to kidnap her. Had Bob underhandedly recruited Frank as an alternative kidnapper? In Don's mind, the idea grew like a monster. Everyone became suspect. Had Bob and Pierre promised to pay Frank a specific amount of money, conveniently forgetting the initial deal the three had made? Had his two joint-venture buddies willfully turned against him?

Surely, Pierre wouldn't do something like that. But Bob was a different matter.

Well, he'd show them. He would successfully carry off the kidnapping then hold out for a larger percentage of the ransom money. After all, he was the one taking all the risks. His share should be more. Bob and Pierre would learn they couldn't double deal with him.

Earlier, at the Holy Springs Temple, Don had felt in control of the situation. He had seen Frank get off the coach and stick with the group during the tour of the temple. So when had he disappeared? Where was he now? Was he with Janice?

He hurried past more tents and peeked inside. Children touched his arms and legs and showed him their wares. Men held up beautifully carved chess sets. Women drew close to him and in soft voices tried to lure him into their tents. He strode forward, carelessly brushing them aside. Ignoring both the merchants and their merchandise, he continued his search.

As he walked from a small tent he caught sight of Janice dashing out of a larger one. He froze in surprise, then he sighed with relief—Frank had not kidnapped her. Don ran after her at break-neck speed.

"Janice," he called. "Janice, wait for me."

The cacophony of sounds seemed to prevent her from hearing him. He ran faster, called louder, and, finally, she glanced back and saw him. She slowed her pace and stopped. Catching up to her, he saw the expression on her face. It was either sheer terror or primitive anger. He wasn't sure which.

"Are you okay?" he asked.

"Oh, Don. I just had the most dreadful experience."

He moved closer, put a hand on each of her shoulders, and gazed questioningly into her eyes.

"A woman enticed me into the back of her tent and latched onto me." Janice held up her left arm and he saw dark finger marks coloring the skin of her wrist.

"My god," Don said. "What happened?"

"The saleslady clutched my wrist and a man stood guard at the entrance to ensure I couldn't get away." She held up a flimsy piece of material. "For this piece of junk I gave her all the money I had. Four American dollars, one Australian dollar, and five hundred Indonesian rupiahs. Then she let go of my wrist and then the man at the entrance of the tent stepped aside and let me leave."

"I'll go back there and tell them a thing or two."

"No, don't. Why create an incident? I wasn't hurt and, fortunately, I didn't have much money with me."

"At least you're okay," he said.

"Everyone will be waiting for me. I'll be in the doghouse again." She gazed at him wistfully.

Noticing a stone bench nearby, he said, "You've had a bad experience. You need to rest before facing the annoyed group on the coach."

She followed him to the bench, sat down, and took a few deep breaths. "My heartbeat's finally slowing down. You're a great comfort, Don."

He sat beside her, put his arm protectively around her shoulders, and watched her close her eyes. He felt confident that she was putting all her trust in him. What better time for the two of them to take off from the tour group?

"*Bon jour.*"

The two words jarred him like an earthquake. He

looked up at Madeline Bouchard who stood in front of the bench. Her sparkling white teeth, beaded top, and bright skirt almost blinded him. He felt annoyed, almost angry.

"Am I interrupting a tryst?" she asked and her smile widened.

"Not at all," Janice replied. "We're just resting."

"You like my outfit? I bought the skirt and top in one of those tents and decided to wear them immediately."

"They're lovely," Janice said. "Lots of bling."

"*Merci beaucoup.* Now we go to the coach. We're late."

"Yes, we are." Janice stood up. She looked down at Don who continued to sit on the bench. "Are you coming, Don?"

His lips formed a straight line and, in slow motion, he stood up. Feeling annoyed, he followed the two women and tried to tune out Madeline's enthusiastic chatter. At the parking lot, her voice managed to penetrate his eardrums.

"I had such fun shopping in that market," she said.

"I'm glad someone did." Janice walked up to Philomela and Miranda and stopped. "I apologize, again," she said.

"Oh Janice." Philomela gave her a hug. "Miranda kept reassuring me that everything was okay, and thank goodness she proved to be right."

"Salespeople wouldn't let me leave their tent. It was awful. I'll tell you about it later."

She moved behind Don and Miranda and went up the steps into the coach. Philomela followed.

"You should be ashamed of yourself," the cane-lady admonished, pointing her cane like a long index finger at Janice. "You kept everyone waiting. Again. You're an inconsiderate brat."

"It wasn't her fault," Philomela said, leaning toward the angry woman.

Not mollified or interested in reasons for the delay, the lady continued to wave her cane like a weapon. Janice ducked, to keep from being hit, then hurried down the aisle, apologizing to everyone as she went by them. She plopped down on a seat in front of Don and Miranda.

"Did Don rescue you?" Philomela asked, sitting down beside her.

"No. He saw me run out of their tent. He caught up with me and we sat on a bench to catch our breath. Madeline hustled us to the coach."

"It was un-gentlemanly of him to let you take the brunt of the cane-lady's anger."

Sitting behind them, Don coughed and cleared his throat.

CHAPTER 23

Ten months ago, Kuala Lumpur had been nothing but an exotic name on a map. Now it had an airport arrival area with a large scary sign: *Anyone carrying drugs will be penalized with death.* Janice glanced around. She hoped no one had stashed illegal drugs in her carry-on.

Relieved to get through customs alive, she followed Philomela to a parked coach. On the drive from the airport to the hotel, she listened to the guide explain that Kuala Lumpur means "muddy estuary." She learned that the city is the capital of Malaysia and contains six and a half million people, more population than any Canadian metropolis. Near the city center, she glimpsed the Petronas Twin Towers and heard the guide announce it had appeared in the movie, *Entrapment,* starring Sean Connery.

Inside their hotel bedroom, she admired the attractive

decor and agreed with Philomela's assessment: "Our room is colorful and comfortable. The Shangri-La Hotel lives up to its name—Paradise."

❧❧❧

Next morning, Janice made her way through the high-ceilinged lobby and pinched her arm to make sure she wasn't dreaming. The pinch hurt so she knew she was awake. She patiently followed the cane-lady up the steps of the coach then waited for her to plop her buttocks on the prime front seat. Janice avoided her cane and abusive words by scurrying down the aisle and midway settling on a seat beside a white-haired lady who seemed the inverse of the cane-lady. Through the window, Janice glimpsed Frank maneuver amongst a group of fellow travellers then she turned and saw Don sit down on the seat across the aisle from her. Glancing over at him, she noted his clenched jaw and wondered if he was recalling Philomela's remark about his ungentlemanly behavior. Or maybe he was still fretting about Frank taking her kangaroo hunting. Peripherally, she saw Frank walk down the aisle of the coach, stop and chat with a lady, and sit down beside her. Don's body bent forward as if trying to catch Frank's words.

"Don," she said, leaning across the aisle. "I think Frank got the last seat."

"Too bad he didn't get to sit with his main target."

She looked at him, puzzled.

"You. You're his main target. He knows your dad is a wealthy oilman."

Janice's spine stiffened and she felt indignant. "My dad isn't wealthy. He's fairly well off because he works hard and is a good oil finder." She glared at him.

Don shrugged.

The coach moved forward and she turned away. Gazing past the white-haired lady at the window, she pondered the connotation of Don's words. What did he mean? She didn't know. For a few minutes, she concentrated on impressive skyscrapers then her thoughts flitted back to Don. Did he know something about the veterinarian that she didn't know? Had he implied that Frank was a fortune seeker? Ridiculous. Frank had assumed that she and Don were an item, but she had quickly squashed that idea. After their evening stroll in Perth, her contact with Frank was nil, until last night.

Though their pleasant walk had ended on a sour note because of Don, for the last three days Frank had steered clear of her. Too bad. She would have enjoyed hearing his impression of the Balinese artist's village, the wood carver's village, and the silver smith's village. She wondered what he would say about her encounter with the aggressive saleslady with the vice-like grip.

Automatically rubbing her wrist, she recalled the nerve-wracking experience. Even now, she felt her heart beat faster and her palms grow moist. She doubted the woman and her male partner would have inflicted any serious harm, but they certainly scared her. Oh well, she now owned a tacky piece of rayon, not even true batik, as a memorabilia. Her annoyance with Don softened as she recalled how kind he had been coming to look for her. He really did have redeeming qualities. She wondered if they would have missed the coach if Madeline had not hurried them along.

Yesterday, the situation had been similar. In Kuala Lumpur's open air market, their intrepid flight captain tried on blue-jeans while she and Don wandered off to view fake designer purses and watches. They would have missed the coach again if not for Madeline. She tracked them down and told them to hurry because fellow-travellers were already boarding. Janice thanked her profusely, trying to compensate for Don's sulky lack of appreciation.

Again, she glanced across the aisle at Don's neatly trimmed brown moustache and chin beard. He seemed to be watching Frank, so she cocked her head to get a better view of the object of his attention.

As Frank chatted with the lady beside him, Janice focused on his curly hair and straight nose. She could imagine him healing a sick animal. Then she chastised herself for letting her thoughts dwell on him. She hardly knew the man.

Last night at the captain's party at the Shangri-la Hotel, she had noticed Frank converse amicably with other guests. He chatted with good grace and seemed a sensitive listener. When Don wandered over to the bar, Frank appeared at her side. He gallantly obtained a drink for her and then Don reappeared. The string quartet soon made Don restless so he wandered off and ended up chatting with the bartender. She and Frank listened to the four musicians.

It was during their rendition of "Moonlight Sonata" that she experienced a sudden feeling of faintness and had to sit down. Unable to explain the exact cause of the feeling, she was inclined to blame it on stronger than normal alcoholic drinks. Don had gotten her a gin and tonic and Frank had obtained another. Could either of them have ordered a double or a triple?

Her rumination ceased as the coach came to a stop.

"The Batu Cave," the guide said, "has two-hundred and seventy-six steps. Anyone who has health problems or tires easily in heat and humidity should climb slowly—or stay inside the coach—or wait in that little cafe over there." He pointed to a small eatery. "Monkeys play on the stairs and climb on the railings. They will try to get anything shiny, especially spectacles. If you are wearing sunglasses, you should take them off when the monkeys are nearby. The Sri Subramaniya Swamy temple was established in Batu Cave in 1891. Many symbols of Hindu gods may be seen there. Religious services are often held at the cave."

When the guide's informative spiel came to an end, Janice made her way along the aisle just in front of Don. Outside, he stayed close to her and they walked side by side to the stairs. His sulky attitude was replaced by a cheerful one.

The temperature grew hotter and muggier as they ascended the steps. Their breathing grew labored. At a wide landing, they stopped to rest.

"I'd hate to walk up these steep stairs in the middle of the day," Don said, taking a tissue from his shirt pocket and wiping his brow. "It's bad enough now, and it's not even ten-o-clock."

"Maybe Philomena was wise to stay at the hotel for her dress and coat fitting. Can you imagine having a tailored outfit made in one and a half days?"

"No," he said, "I can't."

"The silk fabric she chose is awesome. The price is so reasonable, I was tempted to order one, too, but I wouldn't wear it enough to make it worthwhile. Besides, I'd rather go to the Batu Cave than hang around the hotel, waiting for a fitting. Oh, look." She pointed up the stairs. "There are a couple of monkeys with those school kids."

Don followed her gaze and they watched children feed two chattering monkeys. The animals jumped on the railing, grasped food from their hands, tasted each morsel, and gobbled it up.

Don chuckled. "Just like cattle on the ranch."

"Pardon?"

"The monkeys remind me of cattle eating grass."

Not seeing the connection, she said, "At least you don't have to worry about cattle snatching your sunglasses." She took off her sunglasses and put them in her purse. "Just to be on the safe side," she said.

The monkeys studied Janice and Don but apparently found them un-glittery and uninteresting. There were no monkeys at the next wide landing so Don and Janice paused to catch their breath.

They put their sunglasses back on, admired the panoramic view, then continued up the stairs. At the top they stopped.

"This must be the two hundredth and seventy-sixth step," Janice said.

"Were you counting?"

"I lost count about a hundred steps ago."

They entered a greenish cave. In its deepening interior, she saw splatters of water on the floor and moisture oozing from ceiling and walls. The floor was slippery and in a few areas puddles of water had formed. She took off her sunglasses, stepped around the puddles, and continued deeper in the cave.

Off to one side in a small alcove, a Hindu religious service was being held. They watched surreptitiously for a few minutes then moved on. In an adjoining room, colorful stalactites hung from the roof and stalagmites shot up from the floor. They walked around them and saw sun beaming like a searchlight through a hole in the ceiling.

"The cave is huge," Janice said.

"Look, here's another room." Don walked around a wooden barricade and peered at a tiny arched opening. "Let's go in." He crouched down to avoid hitting his head and walked through the small opening.

"Why is the barricade here?" Janice asked.

"I don't know. But there's no warning sign of danger, so it must be safe."

Janice walked around the barricade, eased under the narrow arch, and entered a large area so full of stalagmites that she had to watch every step. They penetrated farther inside the cave and it grew darker. Janice's face brushed against something that made her freeze in her tracks.

"Let's go back," she whispered.

"Not yet. Come on."

"My face just brushed against something."

"Probably a stalactite."

"More like a spider web," she said. "We're far from the main thoroughfare and the barricade was there for a reason. Maybe the floors are weak. Maybe the walls or roof might cave in."

"I doubt it, Janice. The area wasn't totally blocked off, so it can't be too dangerous. Come on. Let's go." He took hold of her hand and led her forward.

The dimness made it difficult to see the lime deposits in front of her and she tripped but regained her balance. She stopped and tried to pull her hand from his.

He clutched her hand tighter. "Come on, just a little farther."

"We have to go back. The coach will leave without us."

"We've got lots of time." He pulled her deeper into the tunnel-like cave.

Hearing a noise, she looked around and saw only darkness.

The noise came again and, this time, it echoed eerily off the walls.

She could not identify what the sound was or where it came from. "Did you hear that?" she asked.

"Yeah."

To her relief, he stopped moving forward. The noise

came again and she listened intently. "It sounds like footsteps. I think someone's following us."

"Damn." His voice twanged with irritation.

"Maybe it's a robber." Janice peered toward the opening and her free hand clung nervously to her purse. "Imagine being beaten up by a mugger while a religious service is going on around the corner."

In the dimness, she saw nothing untoward but the sound grew in intensity. It quickly materialized into definite footsteps.

"It's just one person," she said and then called out, "Who's there?"

"Janice, is that you?"

She burst out laughing. What a relief to hear a voice she recognized. "Frank, what are you doing here?"

"Same as you. Sightseeing."

"There's not much to see," Don muttered. "This area's closed off."

Like a shadowy ghost, Frank appeared and moved closer. "I was told they put up the barricade because the walls here are unstable. This is quite a place." He walked over to one wall and felt it. "I wouldn't want to spend the night here. No floor space for stretching out."

"And cold and wet," Janice said.

"Do you realize it's nearly departure time?" Frank asked.

Don let go of her hand and moved to the narrow entrance. She and Frank followed him. Squeezing under the archway and walking around the barricade, she felt relieved that a wall had not collapsed on them. Inside the large, greenish cave, she glanced over at the Hindu religious service then looked back at Frank. He smiled encouragingly. Don strode ahead toward the main entrance.

Outside, she watched Don stride down the steps. "Don, what's your hurry?" she called.

"We don't want to miss the coach," he said over his shoulder.

She opened her mouth to remind him that a few minutes ago he had been unconcerned about missing the coach. Thinking better of stressing his inconsistency, she closed her mouth and slowed her pace. Frank caught up with her and together they started to descend the two hundred and seventy-six steps.

At the bottom of the stairs, Janice looked around. No one from their group was in sight, not even Don. "Omigod," she said, "Am I going to be a pariah again?" She grabbed Frank's hand. They dashed to the coach and climbed aboard. They greeted the guide and the driver.

"You're late again," the cane-lady yelled at Janice.

"You're not late," Miranda Gordon said. She was sitting two rows behind the cane-lady. "You're four minutes early."

Janice smiled at her gratefully and continued down the aisle. She sat down beside the pleasant white-haired lady who murmured, "You just made it. You have trouble being early, don't you?"

Janice nodded. "It's not always my fault."

"What happened this time?"

"I'm afraid we went too far into the cave."

"All three of you?"

"Yes. I apologize if we made you wait." She glanced at her watch and realized that Miranda's time was close to the mark. She really was on time.

Two other passengers came aboard and a few minutes later the coach moved ahead.

CHAPTER 24

"Get out. Get out."
"No no no no!"
"Hiyihiyi."

Janice stared through a stone archway at a sea of angry male faces. From inside the small courtyard, she could see eyes glaring at her, mouths moving up and down, heads shaking vigorously, and clenched fists hitting at the air. What had she done to deserve their anger?

"Out, out."

"No go, no go."

"Unclean, unclean."

"No, no, no!"

"Hiyihiyi."

One voice filtered through the male cacophony. It stood out because of its higher pitch and because the words instead of being angry and negative were clear and positive.

"Janice, come over here."

She gazed desperately at the mass of Nepalese males, all angry and drawing closer and closer to her. Trying to ignore their encroaching movements and threatening sounds, she desperately sought the owner of the higher-pitched voice. Finally, she saw her.

Philomela stood on the far side of the madly gesticulating crowd of unfamiliar men and on the near side of the group of familiar world tourists. Her five-foot-three figure dressed in a Kelly-green pant suit appeared like a small haven of peace. She made Janice think of a verdant miniature park in the middle of a large stone square.

The yelling increased in volume and the fist waving grew closer and more frenzied. There was no question— the angry yelling and menacing fists were directed at her. Fear gripped her. What was wrong? She had touched nothing. She had said nothing. She had simply walked through a stone archway into a small courtyard filled with lifeless statues and stone benches.

The angry men drew closer and their voices competed with the wild drumbeat of her heart. She glanced briefly back at the small courtyard, took a deep breath, then strode bravely through the archway toward the crowd. She scurried off to the side around the men and the angry noise lessened. A dim light of understanding dawned on her—was something religious involved?

After bypassing the men, she flew down a slope to Philomela. Her mentor's arms enfolded her and the angry noise subsided. Feeling like an injured bird, Janice felt her rapid heartbeat slow and her breathing grow less shallow. The warmth of Philomela's embrace assured her that all was right with the world.

"Well, Janice, you did it again."

She gazed into her mentor's green eyes. "What did I do wrong this time?"

"You stirred up a lot of excitement. The guide warned us—the courtyard up there is sacred for Hindu devotees, males only. Women are forbidden to enter. If a woman even looks inside, it is a bad omen. And you strode right in."

"Omigod." Janice's hands flew up and covered the lower part of her face. "I didn't hear him say that. I must have been gawking around and not paying attention."

"You certainly made those local men pay attention." Philomena grinned and glanced at the crowd of males who continued to jabber and stare with malice at Janice. "Your short skirt probably didn't help either."

"I wore this dark skirt because it touches my knees."

"Not modest enough," Philomela said.

"What's so almighty important about that small courtyard anyway? It only contains stone benches and statues."

"It belongs to a patriarchal religion. It's designed to help power-hungry males dominate and demean females."

"Philomela!" Janice exclaimed. "You're a female chauvinist pig."

"Occasionally." Philomela's face registered mock seriousness. "Have you ever noticed how most of women's problems start with men?"

"In what way?" Janice asked.

"Mental illness. Menstrual cramps. Menopause. Menace."

"You're incorrigible." Janice giggled, feeling better already. Then she glanced over at the men who were dispersing. "You know, I really was scared. Those men looked angry enough to stone me to death."

"That might have happened had you not been with a large group of tourists." Philomela's green eyes flashed as she peered at some of the men. "Those fellows envy the insatiable power of the vagina."

"Philomela." Janice giggled again. "You're reversing Freud's theory of penis envy."

"Do you think I can compete with Freud?"

"Of course, you can," Frank said. Unnoticed by the two women, he had extricated himself from the tourist group and walked over to them. He smiled. "Janice, you always manage to spice up our tours."

She didn't know whether to be flattered or offended.

"We're at the mercy of male devotees," Philomela said. "It's time to go. Besides, our group is leaving."

Frank nodded and his clear gray eyes shifted from Janice's blue eyes to Philomela's green ones.

"Janice didn't hear our guide warning us about that little courtyard," Philomela explained as they walked through the square to a large entrance gate.

"That explains everything," Frank said.

Philomela led the way through the gateway. As they reached the other side, a small man magically appeared. From under his shirt he pulled out a large, sheathed knife.

Janice gasped, terrified. The man was going to kill her for her indiscretion. She clutched Frank's arm. He moved between her and the man, as if protecting her from unwarranted violence. Her heart thumped wildly beneath her ribs.

"Ten American dollahs," the man said.

Frank looked down at his face and grinned. Janice sighed with relief—the man was not an assassin, he was a merchant trying to make an honest living. She watched Frank take the curved knife from its sheath and study it first with his eyes and then with his fingers.

"Okay," he said and put the knife back in the sheath. He opened a Velcro pocket in his pants, pulled out his money clip, and extracted a ten-dollar American bill.

The man leaned forward, scrutinized the money, and then accepted it. Both men smiled, happy with their business transaction. The Nepalese man disappeared as magically as he had appeared.

Philomela, who had turned and witnessed the transaction, seemed astounded. "He came and went like a jinni in a jar," she said.

"This," Frank said, holding up his new purchase, "is a Ghurkha knife. I didn't expect to buy a lethal weapon at the gate to a temple square."

"I wonder what the priests would say about this little business deal," Philomela mused.

"Nothing," Frank said. "Janice's crime was far worse than a man selling a knife."

Philomela snorted but held her tongue.

As they strolled toward their tour group, standing in

a square bordered with shops, Frank glided his fingers over the shiny blade. Janice saw Don staring at it as if mesmerized.

"You have a knife," he said to Frank.

Frank nodded and dramatically replaced the knife in its sheath. "I just bought it." Before he could tell Don about his deal, the guide began to speak.

"Worshipers in many of these temples combine Hinduism and Buddhism. Both religions focus on Allah." The guide pointed toward the majestic mountains. "Observe the Himalayan mountains and note the two middle syllables of Himalayan—al-a."

"Could Allah on the Himalayas compare with Zeus on Mount Olympus?" Philomela whispered,.

"No one worships Zeus," Janice replied.

"That's his best feature."

"You have thirty minutes to shop," the guide said. "Then you will return to the coach for a drive to Dhulikhel, a beautiful mountain resort on the road to Tibet. There we will eat lunch."

They admired merchandise displayed outside the tiny shops and watched cows wander freely between the tables. They moved aside as one of the animals walked toward them.

"Holy cows have more freedom around here than unholy women do," Philomela said and gently patted the cow on its shoulder.

CHAPTER 25

The coach snaked up a twisty, narrow road. Philomela cringed at the hairpin curves and steep drop-offs, yet was in awe of the majestic mountains and neatly terraced rice fields. When meeting local coaches, she couldn't believe how many people were packed like sardines inside and how almost as many clung for dear life outside. At each viewing stop, she and other tourists climbed from their coach and were bombarded by young children calling, "gum" and "one American dollah." Every so often, the coach passed men and women whose backs were laden with hay, sticks, or straw.

Philomela pointed to a woman bent forward with a gigantic load of sticks on her back. "There's an example of equality of the sexes," she said.

Janice stared at the woman who walked sedately, bearing her huge burden.

"Going uphill must double the weight of her load," Philomela said.

"Her hair's gray, her skin's weather-beaten, and her body hasn't an ounce of fat. She must be eighty years old."

"Or perhaps fifty."

"Your age?" Janice shook her head. "You have smooth skin and radiant red hair. Could you carry a load of sticks like that?"

"Yes, if I'd practiced it all my life."

As they entered the town, Philomela repeated the guide's earlier comment: "It is a beautiful mountain resort." She gazed at clean and attractive buildings, tables set up outside for lunch, and rice fields forever climbing the ascending foothills.

Everyone left the coach and silently gazed at the stunning vistas. The guide once again beckoned for them to gather around.

"Anything under fifteen thousand feet is called a foothill. These lordly mountains are the great wonders of Allah. You may stay here and admire them or go over there and purchase beer and soft drinks." He pointed to a table laden with bottles and cans. "Then you may help yourselves to the buffet of Nepalese dishes. Please sit at any table you wish." He flashed a smile, waved his hand, and walked away.

Standing beside Janice, Philomela saw Don come toward them. It occurred to her that all morning he had avoided her, doubtless annoyed with her un-lady-like remark on the coach last evening. Now, however, he walked up and smiled at her as if all were forgiven. He hooked his arm through Janice's. Philomela found his possessive action irksome.

"Could I buy you beautiful ladies something to drink?" he asked. "Maybe a beer?"

"Thanks for the offer, Don," Philomela replied. "But we'll join the queue and buy our own."

"Forever independent." He grinned at her then guided Janice to the food queue and stopped behind the cane-lady.

Philomela moved behind them and Frank joined her.

"See those paths on top of the dikes in the rice fields?" Don said to Janice. "They're trekking trails. There are similar trails behind our hotel in Katmandu. Maybe you and I could follow one up to the white and gold temple, the one they call the Monkey Temple."

"What a good idea." She turned and looked at Philomela and Frank. "Would you two be interested in doing that?"

"Possibly," Frank said.

Philomela did not reply because her attention focused on the cane-lady who stuck her walking stick in front of Miranda Gordon's ankles. Miranda, who was carrying a plate laden with food, lost control. She stumbled, but miraculously she did not fall down. Her plate, however, flipped forward, tossing food on herself and on the grass.

"You idiot," she screamed at the cane-lady. "You tripped me on purpose."

The cane-lady stared at Miranda and held her cane high in the air. "I did not."

"You stuck that miserable stick in front of my foot. I'm sick of you waving that stupid thing at everyone. I'm also sick of the way you always demand preferential treatment and never let anyone else sit in the front seat of the coach."

The cane-lady's face grew red. "You think you're so classy with those fancy clothes and that fancy hair."

"I hope I'm not as tacky as you."

Philomela stepped from the line and picked up Miranda's plate and some of the scattered food. Their guide ran over, took the plate from her, and, with a cloth, dabbed the front of Miranda's outfit. He cleaned up the mess on the grass and thanked Philomela for her help. He guided Miranda back to the buffet table.

"To answer your question," Philomela said to Janice, "I'll pass and let you young people trek up to the temple with the big eyed Buddha."

CHAPTER 26

Later that afternoon Janice and Don began the trek to the white and gold temple. They walked behind their hotel on a well-travelled road and passed a variety of buildings. Some were obviously residences and they became smaller and smaller as the road grew narrower and narrower. The road turned into a double footpath then narrowed into a single path. Don briskly led the way and Janice followed, wondering if they were trespassing.

"Look," Don said. "The footpath goes onto a dyke between two rice fields. Do you want to continue?"

She gazed at the path and noted an eighteen inch drop at each side. "How's your balance?"

"Okay."

"So is mine." She looked up the hill but, from this vantage point, could not see the temple. No one came out of the houses, so she said, "Let's go a bit farther."

They followed the path across rice fields and around more houses. She was ready to give up and suggest retracing their steps when the path met a paved road. The road curved and rose steeply toward the temple, now towering above them.

Side by side, they walked on the road and moved quickly aside whenever a vehicle approached. A few people stood outside the doors of their homes and watched them. After going up a sharp switch-back, they reached a parking lot. Off to one side, they saw a stone staircase with a metal railing leading to the all-seeing Buddha. The painted eyes stared at them.

"It's awe-inspiring," Janice said. "I can see why religion engulfs these people."

They walked up the stairs under leafy trees. Monkeys darted back and forth on branches and on railings and extolled them with loud chattering. Janice tucked her sunglasses in her purse, just in case. They met more monkeys playing on the railings then met several religious devotees dressed in long robes coming down from the temple.

Reaching a large plateau on which a market was located, they ignored vendors selling souvenirs. Arm in arm, they reverentially approached the gigantic Buddha.

Janice stared as if in a trance. When she finally spoke, her voice was little more than an awe-inspired whisper. "His eyes truly are all-seeing, all-protecting, and all-embracing."

"His eyes are made of stone," Don said.

She remembered her experience with the male devotees in the temple square. Like the stone statues and benches in the sacred courtyard, the eyes were hard and unnerving. Had her mishap just happened this morning? It seemed days ago.

Apparently more interested in the view, than religion or philosophy, Don walked to the railing and leaned over it. "Wow. Look at this."

Pushing aside memories of her disconcerting experience, she looked over the railing at the hill dropping steeply away. It contained trees that were in fact rhododendrons. Monkeys jumped and chattered nearby but their caterwauling did not stop the scene from imparting peace. She glanced over at Don who pensively stared at the hillside. She was surprised at the expression on his face. His happy-go-lucky manner seemed to have deserted him.

"A penny for your thoughts," she said.

He turned to her and shook his head. "They're worth more than a useless penny."

"Are they worth one American dollah?"

He laughed, turned, and leaned his back on the railing. Gazing up at the all-seeing Buddha, he asked, "Would you like to spend extra time in Katmandu?"

"I would. How about you?"

"Three days will be long enough. I find the place dirty, full of beggars, lice, lepers, and way too religious. Fancy temples don't remove the poverty."

She did not argue with him, though some of the things he found repugnant were the things that fascinated her. "The people may be poor," she said, "but most don't seem to know it. They look happy and well fed, and have a roof over their head. They're extremely polite—unless their religious rules are violated." Don did not reply, so she asked, "Did you see what happened to me this morning in the temple square?"

"Some of it. I was chatting with Miranda Gordon."

He seemed more interested in gazing around at the mountains than in discussing her distressing experience.

"The Himalayas," she said, trying to tune into his mindset, "are as spectacular as our Rockies. Of course, they're younger and have Mount Everest—a mountain that challenges climbers all over the world." Again recalling her recent experience with the irate male worshipers, she said, "As a woman, I have no desire to live here permanently."

Don made no reply.

She waited a bit longer. "Let's start back. Tonight there's a cocktail party, a group dinner, and some entertainment."

They descended the long stairway and she glanced back at the Buddha. Turning to Don, she intended to ask if he thought the all-seeing, stone Buddha could see both good and evil, but the words dried in her mouth. All frivolity left her—his facial expression seemed to express intense worry.

CHAPTER 27

Don passed through the main lobby of the exotic Seychelles Hotel and walked directly to the front desk. Recalling that a flight attendant on the 737-400 had equated forty-five Seychelles rupees with one Canadian dollar, he stopped at the counter.

"May I help you?" a clerk with a faint English accent asked.

"I need some local money. Is there an ATM nearby?"

The clerk pointed to an alcove off to one side. Don walked over to the machine, inserted his credit card, read the printed instructions, and punched the appropriate keys. After the machine spit out rupees, he put them in his pocket. Glimpsing a girl's tawny legs under a pair of white shorts, he was reminded of Lola's graceful walk.

Back in Calgary, with his jeans full of ransom money, he intended to take Lola to the best restaurant in town for dinner and dancing. He also intended to take her for a walk on his newly acquired acreage. Before any of that could happen, however, he had to complete his kidnapping job. This time he intended to succeed.

The Seychelles was a perfect spot to hide with a kidnapped girl. It was more appealing for an extended stay than Nepal. The weather was warmer and most of the buildings were new and modern.

He turned his head and saw the tawny-skinned girl disappear through the main doorway. He nodded to the clerk at the counter, left the cool air-conditioned lobby, and stepped outside. Enveloped by humid warmth, he walked past two taxis parked on the drive in front of the hotel and saw the young girl stroll arm-in-arm with a young man.

So much for her, he thought, they're probably honeymooners. No matter, his twitching leg muscles needed exercise. Sitting in airplanes and coaches did absolutely nothing to stimulate circulation or exercise muscles. The best workout he'd had during the whole trip consisted of walking though large airports, up and down the steps at the cave in Kuala Lumpur, and at the Buddhist temple in Kathmandu. He had done his fair share of elbow bending, but that didn't induce physical fitness, if anything it contributed to flabbiness.

This place was so different from Katmandu. No snow-capped mountains and no gigantic foothills. He noticed a group of palm trees, a bed of bright tropical flowers, and heard birds sing to the accompaniment of surf faintly pounding behind the hotel. To hole up here with

Janice for three or four days would be pleasant. For the first time, he felt pleased that his efforts to detain her on the island of Mana had failed. His failures at the temple market in Bali and in the cave and market at Kuala Lumpur also proved for the best. They allowed him to see more of the world and now plan a new attempt on this lovely island.

The failures of course were not his fault. Two of his efforts had been foiled by Frank. The first incident had occurred when Janice invited him to join their foray into the Mana gift shop. The second had happened when Frank suddenly walked into the condemned cave in Kuala Lumpur. Don still wondered if Frank's appearance had been a coincidence or if Frank had secretly been employed by Pierre and Bob to watch over him. Frank's purchase of a knife worried him.

In Bali, he had successfully enticed Janice to sit down and rest after her ordeal with the aggressive saleslady. The coach would have gone without them if that nosey French woman hadn't appeared and, like a mother hen, urged them to hurry back to the coach. At the street market in Kuala Lumpur, she had done the same thing. However, it was unlikely that she was in secret cahoots with Bob and Pierre.

Don shook his head. Madeline Bouchard was a classy looking dame but, having ruined two good opportunities to kidnap Janice, she was a big pain in the neck. Almost as big a pain as the cane-lady. Miranda Gordon, on the other hand, had encouraged the two young people to get together.

Then, of course, there was Philomela Nightingale. She was still a puzzle.

If he failed to kidnap Janice in the Seychelles, he would have four other chances—in Jordon, Turkey, Austria, and Ireland. There was no need to worry.

In this beautiful setting, he could easily entice Janice away from their fellow travellers. Once that was accomplished, he would lure her into a hotel, any hotel, and the rest would be a snap.

He followed the tawny young girl and her boyfriend down a hill. His leg muscles stopped twitching and he gained a steady rhythm. His stride and momentum increased and he quickly reached the couple when they stopped to look over a railing. The young man heard him and turned around.

"Have you seen these giant tortoises?" he asked.

Don walked over, stopped at the railing, and looked down into an enclosed grassy area. At first glance, he saw what appeared to be two large rocks. One rock began to slowly move on the grass. "Cripes," he exclaimed. "They're huge."

"People actually ride on their backs," the girl said.

"I can believe it." Don stared at the larger tortoise as it laboriously started to move toward the smaller one. "They're bigger than the western saddle I use on my horse."

The girl laughed.

Don gave her an appreciative glance. "Is there a scenic place to walk around here?"

"Follow this sidewalk," the young man said, "until it

stops. Then go on the driveway for a bit, turn left and follow the path to a rocky island. That's an interesting place
and you can easily walk to it."

Don thanked him and continued on his way. When
the sidewalk ended, he walked on the driveway then
turned and followed the path. The corner of his right eye,
noticed something hanging between two trees. He turned
his head and gazed into the eyes of a gigantic spider. It
sat in the middle of a gigantic web.

For a second, he felt panic stricken. He knew the
spider wasn't a black widow and he suspected it was bigger than a tarantula. Would it jump from its web, grab
him, and drag him into its parlour? He shook away the
nonsensical thought and walked on. On both sides of the
path, he saw more huge webs and more huge spiders.
Even in paradise, things could be bad. Why didn't the
locals kill them?

Seeing the rocky island, he hesitated, fearing there
might be more giant spiders. He braced his shoulders and
courageously wound his way amongst shrubs, all the
while watching for creepy crawlies. At the seashore, the
view widened, allowing him to see the hotel to his left,
open water to his right, and the rocky island straight
ahead. Actually, it was not an island. It was a small peninsula. A string of black rocks and gravel formed a natural causeway out to it.

"Hi, Don." The voice came from a girl in pink shorts
climbing over one of the causeway rocks. She waved her
hand at him then scrambled over the last rock and walked
briskly on the sand toward him.

"Janice. Hi. Did you see those awful spiders?"

"I was told they're completely harmless. People who live here consider them good luck and treat them like pets."

"Pets? That's weird." He glanced around. "Are you alone?"

"No. Philomela's somewhere back on those rocks."

This dashed any kidnapping hopes. But he perked up and asked, "Are you going on the coach tour tomorrow?"

"Yes. Are you?"

"Might as well. The only other way to get to the town of Victoria is by taxi."

"Here comes Philomela now." Janice watched her friend make her way over the causeway.

Philomela joined them. They discussed the lovely weather and the beautiful scenery while retracing their steps past the spiders and their webs. Nearing the tortoise compound, they saw Frank leaning on the railing. He paid no attention to their approach.

"Well, if it isn't the horse doctor," Don said.

Frank turned around and grinned. "Hello. I was just thinking how difficult it would be to treat one of these critters."

"How would you turn one on its back?" Philomela asked.

"With great difficulty. I think I'll stay in Alberta and doctor cattle, horses, and household pets."

Philomela laughed. "Like most of the places we've stayed at, this island is a wonderful place to visit."

"But," Frank said, "I wouldn't want to live here."

"I think I could handle it," Janice said.

"Me, too." Don grinned at her conspiratorially. "Shall we try it for a week or so?" He moved close to her.

"Right now, I'd like to swim in the pool—before the reception."

The four of them chatted amicably then, at the hotel, dispersed to their rooms. They later met at the pool for a swim and, once again, dispersed—this time to prepare for the reception. At five-thirty, they reassembled near the pool and enjoyed the party hosted by the staff of Terrific Travel.

Philomela had embellished her fabulous fantastic frock with bright beads and earrings, and Janice wore a cheerful yellow dress. Frank complimented them on looking like two beautiful tropical birds.

"Are you enjoying the Seychelles?" Captain Sanderson asked as he and his wife, Rose, wandered over to them.

"Very much," Philomela replied.

"Captain Sanderson," Frank said, "I must compliment you on maneuvering the plane out of Katmandu's bowl of high hills."

"Actually," Philomela said. "I was terrified."

"I've practiced that take-off in a simulator so often I could have done it with my eyes closed and one arm tied behind my back."

Philomela shook her head in disbelief.

"Were you travelling much over stall speed?" Frank asked.

"We had enough leeway in that regard."

"When you made that steep turn," Philomela said, "everyone in the cabin gazed at the ground and gasped. We all thought we were falling."

"I probably should have warned you," Captain Sanderson said. "Those foothills are so high it is the only way we can gain enough height to fly over them."

"That take-off was one of the highlights of the trip," Frank said.

The reception lasted an hour, then Frank and Don joined Philomela and Janice in a nearby restaurant. They ate a light meal, and when finished, Don suggested they take a walk.

"I need sleep," Janice said.

No one tried to convince her otherwise. The other three seemed to think sleep was a good idea, too.

҂৩҂

Back in their hotel room, Philomela sat down, opened her i-Pad, and read three messages from Brent. The first two were chatty and mundane.

In the first, he described his activities at work and his jaunt to look at a car for sale.

In the second, he gave a detailed weather report and confessed he missed her. Then she read the third message.

"Good grief." With eyes wide, she stared at Janice.

"What's wrong?"

"Lola Grieve is dead."

"Omigod." Janice's lower lip trembled and she

stared at her employer. Finally, she asked, "Was it cancer? A car accident?"

Philomela knit her eyebrows together. "Brent says the police are investigating."

"Why are the police involved?" Janice asked.

"Exactly. Why are the police involved?" Philomela lowered her eyes then slowly raised them and looked pensively at Janice. "First Pierre. Now Lola. What in the world is going on?"

CHAPTER 28

Next morning, Janice had trouble putting aside the shocking news of Lola's death. What could have happened to her? Where and why did she die? Sitting on the coach, she struggled to push aside the sad news and listen to the driver/guide's informative spiel about the Seychelles Islands.

Suddenly, the guide stopped speaking and parked the vehicle on the roadside. He opened the door and hopped off. Was he abandoning them? No. In a matter of seconds, he climbed back on the coach carrying a sprig of greenery that had been growing in the ditch. He held the sprig above his head so all passengers could see it.

"This," he announced, "is lemongrass. As you know, the Seychelles are called the spice-islands." He plunked himself behind the steering wheel and concentrated on his role as driver. A short distance later, he again stopped the coach, hopped off, and returned with another sprig of greenery. Wearing his guide hat, he explained that the sprig was mint. He repeated the process with vanilla, cinnamon bark, and then pointed out a tree called *coco de mer*. "Its flower resembles a male sexual organ and its nut-like fruit resembles a female bottom." He casually commented that local people put the fruit and flower to practical use. Janice did not know what he meant and he failed to elaborate.

Shortly after the coach stopped in the town of Victoria, the practical use of the tree became apparent. At the necessary rooms, Philomela, Janice, and Frank discovered a phallic-like flower above a door designating males and a buttock-like nut above a door designating females.

Gazing at the objects above the two adjacent doors, Philomela said, "They're more descriptive and less boring than silhouettes of a man wearing long pants and a lady wearing a skirt."

"Also less confusing," Janice said, "because today so many women wear pants."

"And," Frank added, "Scottish men wear kilts and Balinese men wear sarongs."

Philomela chuckled, took hold of the doorknob, and looked up. "I hope that two-cheeked coconut doesn't fall on my head." She opened the door and walked safely into the lavatory.

Several minutes later, all three basked in the sunshine and strolled to a large, open-air market. With other members of their group, they sauntered amongst tables displaying local handicrafts, attractively boxed spices, and products made of the interesting tree.

Frank stopped to contemplate dozens of flowers and fruits.

"Are you going to buy a large *coco de mer*?" Philomena asked him.

"Each one is worth two hundred American dollars. I think I'll buy a tiny replica. Only two dollahs."

Philomena and Janice chuckled and left him to make his purchase. At another table, they studied clothing and spices. While Philomela checked various spice packages, Janice strolled over to a table displaying small wooden carvings made from the nut of a *coco de mer*.

Don suddenly appeared beside her. "Janice," he whispered, "how about breaking away from the group for a short walk. I found a cute bar near here."

She glanced over her shoulder at Philomela who was deep in conversation with the spice clerk and at Frank who was talking to the clerk selling *coco de mer* replicas. At that moment Miranda Gordon came up to her and stopped.

"Hello, Janice," she said. "These carvings are attractive. Are you going to buy one?"

"I don't think so," Janice replied.

Miranda glanced around at fellow travellers and, as if a mind reader, said. "Sometimes I'm tempted to slip away from the group and wander around on my own."

"That's a good idea." Don spoke as if he hadn't thought of it himself. He grinned conspiratorially at Janice. "What about it? Are you game?"

Before Janice could reply, Miranda said. "You'll give Philomela a few minutes to herself."

"We won't stay long," Don said. "Nobody will miss us. The coach doesn't leave to take us for lunch until one-o-clock."

Janice glanced at the fake Cartier watch she had bought in Kuala Lumpur. "It's almost twelve-fifteen."

"See, we have at least forty-five minutes."

Grinning at Miranda, he grasped Janice's hand and led her from the market to the street. Traffic was light so they jay-walked to the other side and hurried along the sidewalk for a full block. They turned a corner and went another block.

"The bar is farther away than I expected," Janice said. "And the area seems to be getting seedier."

"There should be one nearby."

"I thought you said you had found a cute bar."

"Well, sort of." A minute later, Don stopped. "Here we are." He opened a nondescript door and ushered her into a nondescript bar. "I think it's part of a hotel."

Compared to the brilliant sunlight outside, the room was dim and murky. She took off her sunglasses, but the dimness remained.

As the pupils of her eyes adjusted, Don guided her to a small table at the back of the room.

"You think this bar is cute?" she asked, sitting down. "You need to have your eyesight checked."

"It's a real Seychelles bar, not a tourist trap. This is something most of our group will not see."

"They aren't missing much. It looks exactly like a tacky bar back home."

He laughed. "But it's not back home. Tacky or not,

we're at the other side of the world. Let's try a beer or maybe something stronger. What do you say?"

"I don't drink alcohol at noon."

"Come on, it's past noon. Live a little. We're on holidays."

"Well, maybe a light beer. Do they have a local brand?"

"I'm sure they do."

A young waiter came over to their table and Don asked for two locally brewed beers. A few minutes later, the waiter returned and set two cans of Coors Light and two glasses on the table. He filled both glasses.

"It's ordinary American beer," Janice said.

"Who cares? Here's to us." Don touched his glass against hers then took a long drink. "Local or not, it's a thirst quencher."

Janice took a tiny sip and looked around at the near-by cliental. They, in turn, seemed to study her, probably, she thought, because of her long blonde hair. Of course, she saw no one she recognized. "It is rather fun to get away from the group," she admitted. "Not that I don't enjoy most of our fellow travellers. It's just nice to be on our own for a short while."

Don agreed and took another swig of beer.

"Generally speaking, this has been a great holiday. And we only have four more stops. The cities of Aqaba, Istanbul, Vienna, and Dublin. Then it's over."

"This island has perked me up," Don said. "Do you like it here?"

"Not this bar," Janice replied, glancing around. "But

I like the town of Victoria, and our hotel is spectacular. Early this morning, Philomela and I walked down to that little bay beside the hotel. You know, near the rocky peninsula. We swam there and the ocean was warm as soup."

"Doesn't sound very refreshing." Don drained his beer and beckoned to the young waiter for another round. "Drink up, Janice."

She glanced at her fake Cartier watch. "Time's flitting. We should get back."

"We have time for another beer, a quick one."

She shook her head.

"Ah, come on, enjoy."

The waiter set two full cans on the table and Don paid him for all four. After filling his own glass, he added beer from Janice's new can to her partly empty glass.

"To us," he said and raised his drink.

Her eyebrows rose questioningly. "To us?"

"To us and the awesome holiday."

She smiled and they drank again.

"You know," he said, "I think Kuala Lumpur was my favorite place. I'd like to go back."

"I'd like to return to Kathmandu."

"Why would you want to go back there?"

"Because of the contrasts, I guess. The contrast of lordly hills and rhododendron forests, snow-capped mountains and valleys crowded with people. Besides, I found the culture so different from ours at home."

"If you went back, you might end up getting stoned for violating a religious rule."

She laughed spontaneously. "It almost happened,

didn't it?" She sipped her beer then set her glass on the table. "Why would you want to go back to Kuala Lumpur? So you could buy more knock-off stuff?"

"Just what I need." He held up his left arm. "See, I'm wearing my fake Gucci watch. It's still working."

"So is my fake Cartier watch, though my wrist is turning black. Philomela is very happy with her real silk dress and coat. There's nothing fake about them."

He watched her place her glass on the table. Then he tipped the can and filled her glass to the top.

"Seriously," she asked, "why would you want to return to Kuala Lumpur?"

"I liked the activity, the modern skyscrapers, and the cleanliness. I felt comfortable there."

"So the ambience suited you."

"Ambience?"

"Atmosphere," she said.

"Absolutely. It suited me fine. I felt at home and nearly everyone could speak English."

"It was more materialistic than Kathmandu."

"I'm a materialistic man."

She smiled. "I suppose most of us are materialistic, at least to a degree. If we weren't, we'd have trouble surviving."

"I like the best that money can buy."

"Around the World in Thirty Days has provided us with that. Delicious food, luxurious accommodation, excellent service, comfortable transportation, and fabulous sights."

"I'll drink to that." He held up his glass and waited

until she raised hers. "To luxury in travel and in every-thing else."

She sipped her drink then raised her left arm and glanced at her fake watch. "Omigod, it's ten after one. We have to go." She leaped to her feet.

"Janice, you might as well sit down again. We'll never get back to the market in time. We've already missed the coach."

"What will we do?"

He burst out laughing. "I'll buy you lunch."

"How will we get back to our hotel? It's on the other side of the island."

"We'll take a taxi. No big deal. I'll pay. Relax and enjoy the adventure. Everything will be okay."

"Philomela will be sick with worry."

"She knows you're a big girl and can take care of yourself. Besides, Miranda will tell her you're with me. Surely, she'll realize we can get back to the hotel on our own."

"I hope so. I don't want her to worry unnecessarily."

"There's nothing we can do about it now. Let's just enjoy our beer then decide where to eat lunch."

She agreed, albeit reluctantly. When Don announced he had to see a man about a horse, she said, "Look for the flower of the *coca de mer*."

While he was gone, she studied the room. There were two people at one table and four at another. She was unable to tell if they were tourists or locals. The waiter was not in sight and the bartender stood behind the bar, vigorously drying glasses with a large dishtowel. Janice picked up her glass and took a slow lingering sip of beer. After setting it down, she glanced in the direction of the necessary rooms. No sign of Don. All she needed now was to lose him. Feeling a bit nervous, she took a bigger sip.

After what seemed a long time, he entered the bar through a side door.

"I wandered around and peeked at the hotel restaurant," he said, apparently explaining his long absence. "It didn't look good." He sat down and picked up his glass. "The hotel desk clerk recommended a restaurant around the corner. We can walk there." He smiled reassuringly and took a long drink of beer.

She smiled, getting into the swing of the adventure. "If the restaurant is nice, we'll eat there, and if it's tacky, we can look for something else."

Don nodded, obviously pleased with her suggestion.

CHAPTER 29

Philomela stood by the coach, looking for Janice. The people milling nearby reminded her of crows, gathering to fly to their evening roost. Her employee's non-appearance had prompted her to ask individuals if they had seen the young girl with blonde hair. No one had.

"She's only ten minutes late," Miranda said, looking at her wristwatch.

Ten minutes or not, Philomela was annoyed with Janice's tardiness. Had she learned nothing about getting to the coach on time? The annoyed remarks of fellow passengers must have registered with her. She was usually considerate of others and a model of punctuality. In fact, those very traits had occasionally worried Philomela. Would Janice's empathy for others make her lose her own identity? Her own ego?

Ridiculous. Of course, Janice wouldn't lose her identity. She was normally considerate of others but she was also capable, intelligent, and her own person. Why in the world worry about her? The girl was free, white, and over twenty-one.

The cliché was unintentionally racist. Philomela changed her thoughts to free, black, and twenty-one, then to yellow, and then to red. Political correctness was too stupid and silly to ever replace polite common sense.

She mentally slapped herself. How could she dwell on such things when the person she loved most, next to her husband and her sister, was not here when expected? She could not distance herself from Janice, nor could she evade feelings of responsibility for her.

After all, the girl was her employee. More important, she liked her and looked upon her as the daughter she never had.

"Philomela." Miranda's voice interrupted her thoughts. "Stop frowning. Janice and Don are together. They're probably having such a lovely time that they lost track of time."

"Are they together?" Philomela asked, looking around for Don.

"Yes, they went off to visit a nearby bar. They'll take a taxi back to the hotel if necessary."

With a deep sigh of resignation, Philomela nodded. Less than fifteen minutes ago, she had been a happy, carefree tourist, breathing the soft moist air and gazing with enjoyment at the array of crafts, spices, and the variety of people in Victoria's open-air market.

She had paid little heed to what Janice was doing, assuming she too was chatting with locals and studying the interesting merchandise spread out before her. It was when she wanted to show Janice a cute sundress that she first noted her absence. But it wasn't until her watch registered one o' clock that she really started to worry.

Turning from Miranda, she spotted Frank sitting on a wooden bench under a big shade tree. She walked over to him and asked when he had last noticed Janice.

"Shortly after we first arrived at the market," he replied.

Philomena sat down on the bench beside him. "She's late again. I don't understand her."

"You have to admit, Philomela, none of Janice's previous late arrivals were entirely her fault."

"I know that."

"I hope she's okay," Frank muttered.

Philomela looked directly into his gray eyes and her own eyes widened in dismay. He seemed sincerely concerned. "Oh, Frank, I hope nothing untoward has happened to her. According to Miranda Gordon, she's with Don Webster."

"Oh." Frank frowned. "They seem to get on well together."

"Yes, they seem to." Philomela stared pensively at the people in the market. Suddenly, a disturbing thought jumped to the fore of her mind and she turned to Frank. "Why do we both say 'seem to'? Don't we know for sure that they get on well together?"

"Can we really know anything for sure about another person?" He gazed again into her green eyes and, without waiting for an answer, said, "Philomela, do you have qualms about Don?"

"That's a provocative question, Frank." She hesitated for few seconds. "I have to answer, yes, though I can't put my finger on a specific reason. Perhaps I think he's immature. Perhaps I don't think he's good enough for her. That's a natural reaction for a mother, and I look upon Janice as a daughter."

Frank put his hand under his chin and, in traditional thinker fashion, leaned into it. He gazed down at the earth, as if expecting the soil to exude gems of wondrous knowledge. "What time did you last see Janice?" he asked.

"I don't know for sure. She was with me when I was checking out spices at the market. Almost an hour ago"

"Have you seen Don since then?"

"No. But I wasn't looking for him."

"And they're both missing."

Philomela cringed at the word, missing. She could easily forgive Janice for being late. Being missing was a new mindset. A terrifying one.

"Go back to the coach and ask again if anyone has seen either of them." Frank gave her a smile of encouragement. "I'll go around the market and ask the same question."

Philomela went inside the coach and asked all the passengers if they had seen Janice or Don. Miranda was the only person who displayed no annoyance. "Don't worry," she said. "They'll be fine."

"That girl is holding us up again," the white-haired

lady said. "It's rather aggravating for those of us who get here on time."

"I agree." Philomela bit her lower lip. "But Janice's past tardiness was not entirely her fault."

The white-haired lady nodded and her eyes softened.

Miranda walked up to Philomela and placed a hand on her shoulder. "Take heart, Philomela. Don and Janice are young and in love. Why shouldn't they wander off together?"

"In love?" Philomela soundlessly added the adjective, *not*. As far as she knew, they were not in love.

The driver/guide, who had been listening, politely said, "I'll wait another five minutes. If they don't show then, I'll assume they either forgot the designated hour or wandered too far to get back in time. It will be up to them to make their way back to the hotel. Taxis are available, but expensive. If they are healthy and energetic they could walk."

"Instead of being coach passengers, they could become hitch-hikers," Frank said.

The driver/guide gave him a weak smile. "That's about it."

"Maybe I should stay behind and search the nearby area," Frank said.

The driver/guide shook his head. "In what direction would you start? They may already be in a taxi driving back to the hotel."

"Yes," Frank said. "It would be a waste of time."

Philomela looked down at her hands and was annoyed to see them automatically wringing against each other. She was behaving like someone in near despair. *Come Janice*, she willed, *please come right now*. She hoped with all her heart her mental telepathy would work.

It did not. Philomela was the last person to take a seat in the coach.

CHAPTER 30

Janice's heart banged rapidly against her ribcage. Was the quick thudding caused by their two block jaunt or by the appearance of seedy looking bystanders? The scruffy attire and surly manner of three males lounging in a shop doorway made her feel especially uneasy. The tallest man stared at her so intently that she quickly averted her eyes and looked straight ahead. She walked faster.

"Do you think those fellows will mug us?" she asked.

"No," Don replied. "They're just giving you the once over. It's not every day a good looking chick with blonde hair strolls by."

Janice wanted his words to be reassuring, but they were not. Two more scruffy men stared at her. She shivered, though the temperature must have been at least thirty-five degrees centigrade.

With a sense of relief, she saw an eatery that looked promising. "Look over there." She pointed at a bistro across the street. To her, anything was better than enduring the stares of seedy looking men.

The street lacked steady traffic, so they jay-walked across it and entered the bistro. She felt the temperature cool slightly and noticed that the clientele appeared neater than the fellows lounging on the other side of the street. Her heart muscle beat less vigorously.

"Do you think they have air-conditioning?" she asked.

"Absolutely." Don looked up at the ceiling. "Those fans are it."

A waiter directed them to a table and, in butchered English, asked if they would like anything from the bar. Don ordered a beer and Janice asked for coffee. Don tried to persuade her to have something stronger.

"No thank you." Her emphatic decline seemed to bring a cloud across Don's face, but she didn't care. She had drunk enough alcohol for one day and wanted no more. Glancing around the room, she mused aloud about the other patrons. "The guide told us the Seychelles has a real mix of cultures—French, Russian, American, Cuban, and Canadian. Quite a few of them seem to be right in this room."

Before Don could respond, the waiter returned and placed water, beer, coffee, and two menus in front of them. They perused the daily fare then both ordered curried chicken. In a short space of time, the waiter delivered it.

"That was quick," Don said and picked up his fork. He tasted the chicken, sipped his water, and, with a nod of his head, said, "It's spicy."

Janice sampled a portion and agreed with him. "There's no mistaking that we're eating curry. And I must say it's delicious." She took a few more bites then cooled her throat by gulping down some water. When the meal was finished, she set her knife and fork neatly on her plate and sipped her coffee.

The waiter appeared. "More coffee for the lady?"

She nodded and he topped up her cup then took her empty plate away. She sat back, feeling content. She no longer felt panic stricken about missing the coach and even her earlier apprehension of the seedy neighbourhood had subsided. The food and the attentive waiter had helped revive and relax her. She felt confident that getting back to the tour-group hotel would not be a problem. Then she saw Don gazing intently up at the ceiling.

"What's wrong?" she asked.

"Do the blades of that ceiling fan look lopsided to you?"

She looked up, cocked her head from side to side in order to study the fan from different angles. "I don't think it's lopsided. Are you afraid a blade might spin off and hit us?"

"The blades just look crooked to me." He smiled amicably and finished his beer.

Noting that the newly topped up portion of coffee tasted slightly different from the first part, she drained the mug. *Probably brewed in a different pot*, she thought.

She watched Don pay for lunch and followed him out the door. He stayed close to her as they walked past the scruffy men toward the hotel bar they had recently patronized.

"If we're going to walk," she mumbled, "shouldn't we go in the opposite direction? I think our tour hotel is that way."

"Too far to walk. There are taxis near the hotel where we had our beer."

"Oh? I hadn't noticed any." She stumbled but quickly regained her balance.

"You okay?" he asked.

"I feel drowsy."

By the time they reached the hotel, her vision was blurry and she could hardly walk. "I can't stay awake," she said. "Too much beer before lunch, I guess."

"Plus a combination of worry and heat. You can rest while I find a taxi."

He helped her into the hotel and she vaguely saw him nod at the clerk behind the reception desk. Before she knew it, they were in an elevator. After a short ride, he picked her up and carried her down a hall. It seemed normal because her legs and brain had turned to mush.

"You'd think we were a bride and groom," he said.

His words drifted to her ears as if coming from afar. When she stretched out on a soft cloud, it felt good. "What's wrong with me?" she mumbled.

"Nothing's wrong. You're just tired. After a short rest you'll be up and running."

Her eyes closed and his words faded.

cσɔcσɔ

Up and running after a short rest proved to be a misnomer. When her eyes finally opened, she could not get her bearings. She glanced around in dismay. Where was she? The double bed was strange. The room was strange. The colored lights shining through the window were strange. Was it night time? Rubbing her forehead with her hand, she stared out the window at a neon sign sending shards of red, white, and yellow into the room. What was this place? How had she gotten here? Feeling groggy and confused, she raised her head and looked around at the basic furniture—chest of drawers, chair, bedside table. Nobody else was in the room. She was alone.

She noticed an open door and, beyond it, saw what resembled a sink. She sat up slowly and looked down at her body. Although her shoes were gone, she still wore her yellow cotton walking shorts and tee-shirt. Obviously, no one had stripped off her clothes and abused her. Thank goodness for small mercies.

The coach tour. They had been at the market in Seychelles' capital city and she and Don had wandered off. Memory was coming back. They had lingered too long at a hotel bar and missed the coach's departure deadline. Then they had walked to a bistro and eaten curried chicken. She looked at her wristwatch: eleven o'clock. Her mind counted backward—about eight hours since they had finished lunch.

Her memory started to fail her. Had they walked back to the hotel bar to find a taxi? She had no clear recollection of doing so. Was it still Tuesday? On Wednesday at noon they were scheduled to fly to Jordan, the fourth to last stop on their trip. How many days had gone by? Had the plane gone without her? She felt too exhausted to worry.

If she had slept for eight hours or more, why was she still so tired? She again tried to remember the sequence of events. She drank one and a half beers with Don in the bar. At lunch in the bistro she ate curried chicken and drank water and coffee. Her heavy sleep could not be blamed on too much alcohol. What else could it be? Simple exhaustion? Was she coming down with a virus, a flu, or something worse?

She lowered her feet to the floor, slowly eased off the bed, and stood up. Hanging onto the edge of the counterpane, she gingerly took a step. Her bare feet moved silently on the carpeted floor from the bed to the open door. She peered into the small room and switched on a light. It was definitely a bathroom. The cracked fixtures lacked the sparkle of Mr. Clean, but she had seen worse. She took off her fake Cartier watch and, while washing her hands, noticed a blackened area on the skin of her wrist. It was not the wrist the merchant lady had clenched. It was the one that her fake watch had encircled. The watch, she knew, contained no gold, just cheap, painted metal.

After returning to the bedroom, she walked to the window and read the neon sign: *Res Ezee*. What did it mean? Then she realized it was the name of the hotel with the letter T missing. She searched the room for a phone, but found none. That meant going down to the desk and asking the night clerk to phone a taxi for her.

She needed her sandals. Where were they?

She looked around the room and under the bed. No sign of anything resembling a shoe. Nor, she suddenly realized, a purse. Her purse was more important than her shoes because it held her money and her credit card. She opened the door of a small closet and saw three empty coat hangers. She went to the dresser and pulled out three rickety drawers. All were empty.

CHAPTER 31

Philomela changed into her brown jogging outfit. Though a comfortable garment to wear, its dull color corresponded with her emotional outlook. She felt tired, sick at heart, and wanted to talk with someone, preferably a woman. But who? Miranda Gordon popped to mind. Miranda would be optimistic, confident that Don and Janice had purposely run off together. Philomela didn't believe it, though she'd rather have them doing that than being the victims of assault, rape, white slavery, or organ theft.

She opened her iPad in hopes of being cheered by a message from Brent. Three messages awaited her perusal—all from her husband. The first was a Calgary weather report. The second was a brief account of his work. The third was a police announcement: Lola Grieve's death was no longer suspicious—she had been murdered.

Philomela read the last message three times. Comprehension was beyond her. Who killed the young girl? What was the motive? Feeling distressed and appalled, Philomela tried to remain calm. It was difficult to slow her heartbeat and keep her thoughts from flitting from Lola to Janice—one girl murdered and the other missing.

At ten after eleven, she looked out the window at the blackness of the sea and decided who to call. She dialed and put the phone to her ear. The operator answered and she asked not for Miranda's room but for Frank's. On the second ring, he picked up and said hello.

"Frank," she said, "Janice is still missing. I'm at my wit's end. This is so unlike her."

"Do you want to see me?"

"I hate to impose—"

"What's your room number?"

She gave it to him, thankful for his thoughtful response. After closing off the phone, she glanced in the mirror. Her reflection shocked her. She looked haggard, worried, and a hundred years old. She touched her lips with lipstick and combed her hair. She still looked dreadful.

Frank's arrival made her feel better, but not look better. They sat down on two chairs, facing one another, and he seemed as worried about Janice as she was. They discussed the one important issue—how to locate the missing girl.

"There's no point in wandering aimlessly around the island," Philomela said, trying to portray more courage than she felt. "That would reveal and resolve nothing."

He nodded in agreement. "Let's start by reviewing what's been done so far."

"I talked briefly with Fran Moleski. She told most of our fellow travellers that Janice and Don are missing and to keep an eye out for them. An hour ago, I notified the police that they are missing."

"What did they say?"

"They were sure she would turn up later this evening."

"That was less than helpful."

"To depress me even more, I received bad news from Brent." She told him about Lola's murder and explained, "She's a waitress at the Coyote Lounge and she modelled for one of *The Integrator* advertisements. She was a year behind Janice in high school. A wonderful young girl."

"Do you think there's any connection between Lola's murder and Janice's disappearance?"

"I have no idea."

Frank's fingers drummed on the arms of his chair and he chewed his lower lip. Finally, he said, "I'll phone the police and see if they've come up with anything." He stood up, went to the bedside-table, and picked up the phone.

Philomela gave him the police phone number then listened to his side of the conversation. She watched his brows knit together and his lips compress. Obviously annoyed, he shook his head and slammed down the receiver.

"They're no help at all. When I said she was with a young man, the policeman burst out laughing. He considers it a romantic getaway. I insisted the girl would not knowingly cause her friends such worry and he said he'd check the hospital to see if anyone fits her description."

Frank and Philomela paced around the room, looked out the window, and tried to make mundane conversation. When the phone rang Frank picked it up.

He said hello and listened then asked if anything else could be done. With a twinge of sarcasm, he thanked the person on the other end of the line. Looking over at Philomela, he said, "They still don't take her absence seriously. The man was almost insulting. But I will give him credit—he did check the hospital and no one fitting her description was admitted today."

"I don't know whether that's good or bad news." Assault, rape, white slavery, and involuntary organ donation again flitted through her mind. Trying not to be downcast, she asked, "Should we continue to phone and nag the police?"

"Let's wait fifteen minutes."

"I have an idea. Let's call all the hotels listed in the phonebook. Maybe a desk clerk will recognize her description."

"Good idea." Frank gazed at her. "Do you suppose they could be in Don's room?"

"I phoned his room earlier, several times. No answer. I managed to get his room number and knocked on the door. Again, no answer."

"Janice may be somewhere not of her own volition. She may be unable to contact you."

"You mean held captive?" Philomela shivered.

"Maybe she's not even with Don. Or maybe they've both been whisked away—"

"Easy Philomela."

"I know my imagination's running riot. To make matters worse, I keep thinking about Don. There's something about him. He's really a nice young man, but my gut feeling tells me he may be up to no good."

"He probably just wants to seduce her."

She laughed, feeling a trifle hysterical. "I hope that's all it is."

Frank looked at his watch then phoned the police again. This time, he spoke politely with no hint of sarcasm. His words slowed and his tone of voice softened, making Philomela think he was experiencing a sense of hopeless resignation. Placing the phone on its stand, he said, "The police have nothing new to tell us, but they promise to keep their names and physical descriptions on file."

"A fat lot of good that will do." Philomela was on the verge of tears.

CHAPTER 32

Janice knew the loss of her purse was more serious than the loss of her shoes. She could make her way without shoes, but how far could she go without money and her credit card? Fortunately, her passport was in the locked safe at the tour group hotel.

Though the soles of her feet lacked the toughness necessary to withstand gravel, rocks, and rough cement, she was willing to risk injury by walking across the island. On the other hand, she could take a taxi and upon arrival contact Philomela for money to pay the driver. Yes, riding in a taxi would be better than walking and risking injury to her feet.

She opened the door, looked down each side of the corridor, and saw no one. In bare feet, she walked along the worn carpet. As she neared the elevator, its bell rang and its door glided open. Don stepped out.

"Janice!" he exclaimed and hurried toward her. "You're awake. Are you feeling better?"

"Oh, Don. I'm so glad to see you. I thought you had deserted me."

"I wouldn't do that." He studied her from head to bare feet. "You're sure you're okay?" When she nodded, he said, "I was really worried about you."

"Maybe the curried chicken was bad or maybe I caught a flu bug."

"I thought you were suffering from heat stroke and just needed sleep."

"That's possible, too, I suppose." She gazed at his face and was touched by his expression of concern. "I was just on my way to ask the desk clerk to call a taxi. I can't find my purse or my shoes."

"Oh, I carried you up here when you couldn't walk and I don't remember seeing them."

"I looked under the bed and in the closet. They're not in any of the drawers either. What happened, Don? I can't remember anything clearly after we ate lunch. I don't even know what day it is. Is it Tuesday?"

He grinned and glanced at his watch. "Yes, it's still Tuesday."

"Thanks goodness. I was afraid I may have missed the flight to Aqaba."

"No worry there."

"Speaking of worry, Philomela will be beside herself. I should get back to our hotel as fast as possible. Or at least phone her."

"Let's go to the room and discuss it."

"What's to discuss?"

"Well, I'll go downstairs and see if the clerk has your purse and shoes. They might be in the lost and found."

She stepped toward the elevator. "I don't want to go to the room. I want to go the lobby."

"Janice, you're in your bare feet." His arm went around her waist. "You don't want to catch athlete's feet or something worse." He eased her back to the room then sat with her on the bed. He kissed her on the cheek. "I'll just be a minute. You wait here."

The door locked automatically behind him. She sat quietly on the edge of the bed and tried to relax. A minute passed. A few more minutes went by. Then she got up and walked to the window and looked out at the *Res_ Ezee* sign. Don was taking too long.

CHAPTER 33

Philomela looked at the hotel section in the phone book. Squatting in front of the bedside table, she punched in the numbers for the first one listed. A clerk answered. He provided no help at all, so she dialed the number for the second hotel. After dialing the third number, she experienced a feeling of faint hope and jotted down the hotel's address.

The search via telephone proved as frustrating as it was helpful. Every time a hotel clerk put her on hold to search the daily record, she tapped her foot impatiently. Most clerks were no help at all, though a couple gave her information that was better than nothing. After completing the last call, she handed Frank the sheet of paper with her jotted notes.

"Here are the names and addresses of four possibilities," she said. "The memories of the hotel clerks may or may not be reliable."

He took the paper, scanned it, then nodded his head and stood up. "I'll go downstairs right now, get a taxi and personally visit all four hotels."

Philomela glanced at her watch. "It's almost midnight. There's no way I'll be able to sleep. I'm going with you."

They hurried through the lobby of the hotel, walked outside toward a waiting taxi and met Miranda.

"Hello, Frank and Philomela. What are you doing up so late?" Not waiting for an answer Miranda continued. "I've just had a pleasant walk. Now I intend to have a nightcap. Will you join me in the lounge?"

"I'm afraid not," Philomela replied. "Janice and Don are still missing. We're going out to search for them."

"Where will you search?"

"In a few hotels," Philomela replied.

"You two are being mother hens," Miranda said. "Don and Janice are old enough to know what they're doing. If they want to have a romantic night away from the rest of us, let them do it in peace."

"Janice would not knowingly cause me such anxiety," Philomela said.

"Circumstances probably encouraged romance so they took advantage of it. They wouldn't even think about causing worry to their fellow travellers. Leave them to it. Stop worrying and have a nightcap with me."

"I can't stop worrying," Philomela said. "I have to do something." She turned from Miranda and hurried to a waiting taxi. Frank followed her.

CHAPTER 34

Retrieving Janice's purse and shoes from the lost and found box, Don heard the desk-clerk talk on the phone about a missing, blonde-haired girl. His ears perked up when the clerk said, "Yes, a lady said two people are coming to the hotel to check on her."

Don felt panicky and suffered a moment of indecision. Then, seeing a bearded fellow sitting on a couch, he had a flash of brilliance. He struck up a conversation with the man and learned his name was Caleb. For a small fee, Caleb agreed to keep Janice in her room for half an hour then set her free.

Don gave cash, room key, and Janice's purse and shoes to Caleb. At the same time the desk-clerk turned over his job to a white-haired gentleman. Don focused on Caleb, handing him a roll of duct tape, and saying, "Don't hurt her." Feeling slightly apprehensive, he watched the bearded man disappear in the elevator.

He knew he must flee before the two people, probably Philomela and Fran Moleski, arrived looking for the blonde girl. He needed a taxi to take him to the tour group hotel. Once there, he would pretend…Pretend what? Pretend he had been there all evening? No, that wouldn't work. Pretend he suffered from amnesia? No, that was no good either. Pretend he had been drugged? Maybe. First he must find a taxi. Time was flitting.

Don nonchalantly walked past the white-haired clerk then picked up speed and dashed out the door. Outside, he looked around for a taxi. None was in sight. He went back inside and strode to a payphone, saw a taxi number on the back of a phonebook, and dialed. Yes, a taxi would be right there. He again hurried outside. Looking up at the *Res_ Ezee* sign, he wondered if Caleb and Janice were looking out the window.

He stood on the sidewalk and waited. A feeling of depression bore down on him—another failure. This one was worse than the others because Janice was beginning to suspect his actions. He longed to chat with Pierre and ask his advice, but Bob had insisted that no contact be made until after the kidnapping was a done deal. Oh well, there were four more tour stops. He still might succeed.

e♥ɔe♥ɔ

Janice decided to go down to the reception desk. As she turned from the window, she heard a key being inserted in the door lock and saw the doorknob turn. The door opened.

A tall, bearded man appeared. He stood still and gazed at her.

"Who are you?" She nervously watched the man enter the room. He looked familiar. He resembled one of the fellows she had seen on the street while walking to the bistro. A twinge of fear sent the beginnings of a scream to her throat.

"Me Caleb," he said and his tone of voice seemed pleasant and reassuring. "These yours." He raised his left hand holding her shoes and purse.

She swallowed her scream and her terror subsided. She felt relieved that her shoes would protect her tender feet from stones and gravel and that she would have her credit card. "Thank you," she murmured. "Where is Don Webster?"

"He held up." The man set the purse and shoes on the floor, closed the door, and walked toward her.

"Held up? What do you mean?" A twinge of fear returned.

Caleb pointed a clenched fist at her. "Pow."

She dashed past him, snatched her shoes and purse, and opened the door. In that instant, Caleb's arms circled her waist. Before she knew what was happening, he kicked the door shut, covered her mouth with duct tape, and held her arms behind her. She almost lost her balance as he taped her wrists together. As she kicked at him with her bare feet, he dragged her to the bed and tossed her onto it.

He grabbed her flailing feet and wound duct tape around her ankles.

She lay on her side, angry, uncomfortable, and terrified. He sat down on a chair and stared at her.

Where was Don? Was he bound in some other room? What did "Pow" mean? Had he been knocked unconscious? Had he been shot? What was going on? Was Caleb a criminal stealing credit cards and money? Or was he someone more ominous?

She tried to sit up but was physically powerless to do so. She felt as if she were swirling in a river, spinning toward dangerous rapids with the shore irrevocably beyond her reach. She wanted to cry out, but because of the duct tape she couldn't.

CHAPTER 35

Philomela noticed a taxi pull away from in front of the hotel but gave it little thought. She was thinking that this hotel was their final destination.

Their taxi driver had driven above the speed limit, probably because the streets were empty of pedestrians. Only an occasional flash of headlights from a passing car had indicated people were out and about. Their driver's first stop had been the Seaside Hotel. Frank had leaped out of the car, asked him to wait, then dashed to the hotel. Philomela ran after him. In tandem, they entered the hotel reception area.

Her first thought, stupidly, was romance. The hotel's spacious, luxurious appearance could enhance a lovers' tryst. Frank was more logical. He spoke with the reception clerk then walked back to Philomela and shook his head in resignation.

"The girl who fit Janice's description checked in Monday afternoon and left today at noon."

"Guess that's that," Philomela said. "Janice was with us until noon today."

"Well, on to the next one." Frank led the way outside and they climbed into the waiting taxi.

The driver resumed his tour of the nearly empty streets and came to a stop in front of another inn. Philomela noted the surroundings with apprehension. They weren't exactly tacky, just a little run down, not very amenable for a tryst. If she weren't so desperate to see Janice, she would hope not to see her here.

Inside the inn, she listened to Frank explain to the clerk that he had phoned about a young, blonde-haired girl.

To Philomela's ear, the man spoke with a French accent. "She's in the bar right now." He pointed to a closed door.

Frank and Philomela hurried to the door, opened it and entered a dull, dingy room. As their eyes adjusted to the dim light, they looked around and, at first, saw no one who fit Janice's description. Then Frank grabbed Philomela's arm.

"Is that her in the second booth on the right?"

Philomela saw a girl with shoulder-length blonde hair. "It could be her, but the man with her doesn't look like Don."

Without replying, Frank strode between tables toward the booth. As he neared it, he slowed to a halt, smiled at the couple, and turned around. He reached Philomela and shook his head. "Not her and not Don."

Back to the taxi and on to the next hotel. It proved no better than the first two. Frank actually had the clerk phone the room and wake up the occupants. After a lengthy explanation, he managed to get their room number and went up to it. No luck. Wrong girl.

Finally, the taxi took them to this, their last destination. As the driver parked in the spot left vacant by the departing taxi, Philomela looked over at the building. Seeing a sign, she said aloud, "Res-Ezee. The T is missing." Climbing out of the taxi and glancing at the dimly lit, rundown area, her emotions were mixed. She disliked the tawdry surroundings yet hoped Janice was here.

Frank asked the driver to wait for them and, with Philomela at his side, strode into the reception area. He leaned against the counter, rang a buzzer, and, after what seemed an eternity, saw a white-haired gentleman appear from a back room and shuffle forward.

"I phoned about a missing young woman," Frank said. "A girl with blonde hair."

The man peered over glasses resting half way down his nose. Looking puzzled, he said in understandable English, "Me know nothing."

"Did you see a young woman with shoulder-length fair hair and blue eyes?" Philomela asked. "She was wearing a yellow tee-shirt and yellow walking shorts."

The clerk shrugged his shoulders. "Me come to work fifteen minutes ago."

"Did a young couple check in this afternoon?"

The clerk ran his finger down a list of eight names.

"Three people here this afternoon. Four o'clock. I no here. I see man this evening. Young." He stared at Frank and absently stroked his chin. "He look like you. I no see no woman."

Philomela leaned closer to the clerk. "Did the man who looks like this man have brown hair, a brown moustache, and a small beard?" She pointed to the top of her head and above her upper lip, and then with thumb and index finger flicked her chin.

"Brown hair." He nodded and imitated her gestures by pointing to the top of his head and his upper lip and chin.

Philomela's heart missed a beat. "Can you tell us his name and room number?"

"I no do that."

"If I phone the police," Frank said, "would you give the number to them?"

"Yes, I have to."

Frank reached over the counter and picked up the phone. "Do you mind if I use it?"

The clerk shrugged.

Frank dug in his pants pocket and brought out Philomela's piece of paper containing the police station's phone number. He quickly punched in the numbers then slowly spoke in the phone. With a look of satisfaction on his face, he handed the phone to the clerk. "The police want to talk with someone working in the hotel."

The clerk spoke into the phone and then hung up. "They think they two lovers."

Philomela bit back a sharp retort. She stared at the clerk. "What is their room number?"

The clerk shrugged again. "Room three one five."

Frank and Philomena dashed to the elevator. At the third floor, they stepped into an empty hallway and ran to room 315. At the closed door, they stopped and looked at each other. Frank tapped gently on the door. They heard footsteps. Obviously, the building was not sound-proof. Frank knocked again, louder this time.

"Who there?" a voice asked.

"Room service," Frank said.

"I order no room service."

"The reception clerk sends two bottles of beer for you, courtesy of the hotel."

"What the—"

The door opened and, before Caleb could close it again, Frank leaped inside, grabbed his right arm, and pinned his left one behind his back. They scuffled and Caleb muttered a string of curses.

Philomela looked into the room and saw Janice lying on her side on the bed. Her shirt was pulled high exposing her brassiere but her yellow walking shorts were still intact. Philomela ran to the bed, grasped the duct tape, and ripped it off her mouth. "Sorry if that hurt, Janice."

"Omigod. Am I glad to see you." Janice's voice cracked with emotion and her eyes filled with tears. "My wrists are tied behind my back. It's really uncomfortable."

Philomela tried but could not get the duct tape from around her wrists. She opened her purse, searched the contents, and brought out a tiny pair of nail scissors. After many snips, she finally succeeded in cutting the tape. With a grimace, Janice moved her arms forward then sighed and rubbed her wrists. The older woman cut the duct tape from around her ankles, allowing the girl to stretch her legs and sit up. Tears of relief streamed down Janice's cheeks and Philomela hugged her. Grunts and groans made them look toward the two struggling men.

It was difficult to ascertain who was getting the better of whom. Caleb punched Frank's stomach and Frank's fist connected with Caleb's jaw. The blow to the jaw was hard enough to make Caleb totter and slowly collapse in a heap on the floor. Frank studied him for a second then moved to the bed. He gazed with obvious concern at the girl's tear stained face.

"Janice, are you okay?"

"I am now. Thanks to you and Philomela."

"Was that man trying to ravage you?" Philomela asked.

In spite of the situation, Janice laughed. "Oh, Philomela, that's such an old-fashioned word."

A noise near the door made all three look in that direction. Caleb was up and moving to the open door. Before his actions registered with the others, he disappeared from the room. Frank dashed after him. A few minutes later, he returned, breathing heavily and shaking his head. "He ran down the stairs and I lost him." Taking a deep breath, he gazed at Janice who was still sitting on the bed rubbing her wrists. "Are you sure you're all right?"

She nodded her head. "I'm so glad to see you."

At that moment, voices and footsteps echoed through the open door from the hall. The sounds grew louder and two policemen strode into the room. They stopped and stared at Janice's tear stained face and at the hunks of duct tape lying in a heap on the bed beside her. Then they looked at Philomela and Frank.

"What kept you?" Philomela asked sarcastically.

Either missing or ignoring her sarcasm, the elder policeman asked, "So what is going on?"

Frank told them his name and introduced the two women. The police acknowledged the threesome with polite nods. Frank described what had recently happened while the policemen continued to stare at Janice's tear stained face, her reddish wrists and ankles, and the pile of duct tape sitting beside her on the bed. They glanced at each other as if embarrassed.

"On the phone you didn't believe us," Frank said. "What made you change your mind and come here?"

The elder policeman looked sympathetically at Frank but resisted giving him an apology. "We got a phone call from a lady in your tour group. She said a young man had been assaulted but was okay. They were worried about a young lady in room 315 in this hotel. They thought she might need help."

Philomela and Frank looked at each other, puzzled.

"Who would have phoned?" Frank asked.

"I don't know," Philomela replied.

"It's all my fault," Janice said. "I should never have left the group. When Don and I realized we couldn't get back to the coach on time we wandered over to a nearby bistro and ate lunch. We intended to take a taxi back to our group hotel, but after lunch I started to feel weak and fuzzy headed, so Don kindly rented this room and carried me up to this bed. I slept for about eight hours." She concluded by describing how Caleb had taped her mouth, wrists, and ankles."

"That's all he did?" Philomela asked.

Janice nodded. "He just stared at me."

"Do you know where the injured man is now?" Frank asked.

"He is with the lady who phoned," the elder policeman said. "I understand the young man was forced to leave this girl."

No one spoke until Frank said, "I suppose Caleb could tell us, but he's not here." He described the man's tall, bearded appearance to the police.

"We'll talk with the desk clerk," the policeman said. "Maybe he saw him."

"Will it be okay if I take these two ladies back to our hotel?" Frank asked.

The elder policeman nodded and the younger one shrugged his shoulders. Both again gazed at Janice's tear-stained face. The elder policeman said, "Sorry," then walked from the room.

CHAPTER 36

Don couldn't believe that Miranda had phoned the police and told them he was assaulted. He stared at her, speechless.

"I told them you are shaken up, but not seriously hurt. To explain why you left Janice alone at the Rest Ezee hotel, I said you were knocked unconscious and put in a taxi. I also told them a young girl in room 315 might need help."

His throat felt dry. His hands felt clammy. He shouldn't have left Janice with Caleb, even though the fellow did seem harmless. Miranda was right to ask the police to check on her. He needed a drink. He stood up, wiped his brow with his fingertips, walked to the bar, and ordered a rye whisky and ginger-ale. Carrying the drink, he returned to the sofa, sat down, and took a big gulp. He took another gulp and felt the warmth of the alcohol flow down his throat.

Miranda watched him then picked up her martini glass from the coffee table and took a dainty sip. "You're lucky I ran into Philomela and Frank," she said. "They were beside themselves with worry, especially Philomela. Both were ready to search every hotel in town." She paused then quietly asked, "What happened, Don? What caused the screw up?"

"Screw up?" He gazed at her in wonder. What was she talking about? What did she know? And why did she know it?

"Don, you are supposed to nab Janice then keep her out of sight until after our airplane departs."

Dumfounded, he felt his mouth wordlessly open. Regaining a touch of composure, he said, "I don't know what you're talking about."

"Don't deny it. I know all about the kidnapping plan."

Don almost dropped his glass.

"Bob asked me to take this lovely trip in order to help you. I was only too happy to oblige."

He could not believe what he was hearing. So Bob really had hired someone to help him. He had suspected Frank, but not a woman. Certainly not Miranda.

She gave his knee a motherly pat. "Now tell me everything that happened tonight."

"First of all," he said, "tell me how you know Bob. I thought you said you lived in Toronto."

"I do live in Toronto. Bob is my brother. We phone each other every so often." She leaned back and her faint smile encouraged him to talk.

He slowly related how he and Janice had departed from the group and how they drank beer in a tacky bar. Stimulated by a big gulp of rye and ginger, he spoke faster—described their curry lunch, his dropping a sleeping pill in Janice's coffee, and their walking back to the tacky hotel. In conclusion, he slowly asked, "Is the ransom money to be split four ways?"

"Three. You, Bob, and me."

He tipped his glass and gulped the last of his rye and ginger. "What about Pierre?"

"Don't you know?" She seemed genuinely surprised.

"Know what?"

"Pierre died."

Don dropped his empty glass. It made a loud noise but fortunately did not shatter. His hand trembled as he picked up the glass from the carpet and set it on the coffee table. "Pierre was injured, but he was alive when I left Calgary."

"Pierre's fall caused severe head injuries. He died the next day in hospital."

Stunned, Don stared at her. Pierre had been a good friend and now he was dead, all because of a freak accident. What was the point of trying to nab Janice if his friend was no longer part of the plan? He recalled how he and Lola had done all they could for the unconscious man lying at the bottom of the stairs. Apparently, it had not been enough. Nothing had been enough. Things had moved beyond human control. He blinked back tears and, with a loud sigh, despondently heaved his shoulders.

"I need another drink," he mumbled.

"Pull yourself together, Don. We're all going to die, sooner or later. Right now we have to make an excuse for your recent behavior with Janice. Tell me again exactly what happened today."

He slowly related everything and added a few more details.

"Now listen carefully. This is how I see it—you're madly in love with Janice and wanted to spend time alone with her. At lunch, she must have eaten something that disagreed with her and made her feel unwell. Forget the sleeping pill you dropped in her coffee. Don't mention it. You intended to get a taxi and bring her here, but she kept falling asleep so you rented a room at the Rest Ezee hotel. While she was asleep, you went downstairs to the bar and had a drink. You went back to the room and she was still asleep so you returned to the bar. You wandered around until she woke up. Then you went down and found her purse and shoes in the lost and found box. On your way to the elevator, a man who had been sitting in the reception area followed and accosted you. At gunpoint, he took your hotel key and forced you to walk outside and climb into a taxi. He hit you on the jaw with the butt of the gun and you woke up in the back seat of the moving taxi. It brought you here and the driver pushed you outside then drove away. You wondered if the driver was in cahoots with your assailant. You suffered a sore jaw and a sore leg. You limped inside here and I saw you. Concerned about your bruised face and severe limp, I invited you to share a nightcap with me. How does that sound so far?"

"Okay. If I can remember it."

She smiled, glanced at the bartender, who was making his way to the washroom. Slowly she moved her right arm backward then suddenly swung it forward. With great force, her fist struck Don's jaw.

He fell back on the sofa, cupping his lower face in his hands. "What the hell?"

"Sorry, Don. But I hope your jaw quickly turns black and blue. It will make an assault look more realistic."

He continued to hold his hands against his jaw then rubbed it to try and soothe the pain. "That hurt."

"Don't forget that your right leg is sore, too." She gave it a sudden kick and he yelped like stricken dog. With amazing nonchalance, she said, "Your leg must have been injured when you were forced into the taxi. Get up now and walk. I want to see you limp."

He stood up and, favoring his right leg, walked a few steps toward the bar.

"Excellent. You could get a job as an actor. We'll buy a walking stick tomorrow. Now we'll wait for the others to return from the Rest Ezee hotel."

CHAPTER 37

Wednesday morning, Janice helped Don board the coach. The cane-lady sat in the front seat and glared at them, seeming oblivious of Don's facial bruise and limp. She swung her cane from side to side, almost causing more bruises.

"She's not a happy soul," Janice murmured more to herself than to Don.

After a short ride to the airport, they climbed from the coach. Miranda came up to them and gave Don a walking stick, explaining she had purchased it at the gift shop in the hotel. He tried to pay her for it, but she insisted it cost too little to worry about. She turned and walked toward the terminal. Janice and Don slowly followed her. Every so often, a fellow traveller came by and expressed sympathy for Don's bruised jaw and injured leg. Janice noted that each sympathetic word seemed to make his limp grow more pronounced. Inside the terminal, he rested on a bench while Janice joined Philomela in a lineup to obtain boarding passes.

Why they needed boarding passes for a privately chartered plane Janice didn't know. It just meant waiting in another lineup. After obtaining the passes, the two women stood in line beside Don, for what seemed like an hour, to go through security. Then they stood in another line and waited to board the plane.

Janice thought that helping Don to his seat was the least she could do. After all, he had been knocked unconscious while trying to bring her purse and shoes up to the room, and he had a bruised jaw to prove it. He also had a sore leg that had been injured while being tossed into a taxi. His description of subsequent happenings had been vague but scary—waking up in a dim world of steady motion then being pushed from the taxi to the sidewalk. It was fortuitous that Miranda was having a nightcap in the lounge. She was the one who phoned and advised the police to go to room 315 in the Rest Easy hotel. Apparently she also had bought Don a rejuvenating nightcap.

Janice sat beside Philomela on the plane and recalled entering the lobby last night. With her two rescuers, she had seen Don and Miranda sitting on a sofa.

Philomela had marched directly to Don and reprimanded him for not phoning and informing someone of their whereabouts. "It was a sin of omission on your part, Don," she said. After noting his swollen jaw and hearing about his sore leg, she softened her condemnation. "All's well that ends well."

Janice also recalled being bound and gagged in the

hotel room. She shuddered. With a sigh, she glanced over at her employer who sat reading a novel. "Philomela, I think I should check on Don."

Philomela nodded and Janice made her way up the aisle. She stopped beside Frank and again thanked him for coming with Philomela to her rescue. She then found Don asleep so returned to her seat beside Philomela.

When the airplane descended onto Aqaba's runway, she gazed with interest out the window at Jordon's sandy countryside. Fran Moleski had promised to help Don disembark.

Philomela breathed in deeply. "The sun's near the horizon and the air is warm and dry."

When their baggage was stashed in the bottom of a coach, they climbed inside. As they moved along, Janice gazed out at dozens of windowless buildings. "Why are there so many unfinished condominiums?" she asked.

"Probably a result of the downturn in the world economy," Philomela replied.

Inside the hotel reception area, while waiting for the distribution of room keys, Janice strolled over to a large map hanging on a wall near the registration desk. She read the names of various countries: Jordon, Saudi Arabia, Syria, Egypt, Lebanon, and Yemen. Puzzled by a large unnamed area, she turned to Philomela. "Is that unnamed area just uninhabited desert?"

Philomela gazed at the map. "Good grief. That's Israel."

"Why isn't it labelled?"

"Maybe the local map makers think Israel shouldn't exist."

Fran distracted them by giving them their room keys. They left the wall map and took an elevator to their third floor room, which proved small but comfortable. They washed clothes, draped them on chairs out on a small deck, and then donned summery dresses. Back on the main floor, they walked down a flight of stairs, passed a gigantic swimming pool, and entered the dining room. They enjoyed a light buffet supper then strolled on a cement path bordering the beach of the Red Sea.

"Just think," Philomela said, "Moses parted the waters of this very sea. You do know that Biblical story, don't you?"

"Of course. I may not be the brightest star in the sky, but I'm not the dimmest either."

Philomela laughed.

Back in their room, they went out on the deck, breathed in the warm air, and touched their laundry. To their surprise every item was bone dry.

"At home, this laundry would take several hours to dry," Janice said.

Later, in bed, she tossed and turned. Nightmares of duct tape over her mouth and around her wrists and ankles tormented her.

CHAPTER 38

Philomela covered her body and arms with a long sleeve tee-shirt then put on a pair of white shorts and a flimsy ankle-length wrap-around skirt. She tied back her hair with a stretchy ribbon and smoothed sun screen on her face, neck, hands, and lower legs. She looked over at Janice who was already dressed in knee-length walking shorts, yellow cotton shirt, and white runners.

"Are you ready for the trip to Wadi Rum?" Janice asked.

Philomela nodded, simultaneously admiring her employee's youthful muscles and lightly tanned skin. Her own skin had lost several battles with wind and sun and her muscles had started to succumb to gravity. Oh well, no one could be forever twenty-six. In the hotel reception area, they mingled with fellow travellers.

Janice pulled out her camera to take a few photos just as Fran walked over to her.

"Don's leg is bothering him," Fran said, "so he decided to stay at the hotel and rest it." She glanced at her watch. "It's nine a.m. Time to board the coaches."

Philomela and Janice moved from the cool, air-conditioned hotel out into the searing, desert heat. It was with relief that they entered the air-conditioned coach. They sat down three rows from the front, directly in front of Frank.

As the coach eased from the hotel, a dark haired man wearing a tan shirt and a pair of tan pants stood up in the aisle near the driver. He held a microphone to his lips.

"Welcome to Jordan," he said. "I am Abdulla from the city of Amman and for two days I will be your guide."

Philomela liked his deep voice and found his flawless English easy to understand.

"Do you find Jordan's climate warmer than Canada's?" Abdulla asked.

"Yes," reverberated from one end of the coach to the other, ending in laughter.

The coach turned from the main highway to a smaller, paved road, and treeless mountains loomed at each side. Abdulla waved his hand toward the rocky outcrops. "*Wadi* means valley and *Rum* means tall mountains. The mountains are made of granite and sandstone and some of the ridges are a thousand feet high." He sat down and everyone concentrated on rubber-necking. A short while later, the driver guided the vehicle into a parking lot and

Abdulla stood up. "This is the Wadi Rum Visitor Center. Feel free to browse. Please return to the coach in twenty minutes. If you stay longer, you'll be left behind. See you in twenty minutes."

Janice and Philomela wandered over loose sand to a sidewalk in front of a long, low building. They entered a shop, pushed their sunglasses on top of their heads, and proceeded to study trinkets, jewellery, and books. Philomela chose a book and took it to a salesman. She finished her financial transaction and caught up to Janice who was approaching the doorway.

Janice, gawking in all directions except where she was going, abruptly smacked into a black pyramid. Philomela saw her employee's blue eyes widen in surprise and gaze at two dark eyes, which were gazing with surprise at her. The dark eyes swept from blonde hair down to bare legs and sandals. The blue eyes swept along black drapery that covered everything except eyes. For a few seconds, blue and dark eyes stared at each other. Then the two bodies shifted sideways and moved in opposite directions.

Laughter bubbled from Philomela's throat—the two women were such a startling contrast in color and clothing. She tried to recall the name of the woman's long black garment. If she remembered correctly it was called niqab.

"Can you imagine wearing a shroud like that?" Janice whispered, easing close to her mentor. Without waiting for an answer, she babbled on, "Doubtless the drapery hides a woman, but who knows for sure? It could be a man under all that fabric."

Philomela listened to Janice's mutterings and mulled over a few questions of her own. Why did males wear heat reflecting white and females wear heat absorbing black? Why did men expose their faces and women did not? Unable to think of logical answers, she said, "I bought a book titled, *I Married a Bedouin*."

"Awesome. That should be interesting. Does the protagonist wear a garment like the person I bumped into?"

"On the cover picture she's wearing a kerchief, a blousy top, and a long skirt."

"Was the person I bumped into wearing a burka?" Janice glanced back at the shop they had just left.

"No. Burkas have mesh over the eyes."

"Omigod. It must be hard to see and breathe, to say nothing of restricted movements." Janice blinked several times as if trying to clear her vision.

"I've read," Philomela said, "that these women develop osteoporosis at a young age. Ironically, they lack the sunshine vitamin."

"Vitamin D." Janice glanced up at the brilliant sun and shook her head.

Their sandals crunched on sprinkles of sand on the sidewalk and then on the tile floor of the restroom. Ubiquitous, pinkish grains sifted everywhere but, otherwise, the room was spotlessly clean.

"This necessary room is better than lots," Philomela said as they walked outside. "We didn't have to straddle a hole in the floor or clean ourselves with an awkward garden hose." She consulted her wristwatch. "Our twenty minute time limit is almost up. We'd better get back to the coach."

ℰᴐℰᴐ

After a short ride, the driver parked the coach beside dozens of other large vehicles in the village of Rum. The cane lady descended the steps first then berated Abdulla for not helping her.

"She's a quarrelsome queen," Philomela whispered to Janice, and they automatically distanced themselves from her.

Frank beckoned and led them to an open-air jeep. All three climbed in the back seat and the driver, who looked twelve years old, grinned and proudly revved the engine. Flaunting his youthful immortality, he raced the vehicle over a barely discernible trail in the sand.

"This underage maniac should be in Alberta," Philomela said, hanging on for dear life. "He'd be a good bronco buster."

The underage maniac abruptly stopped the Jeep near a cleft in a large mountain and his three passengers jumped onto the soft sand. They walked toward the cleft and, with dozens of other tourists, clambered up an embankment to a narrow path. A covering of loose sand made the path slippery and, at one point, Philomela skidded, lost her balance, and was saved from falling by Frank grabbing her arm. After her near accident, she moved with greater care. After examining what looked like graffiti but, in reality, were petro glyphs, they maneuvered their way back through a crowd of oncoming tourists. A jumble of different languages bombarded their ears so the three adventurers were relieved to leave the rocky path and walk in silence to a large Bedouin tent.

The tent was made of black goat hair and, inside, was a bazaar, displaying clothing, trinkets, and food. They watched Madeline Bouchard and Fran Moleski try on headgear while a local merchant explained how to pronounce keffiyeh and how to wrap it securely around their heads. The end result was surprisingly attractive, and both women decided to buy them.

"Would I ever wear one of those at home?" Janice asked.

"Maybe at a costume party," Philomela replied.

Free of the encumbrance of purchases, the threesome again boarded the Jeep. The youthful speed-demon whisked them to the top of a sand dune to a bigger, brighter, and more elegant tent. It was open on one side and its roof and other three sides were made of a canvas-like material colored in stripes of red, white, and black. The same bright material covered mattresses that had been strategically placed on the ground around low tables. The tables were covered with white cloths on which sat white serviettes, shining cutlery, and gleaming glasses. A few elderly travellers with arthritic knees and hips groaned as they tried to achieve the athletic feat of sitting so low to the ground.

A young version of Omar Sharif came up to Frank and asked for drink orders. Frank consulted his two companions then ordered three beers. As the young man walked away, Frank remarked that obtaining alcohol in Jewish and Muslim countries was easy, but finding pork bacon and pork ham was impossible. The young server placed their beverages on the table and invited them to go outside and watch the chefs dig the cooked lamb from a pit in the sand. In unison they rose and, while strolling out to the designated area, they heard the cane-lady yell from inside the tent.

"I can't get up. Someone help me."

"Poor Fran," Philomela said.

They watched two men dig a big hole, lift a huge pot from its sandy grave, and remove the lid. An enticing aroma filled the dry air. With stimulated appetites, the audience returned to the welcome coolness of the tent. Reaching the line of people at the buffet table, Philomela stopped behind Fran and greeted her.

Holding two plates, Fran turned. "I'm not eating for two. One plate is for our friend with the cane. This is easier than helping her get to her feet and move around and sit down again."

"I admire your patience, and your politeness," Philomela said.

"This tour is designed for people who are physically fit." With a wan smile Fran diplomatically said no more.

The large variety of food, including slices of lamb, proved delicious. Sitting at the low table, Philomela admitted to feeling stuffed. Janice agreed and suggested they wear off a few calories by going for a walk. Frank declined but Philomela said okay.

The two women left the inside hustle and bustle and welcomed the outside peace and quiet. Though sunny and hot, they limbered their leg joints and muscles by strolling up a sandy slope. Philomela undid her long wraparound skirt, exposing her white shorts. She dropped her skirt, stepped out of her flip-flops and walked barefoot on the hot sand.

"Ooh. It's hot." She glanced back. "I wonder how long my footprints will last in the sand."

"Until a breeze blows." Janice held up her camera and took five pictures, all showing Philomela and her footprints. Handing the camera to Philomela, she said, "This particular photo is quite artistic. I could incorporate it with an article for *The Integrator.*" She then glanced back at the tent and exclaimed, "Omigod, Omar Sharif is staring at you."

Philomela turned. "I'm staring at the young server who's staring at my bare thighs." She hurriedly picked up her skirt and wrapped it around her lower body. Then she stepped into her flip-flops.

"He probably thinks you're a whore," Janice said.

The young man disappeared into the tent and the hot sun forced the two women to return to it, too. They sat down on the brightly covered mattress beside Frank. The young Omar Sharif pick up their empty dishes and glasses.

"You know," Janice mused, "It just dawned on me. I haven't seen one local woman out here."

Before anyone could comment, a loud voice announced it was time to depart. The threesome climbed into the back seat of the Jeep and, with the twelve year old speed demon at the wheel, flew like a bird across the sand. Roaring past other vehicles heading in the same direction, Janice was tossed against Philomela and Philomela against Frank and vice versa.

"I wonder if our driver has his pilot's license," Janice said as they came to an abrupt stop.

"He could fly with Pegasus," Philomela said. Then, wondering if her companions knew the myth, she added, "Pegasus is Greece's mythical winged horse."

Frank and Janice nodded and jumped onto the sand. Philomela followed, thankful to be alive.

❧❧❧

Back in the coach, Abdulla sedately continued his spiel. "In the movie, *Lawrence of Arabia*, Lawrence traversed *Wadi Rum* on a camel with the Bedouins. "He named those mountains, 'The Seven Pillars of Wisdom.' The wisdom part is debatable. As you may or may not know, Lawrence survived daring desert adventures, only to be killed in a motorbike accident in England."

When the coach stopped at their hotel, Philomela looked at her two friends. They were covered from head to toe with pink sand. Knowing full well she looked just as sandy and just as pink, she grinned at them. In the reception area, their grubbiness was accentuated by the appearance of a clean, well dressed Don Webster. Looking smart in a white shirt and tan pants he studied them then suggested they eat dinner together.

"You can tell me what I missed," he said.

His suggestion was accepted and all three went to their rooms to shower off the day's sandy memorabilia.

Feeling fresh and clean, Philomela followed Janice into the restaurant where she greeted Miranda, Madeline, and Andre. The two women obtained food from the buffet and took it out to the patio where Don and Frank sat at a table.

Though still warm, the air was cooler than during the heat of the day so they enjoyed their alfresco dinner and told Don about Wadi Rum.

"My only excitement," Don said, "was when three people walked into the Red Sea for a swim. All three wore black flowing robes that covered them from head to toe."

"They swam in those outfits?" Janice asked, obviously amazed. He nodded and she asked, "What did they look like when they came out?"

"I got interested in my book and didn't see them come out."

"Oh, Don," Janice said. "The fabric would have clung to their bodies like a second skin. You missed the best part."

He laughed. "I probably did."

They walked together to the elevator then went to their separate rooms. It had been a long, hot day. Preparing for bed, Philomela asked Janice if she had noticed Don's limp.

"I saw him carry his cane," she replied. Her eyes widened. "But I didn't see him use it."

"That's because he didn't use it."
Janice gazed quizzically at Philomela.
"His injured leg is healed. It's a miracle."

CHAPTER 39

Janice stared through the coach window at Jordan's limitless stretch of desert. A dome of clear blue sky loomed above beige flatlands and undulating hills and she found the color combination gentle on her eyes. Every so often, she saw camels, either lazing beside the highway or grazing on invisible plants.

"They must eat sand and hot air," Janice muttered more to herself than to Philomela. "Nothing looks edible."

Where were the fields, the crops, the gardens? And where were the sources of drinking water? To the west of Jordon, lay the mineral-filled Dead Sea and to the south was the salty Red Sea. What did local residents do before the advent of desalinization? This country, though bright and beautiful, was strange and mysterious indeed.

Janice leaned close to Philomela. "I understand why Allah is so important here. If I lived in this forbidding landscape, I'd want an all-powerful god to guide and pro-tect me."

"I'd even welcome a jinni jumping out of a lamp."

Janice giggled. "Me, too."

"We are nearing Petra," Abdulla announced over the speaker system. "As you know, Petra is one of the Seven New Wonders of the World. It was built in the sixth cen-tury B.C. by early Bedouins, called Nabataeans. Their culture, art, and myths were influenced by Greece and Egypt. Between crevices in rocks, they cultivated in-cense, myrrh, and aromatic plants. Their water system was extensive and advanced, containing canals, dams, and reservoirs carved in stone. The beautiful colors in the stones are natural—rose, blue, yellow, turquoise, purple, rust, red, and gold.

"In the second century A.D.," he continued, "Rome took control of Petra. Four centuries later, the city was destroyed by an earthquake and, after that, was never ful-ly inhabited. For almost thirteen centuries, Petra was thought to be a legend like Atlantis and Troy. Then in the nineteenth century, with the help of a young Bedouin boy, a Swiss explorer re-discovered it. For the movie fans amongst you, Petra was featured in the last scenes of *In-diana Jones and The Last Crusade*."

The coach stopped near an attractive hotel and Ab-dulla explained that, on their return from the legendary city, lunch would be served in the hotel dining room.

As usual, the cane-lady left the coach first. Miranda, wearing a wide brimmed hat, followed her. When Janice and Philomela stepped onto the sand, Miranda glided over to them. "I can hardly wait to see Petra," she said. "But this heat is brutal."

"We'll need our water bottles," Philomela said.

The three women followed Abdulla then stopped to watch donkeys and horse drawn carts clatter up and down a roadway. Frank, whose cargo pants seemed laden with water bottles, and Don, whose back-pack fit snugly between his shoulder blades, joined them. Several of the less-fleet-of-foot availed themselves to the clattering carts while those with fleeter feet walked behind Abdullah. He frequently stopped and waited patiently for stragglers. During one of the waits, Don impatiently pulled the sleeve of Janice's shirt.

"Let's walk ahead of these slowpokes," he said.

Anticipating the wonders of the ancient city, she nodded and proceeded to keep pace with him. Janice saw no sign of his limp. He was indeed miraculously cured. They walked quickly and Abdulla and his group were soon left far behind.

As the twosome hurried far ahead, Miranda glided over to Frank and smiled pleasantly at him. "I heard someone say the temperature is 52 degrees Celsius."

"I believe it." Frank grinned. "But it's a dry heat."

"Dry or not, it's incredibly hot. I'm a poet and don't know it." Miranda laughed and turned to Philomela. "Will you be able to walk two or three kilometres in this heat?"

"I hope so. I just sipped some water and slathered on more sunscreen."

"We don't want your fair skin to burn." Miranda

chatted about inconsequential things until Abdulla started speaking, then she joined others and they formed a semi-circle around him.

Far ahead on the cobblestone road, Don, wearing brown Adidas, and Janice, wearing white Nikes that yesterday's sand had turned pink, increased the distance between themselves and the stragglers. They walked with increasing momentum and their quiet footsteps contrasted with the horse and donkey hooves clattering past them. The road narrowed and rocky cliffs towered higher and higher, creating a welcome tunnel of shade and cooler air.

"Look at that cave," Janice said. "And those flowers. They're almost as colorful as the rocky cliffs."

They gaily greeted people making the return trip then Janice glanced behind. "I don't see any sign of our group. We've lost them."

"That's not a problem," Don replied. "We'll meet up at lunch."

A short while later, they walked toward what seemed a dead end blocked by a rocky cliff.

Then they saw a narrow opening, a cleft in the rock. Janice walked through it and stopped, amazed. She stared in awe at a gorgeous building with round pillars carved in a different cliff.

"The Treasury," she said.

"Look who's sitting in front of it," Don said.

She saw her most un-favorite person. Approaching the gorgeous structure, she was unable to ignore the woman. "Hi," she said. "Did you ride a donkey down the path?"

"I took a cart and it was dreadful. The horse went too fast and its hooves kept slipping. I almost ended up on those awful cobblestones. It was terrible."

"But you're okay."

The frown and the accompanying whine continued, as she swung her cane toward the building. "We can't go inside this building. It's a rip-off. It's being restored."

"That's too bad," Janice said. "It's so impressive. Have you looked at the other structures?"

"No. They're probably blocked off too."

Don, standing behind Janice, took her hand. "Let's go and explore."

They waved farewell and walked to the main street, where their shoes sank in dry, reddish sand. Their eyes focused on caves and buildings—all carved in a rocky cliff—and their ears heard tourists' shuffling feet and muted conversations. Caves higher up in the cliff became more noticeable and, seeing a path, they started to climb up. They studied an amphitheatre then walked along a trail that became narrower and narrower. They peeked inside empty caves and, finally, entered one. It was surprisingly large and completely empty, except for a colorful blanket hanging across one end.

"This blanket must be a room divider," Janice said. "Gosh, I can't imagine living here."

"Me neither." Don sat down on a rocky protuberance that was shaped like a bench and set his back-pack on the sandy floor. He patted the space beside him. "Give your feet a rest."

She sat down and gazed through the entranceway to

a cliff on the other side of the street on which they had recently walked. "It's like the end of the world. No one knows we're here."

"That's right." Don smiled, bent forward, and reached into his back-pack. His fingers curled around the plastic red bag containing his emergency supplies.

CHAPTER 40

Miranda, Frank, and Philomela walked along the cobblestone road until they reached the narrow cleft. They hesitated only a moment then walked through it and stopped. Awestruck, they stared at the twenty-six century old building.

"This must be what they call the treasury," Philomela said.

Frank moved toward it. "It's breathtaking."

"You can't go inside," a voice whined. "The whole thing's a rip-off."

Until she spoke, Frank hadn't noticed the cane-lady sitting on a rocky shelf. A camel with a tourist on its back walked between them and, when it passed, the cane-lady glared at Frank. Though less than eager to engage her in conversation, he asked if she had seen Don and Janice.

"Filthy animals," she muttered, staring at the camel. "Do you mean the girl who's always late?" He nodded and she pointed toward the main street. "They went that way. Inconsiderate youths. That's what they are."

Frank thanked her and turned to his two companions. They walked three abreast toward Facades Street. The loose reddish sand floated around their ankles as they gawked at amazing structures carved in the rock. Some had high columns and arched doors and windows, others had rectangular openings, and others just exposed small dim caves. They entered three of the latter then returned again to the bright sunshine and clambered up to the amphitheatre.

"It's amazing so much is still intact," Frank said. "Hard to believe it endured violent earthquakes."

Philomela and Miranda nodded agreement.

"Anyone want to explore this path?" Frank pointed to a trail winding along the edge of the cliff.

"Ancient Greeks may have influenced the Naboteans," Philomela said, "but I don't want to join Zeus and his fellow immortals by falling from that narrow path."

Frank laughed and started to climb around a sharp outcrop. He waved at them then walked a short distance on the ribbon like path. A minute later, he looked over the edge and saw his two companions retracing their steps down to Facades Street. He gazed at the cliff on the other side of the street and admired its rainbows of color. Reds, pinks, and rusts were predominant and they looked magnificent. It made him glad he was not color illiterate, or worse, color blind.

He had seen prairies, forests, mountains, and oceans, but never had he seen anything quite like this. Even though it was mesmerizing and beautiful, he knew he would not want to live here.

"What are you doing?"

The voice shattered his reverie. He looked around and saw no one. Where was the voice coming from?

"Let me go."

The voice sounded frightened. Frank felt anxious because he recognized the voice.

"Who's there?" he called.

No one replied so he moved forward. Seeing a rectangular opening in the rock, he carefully edged along the narrow path toward it.

Coming abreast of the opening, he collided with a figure dashing out of it. Momentum was so strong the figure would have lurched over the rocky cliff to the street below if Frank's body had not formed a barricade. His arms automatically went around the woman's waist and helped her keep her balance.

She leaned toward the steep embankment. "Omigod." Then she turned her head and Frank's gray eyes met her blue ones.

"Are you okay, Janice?"

Her head nodded, but her eyes registered fear. "You stopped me from falling over the cliff. You saved my life."

He responded by drawing her close. She made no attempt to withdraw. At that moment, Don walked from the dim cave into the bright light.

He loudly cleared his throat and stared at the couple. "Well, Frank, are you exploring the gems of Petra?"

"Don, what happened to Janice?"

"Nothing happened. We had a misunderstanding, that's all."

Janice turned to Don but snuggled closer to Frank. "Duct tape."

Frank recalled the Rest Easy hotel and the duct tape that had bound and gagged Janice. He stared at Don, trying to understand what was happening now.

"It's nothing." Don said. "I just keep duct tape in my backpack to repair things like ripped pants and torn shirts."

Janice glared at him and wiped her hand over her lower face. "Then why did you try to stick it over my mouth?"

Don chuckled. "That was just a joke."

She stared at him as if at a ferocious beast. "A joke?"

Frank gazed from Janice to Don, obviously puzzled. "We should walk back to that nice hotel for lunch," he said diplomatically. "Don, maybe you could lead the way."

Don slung the straps of his backpack over his shoulders and started to walk along the narrow path. Frank felt Janice clutch his shirttail as they moved forward in single file. She seemed to rely on his shirttail to keep from falling over the embankment so he reached back and held her wrists until the path widened. Then he walked on the drop-off side of the path while she walked on the inner side. When they reached Facades Street, the walking was easy, almost like strolling on a sandy beach.

Don reached the narrow opening in the cliff first. He

turned around and Frank thought his face registered a mix of anger and disappointment.

"Don, are you okay?" he asked.

Without replying, Don strode through the cleft and disappeared from sight.

CHAPTER 41

The flight to Vienna was uneventful.

Janice sat beside Philomela, who provided just enough conversation and reassurance to make her feel secure. During their periods of non-conversation, Janice thought about Don. He was an enigma. The pleasant, young man she had first befriended now bordered on being a nutcase. Though a few of his earlier actions had puzzled her, and still puzzled her, his recent ones made her wonder about his mental state. At the seedy hotel in the Seychelles and in the cave at Petra, Don's behavior was more than disturbing. It was frightening.

She recalled how pleasant and friendly he had been on the island of Mana, then on the boat trip back to Fiji he became surly. At Pioneer World in Perth, Australia, his loud criticisms of Frank were unwarranted. In the Bali market, he gallantly searched for her then grew sullen and annoyed with Madeline for hurrying them to return to the coach. In Kuala Lumpur's Batu Cave, he'd encouraged Janice to enter a forbidden area and then tried to keep her there. When Frank emerged, he petulantly ditched her. In the tacky Seychelles hotel, he was abducted and, luckily, Caleb, whoever he was, proved harmless. In the cave at Petra, Don wrestled with her and tried to duct tape her mouth. She hated to think what would have happened if Frank hadn't appeared.

Though mental telepathy was not high in her beliefs, it jumped a notch as Philomela turned to her. "Don detained you in the Batu Caves, the Rest Easy hotel, and the cave in Petra. Do you think he had amorous intentions?"

"I was just thinking about Don's actions. They were weird but not amorous."

'Mmm." For a moment Philomela seemed thoughtful. "His swollen and bruised jaw in the Seychelles was real. But in Jordan, I think his limp was phoney."

"It sure healed suddenly. I was never afraid of him until we were in the cave at Petra."

"At first he added spice to your odyssey then he just made it odd."

"Odd odyssey," Janice mused. "That describes it perfectly." She glanced back at the man they were discussing. He sat several rows behind them, reading a magazine. Earlier, she had considered avoiding him by hiding in her Vienna hotel room, but then she thought better of it—she didn't want to miss seeing the Lipizzaner stallions and the Vienna palaces.

"Howdy Janice and Philomela." Frank stood in the aisle, looking down at them. "Am I disturbing you?"

"Not at all," Philomela said. "In fact, Janice needs a diversion. A new companion should do it. Let's exchange seats."

She stood up and he responded with a warm smile. Walking down the aisle toward Frank's empty seat, Philomela surreptitiously studied Miranda Gordon who was sitting directly behind Don Webster. Looking elegant as usual, she seemed intent on reading her book. However, the book must have had boring passages because Philomela saw her briefly raise her eyes then quickly lower them again.

The woman's writhing hair reminded Philomela of their three days in Istanbul. They had toured mosques and palaces and the fifteen hundred year old cisterns beneath the city. It was while strolling underground on the eerily lit walkways above the water that the guide had pointed out a relief of Medusa. Carved on a pillar, the picture accentuated Medusa's snake-hair and Miranda, obviously unaware of the Greek myth, had exclaimed, "How terrible. Who could possibly live with hair like that?"

Philomela recalled how she had to stifle laughter because Miranda's hair so resembled Medussa's. However, her gut feeling indicated that Miranda was not a laughing matter. There was more to the glamorous lady than wild hair and attractive clothes. One thing Philomela had noticed was how she always appeared to be on the scene whenever Janice and Don wandered off together. When they were late for the coach in the Seychelles, Miranda knew they had gone to a pub. When Don was dumped from the taxi at their hotel she was there to help him.

When Don and Janice walked ahead of the group at Petra, she chatted animatedly, as if trying to keep everyone from noticing their departure. Was she a middle-aged woman trying to be a catalyst for romance? Or was she something more sinister?

Philomela recalled how Miranda had initially latched onto her and Janice at the departure gala in Vancouver. Their commonality of dress made the meeting seem easy and natural. But even then, Philomela had briefly wondered if Miranda was trying to be more than a jolly companion, interested only in nice outfits.

Thoughts of Miranda faded as the plane landed in Vienna and coaches took them to their hotel. The small bags containing warm clothes, that had disappeared in the Vancouver airport, now miraculously reappeared in their hotel room. The outside air was cool and crisp so Philomela and Janice were pleased to replace summer garments with sweaters and jackets.

"This hotel is a far cry from the 'Res Ezee' with the missing 'T,'" Philomela said, glancing around the room. To her relief Janice responded with a smile. Her employee's scary experiences were slowly becoming history.

For the next three days, they enjoyed the hotel's delicious breakfasts and the pleasant staff who catered to them. It amazed Philomela how most Europeans flipped so quickly from one language to another. She wished she could to the same. However, in Western Canada, skills in languages other than English were less than necessary.

The highlight of the stay in Vienna was the evening at the Ferstel Palace, where they stepped into a bygone era of elegance and splendour. Crystal gleamed, silver sparkled, and not one pair of blue jeans was in sight. Like a modern day Marie Antoinette, Philomela savored oxtail soup with sherry, glazed leg of veal in herb sauce, and listened, entranced, to a boys' choir. When a band started to play a Viennese waltz, there was only one thing missing—Brent.

Philomela's longing to see, chat, and dance with her husband increased with every lilting tune. The holiday was drawing to a close and she was anxious to see him again. Perhaps it was just as well he hadn't been here during her search for Janice. He would have worried about her wandering around in sleazy hotels.

She noticed Janice move her head in time with the music while Frank sat stiffly beside her. It dawned on Philomela that he did not know how to do a Viennese waltz. She stood up and authoritatively took hold of his hand. "I believe this is our dance, Frank."

"I don't know how," he murmured, looking extremely uncomfortable.

She remained standing so he slowly got up and followed her to the edge of the dance floor, where she proceeded to teach him the basic waltz steps. She counted, "One, two, three. One, two, three."

He was a quick learner and, in no time, they were moving over the floor with only an occasional loss of rhythm and only three violent shoe crashes. When the music ended, she brought him back to the table. The lilting music started again and, this time, he escorted Janice to the dance floor.

As the evening progressed, Philomela began to feel like a third wheel on a bicycle. To give the young people a chance to enjoy themselves and not be concerned about her, she left their table and approached the Sandersons. The captain stood up and greeted her, and his wife, Rose, invited her to take an empty seat. After exchanging pleasantries, they discussed the spectacular Lipizzaner stallions they had seen the day before and then admired Janice and Frank, who were whirling like professionals on the dance floor. During a break in the music, Captain Sanderson brought up the subject of Don Webster.

"It's a blessing nothing serious happened to Janice or Don in the Seychelles," he said. "People's Airline and Terrific Travel would have been up to their eyeballs in investigations."

"You can thank Frank and me for finding Janice," Philomela said, trying not to be too puffed up with pride. "We found her before the police even believed anything other than romance was happening. And, of course, Frank also came to her rescue in Petra—though he said that was more good luck than good management."

"Frank and I discussed it," Captain Sanderson said. "We agreed that Don is a pleasant young man, but he's immature and a bit wrong-headed." He glanced at Janice and Frank, who were again tripping the light fantastic. "I think Don has missed out with Janice."

Philomela nodded in agreement. "Don has superficial charm, but he's emotionally unsure of himself. I suspect he could easily be led to do stupid things."

"Are you a psychologist?" Rose asked.

"No." Philomela chuckled. "But Janice is my employee and I feel responsible for her. As a result, I've given the situation considerable thought. I don't think Don wanted to harm her, but he wanted something. Who knows what?"

"Seduction," Captain Sanderson suggested.

Philomela shook her head. "I think it's something other than that."

"Don phoned me late this afternoon," Captain Sanderson said. "He explained he was suffering from a headache and would be unable to attend the dinner and dance."

"It's just as well." Philomela glanced at a couple of dancers whirling past. "Don's sensitive enough to know a few of us dislike the way he treated Janice."

At the end of the evening, Philomela glided like an aristocrat down the stately curving stairway and thought of the straight stairway at the Coyote Lounge. Looking at the bottom of the stairs, she saw not Pierre Lalonde but Janice. She was approaching the elegantly attired Bouchards.

"Madeline, thank you so much," Janice said.

Puzzled, Madeline took a step backward. With questioning eyes, she gazed at the young girl and asked, "For what?"

"For appearing at the right times."

Madeline seemed speechless.

"I'm truly grateful," Janice said. Then she smiled broadly and walked over to Frank.

As Philomela reached the bottom of the elegant

stairway, Madeline edged over to her. "What did I do to deserve Janice's thanks?"

"I'll explain tomorrow on the airplane." Philomela smiled at her then followed Frank and Janice out to the coach.

Back at the hotel, Philomela breathed in the cool fresh air and left the young couple to stroll outside in the moonlight. Inside the hotel room, she brought out her i-Pad and found one message from Brent. The weather in Calgary was good but the news about Lola was bad.

The police are asking everyone who saw the deceased on the fatal evening to come forward. They want to talk to anyone who was near Central Park Library on the night of the murder, especially anyone who might have seen a gray Datsun with a red interior.

She put on her nightgown and brushed her teeth, but her thoughts dwelt on Lola in Calgary. Why would anyone want to kill her?

CHAPTER 42

After their Boeing 737-400 landed in Ireland, the world travellers' toured Dublin's Trinity College. In the library, they viewed the ancient book of Kells then gazed at busts of, and books written by, Irish literary masters. That evening, they enjoyed a final dinner with local entertainment in an Irish pub.

Next morning, they boarded the plane and Philomela felt a twinge of sadness. This was their last day of travel. The plane, that had become a home away from home, stopped in Iceland for refueling. Then it landed in Toronto where eastern passengers waved friendly goodbyes. The cane-lady lived up to expectations by reprimanding a flight attendant about terrible food and complaining to Fran about the stairs in Trinity College. Her final act, as she departed, was to flick her stick at Janice.

Philomela stepped toward the unhappy woman. "It's been a great trip," she said, "and I wish you well."

"You're just as bad as that awful girl." Her glaring eyes turned to Janice.

Envy? Was the woman envious of Janice's youth? Philomela felt sorry for her but, on the other hand, she felt happy to see the last of her. She suspected most of her fellow travellers harbored similar feelings.

The flight continued to Vancouver, where the remaining passengers hugged each other, bade fond farewells to the crew, and went their separate ways.

That evening in their Vancouver hotel room, Philomela climbed into bed and looked over at Janice. She thought of her hotel searches with Frank during the bewitching hour. That entire episode had been emotionally draining because of her fondness for the girl. She was thankful everything ended well.

Her stomach twisted as her thoughts shifted to Lola. Feeling a twinge of nausea, she wondered for the umpteenth time why Lola had died. Who had done it? And how had it been done?

What could she do to help bring the murderer to justice? Probably nothing.

Next morning, the plane landed in Calgary and Brent welcomed the two women with open arms. He, who usually shunned outward displays of emotion, gave his wife a big bear hug and nuzzled her neck.

"I'm glad you're home," he whispered. "I really missed you." Walking to the car between Philomela and Janice, he asked, "Did you have a good holiday?

"It was great," Philomela said, "though rather animalistic. I ate like a pig, drank like a fish, followed tour guides like a sheep, behaved like a holy cow, flitted around like a flea, and carried souvenirs like a camel." He laughed and she added, "The only thing missing was you."

"I'm not an animal, but I'm glad you missed me."

Two days later, Philomela and Janice visited the Coyote Lounge. After eating a late lunch, there, they offered condolences to the owner.

He confirmed what they already suspected—Lola had been a spectacular employee. Over and over he reiterated, "She was always so pleasant and so efficient. The best waitress I ever had." He gazed at Philomela. "I'm glad she had fun modelling for the advertisement in *The Integrator.* People came to see the attractive waitress. And they still do. I hate telling customers that she died." He looked pensive. "I avoid the word murder because the other waitresses are psyched out by it. They all wonder if they'll be next."

"Good grief," Philomela said. "Why would they think that?"

"They're afraid a nutcase is going around killing servers."

"That's bad. Do you have any idea why Lola was killed?"

He shook his head and blinked his eyes.

Philomela noticed they were moist. "Do you know where it happened?" she asked.

"Inside her Datsun. The rumor is that her throat was..." He trailed off, zipped his hand under his chin from one ear to the other, and ignored Janice's gasp. "An early morning jogger found her slumped over her steering wheel near the Memorial Park Library."

"What a horrible way to die." Philomela swallowed and tried to make her own throat muscles relax. More or less succeeding, she said, "If you find any other details, would you let me know? I think all of us should do our utmost to find the killer." She handed him her business card.

"You might want to contact Lola's mother. Mrs. Grieve is very depressed. She lives on Nineteenth Street NW." He produced a phone book from a shelf under the bar.

Philomela flipped the pages, found the name, and wrote the address and phone number in her tiny notebook. When the manager went about his business, she took her cellphone from her purse and punched in the numbers.

The phone rang three times before a soft voice slowly said, "Hello."

"Mrs. Grieve?" Her query was confirmed so she explained, "I'm Philomela Nightingale. Lola modelled for a Coyote Lounge advertisement in my magazine, *The Integrator*."

"Yes. It was a nice picture."

"I was away when she died, but I am deeply saddened by it. She was not only a beautiful girl but a lovely person to work with. Would it be possible for me to visit you for a brief chat?"

"Well…I'm not very good company."

"I understand, Mrs. Grieve. You've experienced one

of the worst things that could happen to any mother. On my part, I wish to see the culprit caught and punished."

"That won't bring Lola back."

"You're right. But don't you think the person responsible should pay for his crime?"

"I suppose so."

"Could you see me today about four o'clock?"

"Oh…" Mrs. Grieve was obviously taken aback. However, she reluctantly agreed.

Janice listened to the conversation and, when it was over, said, "A one-on-one visit with the grieving mother will be best. I'll take this opportunity to visit Collette and Mrs. Lalonde."

"Good idea," Leaving the Coyote Lounge, Philomela gave the flight of stairs a lingering glance. Could the deaths of Pierre and Lola be related? She concluded they could not.

∽∾∽∾

When the door on Nineteenth Street NW opened, Philomela looked down at a petite, white-haired lady, whose facial expression was devoid of welcome. Like an automaton, her expression lacked pleasure, sadness, or anything else. She reminded Philomela of a zombie but, because of the circumstances, Philomela was taken by her. It was no wonder Lola had developed into such a lovely person. The genes ran strong.

"I'm Philomela Nightingale," she said, and her voice was soft.

"Please come in."

She stepped inside the hall. "Mrs Grieve, thank you for taking the time to see me. And once again, please accept my condolences."

Her hostess gently closed the door and, without looking at Philomela, said, "As I told you on the phone, I'm not good company right now. However, I usually have a cup of tea at this time of day. Will you join me?"

"Yes, I'd like that."

Philomela followed her to a blue and white kitchen. Mrs. Grieve indicated a round oak table with four matching chairs and Philomela sat on one of the chairs. She gazed at oak cupboards and white counter tops, on which sat four blue containers. She thought they probably held tea, coffee, sugar, and cookies. She watched her hostess pour boiling water in a blue teapot, set a blue plate with chocolate chip cookies on the table, and then set the teapot beside the cookies. Like an automaton, Mrs. Grieve set blue serviettes and blue and white cups and saucers on the table. She sat down in a chair across from her guest and, with trembling hands, poured tea into the cups.

"Mrs. Grieve, I'm truly sorry Lola's gone. I was very fond of her. And she was respected by her coworkers. In fact, I think everyone who knew her loved her."

Showing no anger, Mrs. Grieve set a teacup and saucer in front of Philomela. "Not everyone."

With a sigh, Philomela nodded and placed her right thumb and index finger on the handle of the cup. "I keep thinking of the incongruity of everything that happened. Do you recall Lola ever mentioning that someone was annoying her? You know, stalking her or making obscene phone calls?"

"No, she never mentioned anything like that."

Philomela raised her cup and thoughtfully took a sip of tea. She set the cup back on the saucer and cleared her throat. "Mr. Lalonde, who recently fell down the stairs at the lounge, also advertised in my magazine."

"Yes, I saw his advertisements. He was a regular patron at the lounge. His death troubled Lola a great deal."

Philomela raised her cup in midair and paused, willing Mrs. Grieve to elaborate.

"I can't remember Lola's exact words...something about someone putting something in Mr. Lalonde's whisky and accidently bumping against him at the top of the stairs."

Philomela froze. What was this? Was this the connection she was looking for? Trying to appear nonchalant, she asked, "Did you tell this to the police?"

"No. They didn't ask me about Mr. Lalonde."

"Did Lola give you the name of the person who bumped him?"

"I don't recall her mentioning a name."

Philomela wanted to yell, "Think...think...think." Instead, she sipped her tea then carefully set the cup on the saucer. She smiled at her hostess. "This tea is delicious," she said.

"It's green tea." Mrs. Grieve picked up the teapot and added more of the steeped liquid to Philomela's cup. "Please have a cookie."

Philomela took a cookie, ignoring her weight-watching rule of not eating between meals. She nibbled it. "Do you remember if Lola said it was a man or a woman who put something in Mr. Lalonde's drink?"

Mrs. Grieve shook her head and pressed her lips together. This was her first noticeable sign of emotion. "No, and she didn't say if a man or a woman bumped into him at the top of the stairs. She and Don Webster attended Mr. Lalonde after he fell."

Don knew Lola? Philomela was struck dumb. She stared at Mrs. Grieve and it took a moment before she found her voice. "You mean Don Webster, the young importer?"

"No, Don works on a ranch."

Could they be one and the same man? "Did Don bump into Mr. Lalonde?"

"No, I believe Don was part way down the stairs when Mr. Lalonde fell."

"Did Lola talk to you about Don?"

"Yes. Often. She liked him. She hoped he would ask her out, but he never did. He stayed with Mr. Lalonde while Lola phoned the ambulance."

Philomela took another bite of cookie and chewed vigorously. With her little finger curled daintily, she picked up her cup and took a long sip of the warm liquid. Smiling encouragingly at her hostess, she asked, "Do you think it was a regular customer who put something in Mr. Lalonde's drink?"

"I don't know."

Philomela remembered Myron McGill mentioning in the car that Mr. Lalonde was one of his joint-venture partners. She knew that Bob Davis was one, too. "Mrs. Grieve, does the name Bob Davis sound familiar?"

"Mmm sort of…"

Philomela leaned forward and, with anticipation, held her breath.

"Lola was careful not to make any false accusations."

Philomela again concentrated on sipping her tea. Then, as if warming both hands on the cup, she asked, "After Mr. Lalonde died, did Lola consider contacting the police to tell them what she had seen?"

"As a matter of fact, she did. But she decided against it because she couldn't prove anything. Who would believe her?"

"And, of course, Mr. Lalonde's glass had been efficiently picked up and washed."

"Yes. She later wished she had saved it for analysis."

"But, at the time, she didn't know he would die."

Mrs. Grieve slowly moved her head from side to side. "No. That came as a shock later."

Philomela sipped her tea then shifted on her chair. "Can you think of anything that might help put a bit of light on what happened to Lola?"

"Nothing. She kept a diary, but I haven't had the heart to look at it. It's such a personal thing. I suppose it doesn't matter now, especially if it might help find whoever killed her." Mrs. Grieve stood up and Philomela saw tears start to flow over her lower eyelids. As if embarrassed at the sudden show of emotion, Lola's mother hurried out of the room.

Philomela felt her own eyes fill with moisture. Poor Mrs. Grieve—her only daughter gone, and at such a young age. The horrible circumstances made it imperative that the killer be brought to justice. Philomela blinked. Knowing her mascara might be dripping, she plucked a tissue from her purse and wiped below her eyes.

"I'm not up to reading the diary right now," Mrs. Grieve said, re-entering the kitchen. "You can borrow it if you promise to give it back to me."

Philomela watched her hostess place the small book on the table. "I promise."

CHAPTER 43

Don Webster entered the Coyote Lounge. He stopped at the bottom of the staircase and his mind's eye envisioned his friend Pierre lying in a heap. He tried to shake the vision away.

Two days ago, he had arrived home from his trip around the world. His body and mind still suffered from the tiredness and time lapses of jetlag. Worse, he mourned deeply the deaths of his two favorite people. Losing Lola and Pierre put life in a new and different perspective. He wondered if it was worth living.

His failure as a kidnapper dropped into an unimportant pit. He rebuked himself for having blamed Frank, Madeline, and Philomela for thwarting his efforts—now realizing they had helped prevent him from doing something illegal and morally wrong. In comparison with the loss of Pierre and Lola, the loss of ransom money and a home in the foothills paled to nothingness.

Staring at the empty floor, he shuddered. Pierre had been alive and now was gone. Yesterday, Don had heard of Lola's death on the radio. At the time, he hadn't been able to take it in. He still felt numb, disbelieving. The last time he had seen her was when they stood side by side and watched the paramedics put Pierre inside the ambulance.

He glanced at his wristwatch. Four-thirty. He was exactly on time for his meeting.

With a sigh, he started to climb the stairs. Like a tired, lame creature, he reached the second level of the Coyote Lounge and automatically looked for Lola. Since yesterday, he seldom thought of anything else. No other girl had ever attracted him like she had. He felt a pang of regret for having never asked her for a date. Just last night, he dreamt of surprising her with a diamond ring then taking her to see his beautiful new acreage. But none of that would happen. The money was lost and the acreage would never be his. And Lola was gone forever.

He paused, feeling his eyes go damp. What made the situation truly sickening was the way she had died. Some crazed person had murdered her.

At their regular corner table, he saw Bob Davis. But no Pierre. Don took a deep breath, walked over to him, and greeted him despondently. Along with his kidnapping failure, two other elephants filled the room. What should have been a pleasant reunion was a dreary wake.

Don didn't apologize for the kidnapping failure. Instead he said, "I keep thinking of the deaths of my two friends."

Bob magnanimously sloughed off the ransom failure and extolled Pierre's qualities of honesty, loyalty, and hard work. Don agreed with every word. Bob gave his order to a waitress and Don noted that she walked away with less speed and grace than Lola used to do. When the girl returned with his drink, Don was aware that she also lacked Lola's friendly warmth.

Bob raised his glass of single malt whisky and proposed a toast to their lost associate.

Don raised his CC and ginger. "To Pierre and," he added, "to Lola."

They both drank.

Setting his glass on the table, Don gazed down at it. Then he asked, "Why did you think Miranda Gordon would be able to help me?"

Bob cleared his throat. "Because she's capable and intuitive. I thought she'd keep that red-haired bitch busy, thus allow you and Janice to escape from her clutches."

Avoiding Bob's dark eyes, Don sipped his drink.

"As a matter of fact, Miranda phoned yesterday. She described two occasions when she had stopped Philomela and a young chap called Frank from joining you and Janice."

"Yes, I did appreciate her help in the Seychelles. She devised a cover-up plan for my botched kidnapping and made it authentic by giving me a bruised jaw." Remembering how his jaw hurt, he brushed his fingers over the still darkened area below his mouth.

"Miranda said a few people suspected you of seducing Janice."

"It never got that far. Everyone just blamed us for making them wait on the coach." Don gazed into Bob's hawk-like eyes and thought how much they looked like Miranda's. His tall, slim build and dark hair also resembled hers, except his hair was short and hers was long and snake-like. "You and Miranda are similar in appearance," he murmured.

"She's my sister."

Don nodded. Lowering his eyes, he realized the older man still inspired him—with awe, but not respect.

A month ago, he had considered Bob a trusted advisor and, now, he wondered at his own gullibility. It was hard to believe he had ever admired the hawk faced man's ability to twist the truth and manipulate people for his own selfish purposes. Even back then, however, Don had enough insight to compare Bob's deviousness to a dark, devil's food cake and his charm to the cake's white icing. Now the man just seemed dark and dreary. His charm was thin and sickly sweet, something to avoid.

"Miranda told me you promised to cut her in for a third of the ransom," Don said.

"She told you that?"

"Yes. You must have asked her to participate when Pierre was still alive. Our shares should have been a quarter each."

Bob glanced away. "Miranda must have misunderstood me, or else you misunderstood her."

Don knew he had not misunderstood her. They finished their drinks then walked side by side to the stairs. On the way down, Don clung to the railing.

Outside, they bade each other farewell.

"See you around," Bob said.

Don nodded, though he knew this would be their last meeting. He paused by the door of his truck and watched Bob climb into his BMW convertible. As the shiny black vehicle zoomed away, a weight seemed to rise from Don's shoulders. It was as if a bad part of his life was disappearing.

Back at the ranch, he dropped a few toonies in the cookie jar to replace the ones he had borrowed. Then he put on his heavy jacket and went outside. By the light of the stars and the half-moon, he walked to the barn and fed the barn cats, just in case their mouse hunting skills had faltered. Later that night, lying in bed, he wondered how long he would continue working as a ranch hand. He liked the work and he liked the life-style, but the pay was low. It would be years before he could save enough money to buy a parcel of land in the foothills. The more he thought about it, the more he wondered if it really mattered.

On the around the world trip, he had learned of other jobs, inside Canada and outside, that could be interesting. It might be fun to work as a baggage handler in an airport or as a waiter or a deck hand on a cruise ship. Participating in a real import business even intrigued him. Maybe he could gain retail experience by getting a job in one of Pierre's gift shops, provided Collette needed new staff.

The loss of Pierre and Lola made him feel hollow inside. He tried to think of good things—his present job and his uncle's joint-venture investment. Who knew, maybe his personal wells with McGill Oil and Gas had fueled the airplanes and coaches on his world trip?

He rolled over and looked out the window. The countryside was dark, but in the sky millions of stars twinkled.

CHAPTER 44

Philomela sat in the Starbuck's Coffee Shop and waited for the arrival of Detective O'Malley. She sipped the caffeinated brew and watched the door.

Last evening, after reading much of Lola's diary, she weighed the pros and cons of contacting the police. The cons consisted of coping with dangerous killers and of placating Brent, who disliked her involvement with the seedier side of life. The pros were more numerous and rested heavily on seeing justice served. Lola had been intelligent, capable, pleasant, and far too young to die—four good reasons to bring the murderer to trial. The pros won hands down, so she'd phoned the General Investigative Unit and asked for Detective O'Malley. When told he wouldn't be available until the next morning, she left her name and phone number.

Early this morning, he returned her call and they arranged to meet for coffee at Starbucks.

Seeing O'Malley enter the shop, she sat up, as tall as her five-foot-three frame could muster, and waved to him.

He waved back and stopped at the counter. Watching him purchase his coffee, she recalled first meeting him at an outdoor police chorus performance on the Eighth Avenue Mall.

She had intended to write a brief review about the show and, because he was the spark who initially ignited the police chorus, she made a point of interviewing him. He explained how singing and entertaining provided happy contrasts to the grimmer aspects of police work. His enthusiasm for the chorus proved so contagious he became the crux of an entire article for *The Integrator.*

Since then, she had chatted with him on numerous occasions. Once at a military ball, he and his wife sat with her and Brent at the same table. At least twice a year, he came to her office to put a chorus advertisement in the magazine.

"Hi, Philomela." He set his coffee mug on the table, slipped off his leather jacket, and draped it over the back of a chair. He sat down and studied her face. "What is it?"

"First, I must compliment you on the show last August. Brent and I enjoyed the chorus and the jokes. So did Janice, my girl Friday."

"I'm glad. We had fun doing it." He looked directly into her eyes, raised his mug, and sipped the steaming liquid. Lowering the mug, he asked, "What have you got for me?"

"Nothing, actually."

"You mean you just wanted to enjoy my charming company?"

"That's right." She bent down, brought her purse up from the floor, and set it on her lap. Opening her purse, she pulled out a small book. "This is the victim's five-year diary. I promised her mother I'd return it. So without her permission, you can't have it."

"What makes you think I'd want it?"

She opened the diary at a page indicated by a book-mark and leaned toward the detective. "O'Malley, the girl recorded a few incidents concerning her workplace that you might like to consider. I'll use first names only. The first incident is this and I quote: 'I saw Bob drop something in Pierre's drink.' The second incident occurred when she later saw him bump Pierre at the top of the stairs. You probably recall that the latter fell down a full flight and died in hospital the next day."

He nodded and, without taking his eyes from her face, picked up his coffee mug and drank.

"I understand the cause of death was severe head injuries," she said. "But I wonder if something in his digestive tract might have been revealing. Was an autopsy done?"

"I think so. How does all this affect the current investigation?"

She replaced the bookmark and flipped to another marked page. "This was written the day before she was mur—um—died." Philomela glanced at nearby customers, all of whom seemed to pay no attention to her. She proceeded to read: "'Mr D invited me to go out with him for dinner, said he wanted to give me a gift. I declined because I already had a date. I also pointed out that he shouldn't give gifts to waitresses. He explained that he had won a pearl necklace at a fundraiser and wanted to acknowledge my efficient and pleasant waitressing with it. He asked if I could join him for a late supper next evening. Because I was curious and also had a desire to own a pearl necklace I agreed. He asked if we could use my car because his was in a body shop having a dinged fender fixed. We decided to meet near the Memorial Park Library. He is a man of many moods so I hope tomorrow he'll be in a good one.'"

"Mmm," O'Malley said. "A necklace. Interesting."

"Was a pearl necklace found in her car?" she asked.

"No. There was no necklace."

"O'Malley, was her throat cut?"

"Information regarding the cause of death is being withheld."

"That's the rumour going around," she said.

"I know. The jogger who found her started it." He shook his head then grinned. "Sorry Philomela. You're the press. When the information is released, you'll be the first person to know. In the meantime, do you think the girl's mother would permit me to have the diary, provided I guarantee to return it?"

"I think so. I have her number. Do you want me to phone her right now?"

"I'd appreciate it. Tell her I'll come by at her convenience and discuss the details with her."

Philomela dug in her purse again and brought out her cellphone. After a brief conversation she snapped it shut. "O'Malley, you can borrow the diary and visit Mrs. Grieve early this afternoon. She makes good green tea."

"Perfect. I also want to visit another person. Don Webster. I talked with the owner of Coyote Lounge. Apparently Don had worked with Pierre in his suntan salon. He was with him when the accident occurred."

"Mrs. Grieve told me that Don and Lola were the first to reach Pierre after he fell. But I didn't know Don had worked for Pierre. Surely you don't suspect him."

The detective picked up his coffee mug and drank.

એવેએ

That evening at dinner, Philomela listened to Brent cheerfully tell about the successful results of his last drilling venture. She decided his mood was good enough to accept her news. She told him about her coffee date with Detective O'Malley.

"Philomela," he groaned, "not again." His eyes shadowed and his head slowly shook from side to side. "Do you have to get involved with murder?"

"Sorry, Brent. But Lola was such a great girl. I have to help bring her killer to justice."

"Can't the police manage without your help?"

"Of course, they can. But I have bits and pieces of information that will speed up the process."

He gazed into her eyes and again shook his head. "I don't like seeing you put yourself at risk."

"There is no risk, Brent."

"When murder's involved, there's always risk."

CHAPTER 45

Next morning in her office, Philomela casually mentioned to Janice that yesterday she had met Detective O'Malley at Starbucks for coffee. Her employee's reaction was quite different from Brent's.

"Lucky you. I'd love to have coffee with that gorgeous hunk. What did you talk about?"

"I supplied him with information about Lola's murder."

"Information? What information?"

"A few things I had gleaned from Mrs. Grieve. O'Malley and I also discussed Don Webster." She paused, expecting a violent reaction from Janice. There was none, so she continued speaking: "O'Malley hoped to visit him yesterday afternoon at the ranch. After having a chat with Mrs. Grieve."

"Omigod." Janice seemed to have a delayed reaction. "Does he suspect Don of murdering Lola?"

"I doubt it. Don wasn't even here when it happened. But Don knew Lola and he also knew Pierre Lalonde. He had worked in his suntan salon."

"Really? Maybe if I'd told Don of their deaths, he might have behaved differently."

"That's possible. But we had no reason to think he knew them."

"It's all so awful." Janice stared at her boss and her eyes grew moist. Then, as if a revelation flashed, her face brightened. "You're the inverse of your namesake. The mythic Philomena helped commit a murder and you're helping to solve one."

"And none of it will bring Lola back." Philomela remembered Lola's mother making a similar statement.

"Does Detective O'Malley think Don knows who murdered Lola?"

"I have no idea."

Later that afternoon, Philomela answered the phone and Detective O'Malley said, "I promised to tell you the latest developments, so here they are. My chats with Mrs. Grieve and Don Webster were informative. Did you know that on your world trip Don was trying to kidnap Janice?"

"Good grief, no. Was he aiming to seduce her?"

"He aimed to hold her 'til her dad paid a ransom for her return."

"That's unbelievable." Philomela was glad she was sitting down. The news was shocking, but it helped explain Don's weird actions. "He seemed far too innocent to be involved in such a scheme."

"He wasn't the instigator of it."

"So who was?"

"I can't say, not yet, but I'll give you a hint. The diary was a great help." She pondered the puzzle and O'Malley continued. "Don said Pierre was against the kidnapping. He was also against a former plan that involved stealing files from McGill Oil and Gas in order to doctor them for an audit. His aversion to these two plans may have initiated his fatal accident." The detective chatted for several minutes, describing Don's version of the failed theft. "This information should not become public knowledge until the culprit is caught."

"Be sure to catch him before the beginning of next month. That's when the next issue of *The Integrator* is due."

After they said goodbye, Philomela's thoughts lingered on O'Malley's information. Why would smart men put effort into developing illegal ideas? She wasn't surprised that Mr. Lalonde had been against the plans. She found it difficult to believe he was even on the fringe of any shady dealings.

O'Malley said Don had wanted easy money to buy a parcel of land in the foothills. The two schemes were bizarre, dreadful. She gave her head a shake.

She recalled Janice describing a handsome drunk who had gotten lost in the file room at her dad's office. They had laughed over his antics.

Janice would be surprised to learn that the drunk was not drunk.

She would be more surprised to learn he had dyed

his hair and grown a mustache and beard so she wouldn't recognize him on the odyssey. She would also be shocked to learn she had been targeted as a kidnapping victim.

CHAPTER 46

Three days later, Detective O'Malley again phoned Philomela at her office. "Both cases have been solved," he said. "The murderer has been apprehended, thanks in great part to you."

Philomela would have felt a sense of satisfaction if Lola and Mr. Lalonde hadn't been the victims. Though she had a suspicion, she asked, "Who is it?"

"Bob Davis."

"Why am I not surprised?"

"Bob has admitted to dropping a sleeping powder in Pierre Lalonde's drink and he also admitted to bumping into him at the top of the stairs—accidently, he said. According to him the whole thing was accidental. He hadn't wanted Pierre to die."

"What about Lola? That was no accident."

"A couple of Lola's remarks made him suspect she had seen him drop the powder in Pierre's drink and then had seen what happened at the top of the stairs. He decided to cover his tracks by getting rid of her before she told anyone else. It was too late—as you discovered in the diary, she already had recorded the details quite succinctly. Last night, he confessed that he had purchased a cheap pearl necklace from a dollar store and, in Lola's car, pretended to clasp it at the back of her neck. Then with a Swiss army knife, he sliced her from ear to ear. With blood spurting from two arteries, she fell onto the steering wheel and died quickly. He stuffed the necklace in his coat pocket and left. Next morning, as everyone knows, a jogger found her. Not so well known was that the red upholstery was covered with her blood."

"Good grief." Philomela swallowed, hoping to curb a feeling of nausea. "I don't want to remember Lola in such horrid circumstances."

"Try to think of her enjoying being a model for your magazine," O'Malley said.

"Yes, Lola had fun doing that photo shoot."

"When I talked with Don, I got the impression he carried a torch for Lola. Her death has hit him hard. In fact, I'd say he's devastated."

Philomela felt a twinge of sympathy for Don. On the trip, she had found him to be young and naive. Lola would have been good for him. Lola would have kept him on the straight and narrow.

"Because of the illegal audit attempt," O'Malley said, "Don knew Bob was capable of white collar crimes. He had no idea Bob was capable of committing murder. Right now, that young man is in a bad state. Two of his favorite people are dead and someone he once admired is a murderer. I know one thing. He won't be so gullible in the future. He'll be content to work for his money, rather than cheat and steal for it."

"Thanks for letting me know the results of your investigation, O'Malley."

"You're welcome, Philomela. And thanks for telling me about the diary. That was our first good lead. I'll return it to Mrs. Grieve as soon as possible."

Their conversation ended and Philomela thoughtfully pressed the off key of the phone. Hearing a movement behind her, she turned and saw her employee standing in the doorway. The puzzled expression on her face indicated she had heard one side of the conversation.

"Janice, that was Detective O'Malley on the phone. The police have apprehended Lola's murderer,"

"Who is it?" Janice asked.

"Your dad's joint-venture partner. And I don't mean Don."

Janice's hand flew up to her face, and she fell onto a straight back chair. She gazed at Philomela and her face paled. "Bob Davis. It's bad enough that he planned to have me kidnapped for ransom money. But murder? And to think I went out alone with him on several dates."

"Janice, it's even worse. He put a sleeping powder in Pierre's drink and then pushed him down the stairs."

"Omigod!" A horrified expression covered her face. "Two murders."

Philomela got up and filled two mugs with coffee. She handed one to her employee and noticed how the girl's hand shook as she accepted it. Janice raised the mug to her mouth and sipped the hot liquid. It seemed to revive her.

"Maybe I'm lucky to be alive," she murmured. "I guess Bob didn't date me for my scintillating conversation. He wanted to keep tabs on me."

"One thing is sure. You did a good deed in your dad's office. You prevented Don from becoming a thief and participating in an illegal audit."

"It didn't enter my mind that Don was trying to steal files. Nor did I think he was trying to kidnap me during our holiday." Janice shook her head and set her mug on the desk. "Theft, forging documents, and kidnapping are bad enough. But cold blooded murder?"

Philomela was pensive. "A murderer lives with his deed, as if sitting on a two-legged stool. He can keep his balance for a short spell but, eventually, he'll tip and fall over."

Janice nodded and picked up her mug. "I have a dinner date with Frank Smith this evening. I'll tell him that, by rescuing me in Petra, he also helped Don."

"And I'll phone Brent. He'll be relieved to learn the murderer has been apprehended."

"You mean," Janice said, "he'll be relieved to learn you're no longer exposed to danger."

Philomela chuckled and picked up the phone. "That, too."

The End

About the Author

Benni Chisholm grew up on the Canadian prairies. While earning a BSN she discovered that writing light verse (doggerel) served as a release from the sad things she encountered in the hospital. In the shadow of the Rocky Mountain foothills, she worked as a public health nurse, helped four wonderful children raise themselves, and saw the publication of poems, short stories, articles, a biography, and an anniversary booklet. She also served as editor of a newsletter for eight years. She and her husband now enjoy life on the Pacific Northwest. Benni's fondness for travel is apparent in her two mystery novels. *STAINED SAND* is located in Hawaii, and the protagonist in *ODD ODYSSEY* travels around the world.

www.ingramcontent.com/pod-product-compliance
Lightning Source LLC
Chambersburg PA
CBHW062035170626
46813CB00001B/344